RUNNING HOTT

A STEAMY RUSH CREEK ROMANTIC COMEDY

HOTT SPRINGS ETERNAL
BOOK 4

SERENA BELL

JMG
JELSBA
MEDIA
GROUP

1

RHYS

Despite what my brothers—and most of New York City—think about me, I don't swipe right that often.

When I do, I put a lot of effort into making sure everyone's on the same page. I explain my one-night-and-only-one-night intentions up front. I make sure her friends know where she is and that she feels safe. I always, always use condoms.

I'm a divorce lawyer, after all. I know the consequence of rash decisions. And I spent my childhood with men who used, left, and screwed over women—which left me wanting never to be those men.

Still, occasionally things don't go as planned.

Tonight is one of those nights.

We're in the hallway outside my apartment when Kirsten—a tall, willowy brunette with curves for miles, blue eyes, and full lips—says, "How do you feel about role-playing?"

I try to hide my grimace. I've never role-played, but I

did once take an improv class, and it was a total nightmare. I'm at home in front of a courtroom and a judge, but when I have to pretend to be someone else, my brain freezes.

"Not my thing," I tell her.

She runs a fingertip down the placket of my shirt, pausing to caress each button. "Could you make an exception for me?" she purrs, finger reaching my waist and sliding across the top of my belt buckle.

"Uh...okay?"

I'll admit it—this is a dick answer, as in my dick answered while my brain was temporarily offline.

"You can be the high school quarterback," she murmurs. "And I'll be the nerdy girl who didn't get chosen for the cheerleading team."

Okay. I can do this. Right? This is what she needs, and a good one-night stand is all about giving a woman what she needs.

"Your name is Randall Westbrook," she tells me, fingers still playing with the buckle. "And mine is Kristen Patton."

"But that's basically your real name."

She pouts. "No, my real name is Kirsten Payton."

"Right. Sorry."

Alarm bells go off in my head. Years of lawyerly instincts. My gut knows the truth. Something—or someone —is off.

She tilts her head. "You pretend you don't know I exist, but you've been watching me for years. Since we were both freshmen. Wanting me. Wanting to cross all the clique boundaries that keep us apart." She clasps her free hand to her chest. "That time in PE when you made fun of me, you were trying to make a connection with me."

Remarkably specific. Are the hallway walls closing in on us?

"Let's say I'm in the library, searching for a book. You're going to have to make the first move, Randall," she whispers. "I'm too scared. You've never shown me the slightest sign that you care about my existence." She turns her body to face the wall, running her fingertips over it in a way I think she means to be seductive.

The alarm bells have become air raid sirens. "Uh, Kirs—Kris—ack, sorry."

"Kristen," she prompts.

"Kristen," I repeat, and then, unable to stop myself, "It seems like maybe high school was a hard time for you?"

"Shh," she says. "Say, 'You think I don't see you, Kristen, but I do.'"

I wince. "I don't want to bring up any buried trauma for you."

"Rhys," she whines. "Say it."

"You actually want this? You want me to pretend to be some guy who didn't appreciate you in high school?"

"I really, *really* want this," she whispers huskily.

"You, uh, think I don't see you, but I, uh—I do."

Her fingers caress the wall. "Me? Randall, are you talking to me?"

She gives me an innocent look over her shoulder.

"Yes, you. I see you all the time when you're"—my mind goes blank—"you know, answering questions in class. And I don't think you're a nerd—"

"No, he likes me because I'm a nerd," she corrects.

"You know," I attempt, "I think maybe role-play isn't my—"

"You're doing amazing," she tells me and, turning to me, wraps her arms around my neck and kisses me.

With a sense of profound relief—*I've passed the test; we're on to the night's real agenda*—I kiss her back, and *yes*. Now we're on track, kissing, groping, stumbling toward my apartment. I fumble in my pocket and find my key card, opening the door, guiding her inside, turning her around to press her against the door, my front to her back.

"Say, 'You dirty little bookworm,'" she prompts.

No, no, no. Every cell in my body rebels. I open my mouth, and all that comes out is a slow hiss of sad air. Other parts of me—besides my lungs—deflate as well.

"Say, 'You dirty little bookworm,'" she murmurs again, like the problem is that I didn't hear the first time. Or didn't understand.

But the real problem is that Randall Westbrook clearly never had the slightest interest in Kirsten Payton. And yet, more than a decade later, she still fantasizes about him rocking her world.

It's tragic, actually.

Why do women persist in having such romantic, optimistic, self-destructive ideas about love when it's abundantly clear that the world is full of men who will tear them to shreds?

I'm standing there, pressing her to the wall, my mouth open and wordless, when a warbly baritone comes from behind me:

"Rhys Hott. You can't stay cynical about love forever."

Kirsten and I shriek like little kids who've been jump-scared.

Raking a hand through my hair, I glare at the intruder in my living room. "What the fuck are you doing here?"

The short, balding man in his late sixties gets to his feet, waving a single sheet of cream-colored paper. "I'm serving you with the letter from your grandfather's will. Nice place, by the way," he says, scanning our surroundings—the mission-style furnishings, the William Morris–influenced textiles, the Arts and Crafts–era paintings and handcrafts. Heavy, dark, comforting.

Normally comforting. Currently full of invaders.

"Who is he?" Kirsten demands.

I sigh heavily. "*He* is Arthur Weggers, my grandfather's attorney and the executor of his will. He lives in Rush Creek, Oregon, where I grew up."

"Why is he here?"

Weggers puffs up his chest. "I'm here to read Rhys a letter from his grandfather."

"My dead grandfather," I clarify, since that part isn't always obvious. "There's this thing—" I close my eyes, because where do you even start with this? "My grandfather is making me and all my brothers—I have four—jump through arbitrary hoops in order to keep the land we grew up on and save our sister's business, and it's Weggers's job to make sure we all do the things we're supposed to." I glare at him.

"Wait," Kirsten says. "What do you have to do?"

"I don't know yet." I turn to Weggers. "What do I have to do?"

"Do you want her here while I read the letter?"

I've been handed a brilliant exit from at least one of my night's problems. "I think I would prefer for the reading to be private," I tell Kirsten.

"Ohhh-kay," she says. "We could, you know, meet up later? Or tomorrow night?" She pins me with a hopeful, wide-eyed gaze.

"I don't think so," I say, and then, because none of this is her fault and because precision is important in life as in the law, "It was nice hanging out with you tonight, but like we discussed, it was a one-time thing."

I press my hand into her back and usher her to the exit, glaring over my shoulder at Weggers as I do. I maneuver her outside my apartment and tell her, "I wish you all the best." Then I shut the door tightly and lean against it.

"How's the hookup life working out for you?" Weggers asks.

When I look up, he's smirking. "Screw you."

He snickers.

The real miracle of the last fifteen months is that none of us has offed Weggers in his sleep.

"Why are you here?" I demand.

"You know the answer to that."

"Why didn't you summon me to Rush Creek?"

"Would you have come?"

I consider. "No."

"That's why I'm here. I learned from chasing your brother Preston all over creation that it's not worth my effort. So I came straight to you."

"How'd you get into my apartment?"

"Your doorperson was very happy to let me up."

Shit. That's what I get for turning down her generous

offer to share her break in the maintenance room, no strings attached. Since then, she has laser-eyed every woman I bring home—only a few, but unfortunately always on her shift—and she hasn't stopped trying to convince me to change my mind. *Look,* she informed me one evening, *I pay attention. They're upstairs with you for an average of two hours and forty-seven minutes, and they leave here looking dehydrated and glowing. Do you have any idea what percentage of men in Manhattan can get a woman off? Lower than the chance of being killed by a meteorite. For the love of God, Rhys, just once.*

I (gently) told that she was, literally, too close to home… but apparently that didn't save me from her vengeful impulses.

I point at Weggers. "It's illegal for a process server to misrepresent—"

"Save your breath," he says, waving his hand again. "I told her the truth. I told her I was your grandfather's lawyer and that I was here to share your grandfather's legacy with you. I asked if I could wait in your apartment, and I showed her proof of my identity, evidence of my lawyer-client relationship to your grandfather, and a copy of the letter, which she read. She approved of it, by the way," he adds. "Said she thought your granddad's plan for you would have a positive effect on your attitude toward commitment."

"Who cares what my doorperson thinks about my attitude toward— No, you know what? I don't want to hear your answer to that. I don't want to hear anything—"

"Too late!" he crows, eyes dancing. "I already read the first sentence of your letter! 'Rhys Hott. You can't stay cynical about love forever.'"

I sigh. "I'm not cynical. I'm realistic." Marriages succeed at the same rate as coins come up heads. Hardly odds to bet your life on.

Weggers peers through his reading glasses at the letter and carries on:

Let's see if we can turn around your grim view of love by exposing you to a rosier view of romance. At the time of the reading of this letter, your sister is in charge of some number of weddings. A subset of these will take place within the following two months. These will become your responsibi—

"He did fucking not!"

"I wish your brothers were here!" Weggers chortles, almost dancing with delight.

I bury my face in my hands. I'm so fucking glad they're not here. They'd have way too good a time with this.

Eventually, I'll have to confront them. But now is not yet.

"Do you want me to keep reading?"

I snatch the paper out of his hand and read the rest to myself.

You will live in Rush Creek during your tenure and take over the planning of these weddings. All of them must actually culminate with the planned ceremony.

"Technically that was my idea," Weggers crows. "About how they had to actually *happen*. To make sure you didn't infect the couples with your cynical views. Brilliant, right?"

"I don't have cynical views!"

I'm aware I've lost the calm that's the hallmark of my lawyerly success. I never lose my cool in court. I definitely never sound like a whiny teenager.

My fucking grandfather.

"You're a divorce attorney," Weggers points out.

"You make it sound like I'm breaking up marriages willy nilly because it's fun for me," I say. "When in fact, I'm only helping people end marriages that are already disasters for them."

It's why I'm a divorce lawyer. To keep women like my mother and my aunt from getting destroyed by powerful men.

I'm good at it, too. I've only failed once.

"We believe what we want to believe," Weggers tells me primly.

"You know this would *never* hold up in court."

He gives me a sage look. Or, more exactly, a look that he thinks is sage. In reality, it's more constipated. "And you know you would never take this to court."

"Just because I haven't yet…"

The smirk is back. "If you're determined to be the first Hott brother who can't get the job done and lets Blue Mining get its hands on the family land…"

Frustration coils in my belly—not because he's wrong, but because he's right. None of us have obeyed the will because we actually believe it's legally airtight. We've done it because it's a form of atonement. A way to show Hanna that we're sorry—for not being there for her for so many years.

And Weggers, the fucker, knows it.

"What if the people decide they don't want to be married? You can't force two people who have nothing to do with this situation to get married if that's not what they want."

Weggers sniffs. "In the unlikely event that any of the

couples decides they don't want to be married, *and* I can ascertain for sure that your actions had no bearing on the outcome, I'll take that under advisement."

I know it's the best I'm going to do, unless I want—as Weggers says—to be *that* Hott brother.

Even knowing I've lost, I make one more stab at escape: "I can't drop all my responsibilities in New York. I have court dates scheduled."

"And those are more important than helping your sister out of a fix?" he asks.

We both know it's not a real question. My shoulders slump.

He holds out a hand and, mutely, obediently, I return the Asshole Granddad letter to him.

"If I were you," he says, folding and pocketing the letter, the smirk returning, "I'd start postponing some of those court dates."

2

EDEN

"I have to tell you something, and I need you to stay as calm as possible until we talk it through."

These are the first words my wedding planner, Hanna Wilder, says to me when I arrive at her office for our two-weeks-before appointment.

I instantly start dredging up worst-case scenarios: The officiant has taken a last-minute ministerial sabbatical to Bali. The baker dropped the wedding cake, and there's a worldwide shortage of ganache. Hanna accidentally double-booked the venue with one of those teen-wunderkind summer circuses, and we'll be getting married to a backdrop of fourteen-year-olds hanging from scarves.

"Ohhhkay," I manage.

"I promise everything's going to be all right. I'll be there every step of the way, overseeing things from the sidelines—"

"Are you okay?" I ask, gesturing in the general direction of her relatively small but definitely pregnant belly. She'd warned me that her previous pregnancy had been high risk and promised smooth sailing even if she had to go on bed rest.

"Oh, I'm totally fine." She waves a hand dismissively. "It's just—" She closes her eyes. "Have a seat."

Warily, I do, and she closes her office door and sits behind the desk across from me. Photographs of beaming couples line the walls, and favors from weddings she's coordinated clutter her desk. She leans forward. "Have you by any chance heard anything about my grandfather's will?"

"There were some rumors," I say carefully. Now I wish I'd listened more closely.

"Right. Here's the thing." She bites her lip. I realize this is the first time I've *ever* seen Hanna look nervous, and that twists my own nerves into a bundle. "My grandfather's will requires each of my brothers to do something...out of character, or there will be...consequences. To me. Well, to all of us, really. So far, because they're not total dicks—well, about sixty-seven-point-eight percent of the time anyway —they've always complied with the will. And in this case, my brother..." She shakes her head and stops. "I can't believe this is my life," she says and then points down at the floor.

"You're a real bastard, you know that?" she asks the wide planks. "I hope you're enjoying yourself down there." She returns her gaze to me. "I know you and Rhys have a history—"

Oh, *shit*.

To be clear, Hanna's brother Rhys and I don't have a *history* history. He and I weren't an item or anything like that.

Almost the opposite.

Rhys represented my asshole ex-husband in my ugly divorce when I still lived in New York City.

Picture Heathcliff—or better yet, picture a young, short-haired Severus Snape. Tall, dark, broody, and so deeply scornful he barely acknowledged my presence. I think he made eye contact with me once, and when he did, he looked away like I was a sixty-year-old guy who'd exposed himself on the subway.

And meanwhile, he dismantled everything that mattered to me with a ruthless precision.

Savings: gone.

Inheritance: gone.

Business: nearly gone, but for a last-minute save by my lawyer.

And my beloved Milo—my adorable, snuggly rescue pup—in half-time custody with my ex, who didn't even want us to get the dog in the first place.

He deprived me of six months a year with my *dog*.

So whatever Hanna is about to say about Rhys, if it concerns me and my wedding, it's definitely not good.

Hanna's eyes scan my face like she's trying to read something there, and then she heaves a big sigh and says, "I'm so, so sorry, Eden, but because of my grandfather's will, Rhys is taking over the final stages of planning your wedding."

"You're joking."

"I assure you, she's not."

The voice is deep. Smooth. Commanding. It sends a

ripple of sensation over my skin, like a warm breeze at the beach, and I turn. The man standing in the doorway is six foot four of scowling antihero—dark hair, dark eyes, and a slight, cruel curve to one side of his mouth.

And two years later, he still won't meet my eyes. Instead he pins his gaze on his sister, eyebrows slightly lifted.

"This is my brother Rhys Hott," Hanna says unnecessarily. "Rhys, this is—"

"I know who she is."

Right.

He crosses his arms. If someone can sneer without altering the lines of their face at all, Rhys is doing that.

Yeah, this should be fun.

He's wearing—as always—a suit. This one is either linen or light wool—I can't tell for sure—in a gorgeous light brown. The jacket hugs his bulky shoulders and clings to his biceps.

It always felt like adding insult to injury that in any other circumstance, Rhys would be *hot*.

"I can take it from here," Rhys tells Hanna in that clipped, arrogant way he has. Like he won't waste a syllable on talking to anyone who doesn't merit his five-hundred-dollar-an-hour time.

(My attorney cost one hundred sixty-five dollars an hour, sliding scale. You could probably have predicted who would "win" that divorce before we ever stepped in a conference room. Not that she wasn't amazing. She was terrific. But. One of Rhys's suits costs more than her total bill for the entire divorce.)

Money wins.

"I did everything I could, Eden," Hanna says, her voice

unsteady. "I know this can't be comfortable for you. But I'm hoping since there are only two weeks till the wedding—"

"I can take it from here, Han," Rhys grits out.

They engage in a prolonged glaring contest. I'm betting on Hanna, one of the toughest, most unflappable women I've ever met—but in the end, she looks away first.

Even his own sister can't win.

"He'll do a good job," she tells me. "My brothers are pains in my ass, but they love me and want what's best for me, and Rhys will absolutely do what has to be done."

I've definitely seen evidence of that. Ruthless. Relentless. Savage.

"I'll be in the waiting area if you need me," she says, ducking her head.

She leaves the door open, but as soon as she's gone, the office feels—absurdly—smaller. How can a person leaving shrink a room? But it has. Rhys now fills all the available space and takes all the remaining air. My chest tightens.

"Fuck my life," I blurt.

"You and me both," he mutters.

"What do you mean *you and me both*?" I demand. "You're the one who took my money and my dog—"

"I didn't *take*—"

"You reallocated them to my asshole ex-husband! My dog can't even come to my wedding because it's Teller's turn for custody and he won't give me visitation!"

He doesn't try to argue with that. "Point taken," he says in that crisp dismissive way of his. "So let's get through this wedding, and in two weeks we'll never have to see each other again."

"Isn't there another way?" I ask.

He shakes his head. "Believe me," he says, "if there were another way, I would not be in this room with you."

I wince. Even though I was well aware of his feelings toward me, the outright admission stings. I tried, even when we were adversaries, to be kind to him. But I could sense his impatience and contempt in every tight, disciplined line of his body.

I now regret every ounce of decency I showed him.

"I have to plan your wedding, so I'll plan your wedding," he says. "Anything else I do screws Hanna."

"The planning's basically done," I say. "If it weren't, I'd have canceled the contract the instant you walked into the room."

He doesn't react to that, not even a flinch. I remember how implacable he always was. Nothing seemed to ruffle his surface, to put even a tiny dent in his absolute, perfect control.

"Today's meeting was to nail down the last stuff, and then you just have to make sure everything runs smoothly the day of—"

"Which I'll do," he bites out.

"I don't doubt it," I say. "I never doubted your competence. Just your *soul*."

Is that a flinch?

I'm not sure I've ever been deliberately unkind to someone. But then no one has ever taken my life down to the studs with utter, ruthless efficiency while also treating me like I barely existed.

There's a first time for everything.

3

RHYS

What did I think? That she'd be glad to see me again?

Of course not. I'm not an idiot.

The last time I was in a room with her, it was a courtroom. And a judge was delivering her a litany of bad news.

I couldn't look at her, at the grief and hurt and frustration on her face. If I looked, I might've broken all my promises to myself.

All my obligations to my client.

All my ethical principles, the ones keeping me from touching my client's ex in ways I'd dreamed about. The ones that had kept me, all those weeks, from screwing over my own client so Eden came out with more.

The ones that had *mostly* kept me from screwing over my own client...

So I kept my eyes fixed on the judge's bald spot, as I had for weeks. There was a birthmark on it in the shape of Bugs Bunny.

Now I pin my eyes on a point on Hanna's desk where

someone has written too hard and left an impression in the wood.

Footsteps sound in the hallway, and a tall, sandy-haired man stumbles into the doorway, classically handsome in a *Connecticut country club* kind of way. But there's nothing country-club polished about him right now. He's sweating, flustered. He looks like he ran a mile to get to us.

"I'm so sorry I'm late," he says.

He addresses this to me, not to Eden. In fact, he doesn't look at Eden at all.

The lawyerly alarm bells go off.

Squirrelly.

I've met with a few other couples before this. Some are starry-eyed, others fight like cats and dogs. But I haven't seen anyone who couldn't make eye contact.

Don't do it, I want to tell her. *Something's wrong.*

I turn my attention to Eden. Her head's cocked as she watches Paul: She sees it, too. But she doesn't look worried.

Didn't you learn anything from the last asshole? I want to demand of her.

But I think of the terms of the letter—*all of them must actually culminate with the planned ceremony*—and keep my mouth shut. Because no matter what I owe Eden, I owe Hanna and my other siblings more.

"Paul," Eden says. "This is Rhys, Hanna's brother. He's taking over the wedding for her."

"Ah," Paul says. "Everything all right with the baby?"

"Everything's fine. Rhys is just..." She looks to me.

"My grandfather's will has some unusual terms, and one of them is that I have to take on some of Hanna's weddings," I explain.

Obviously, I tried to talk Weggers out of giving me Eden's wedding. Hanna even intervened on my behalf, pointing out that the arrangement would also suck for Eden. But Weggers is like a dog with a bone. And when he saw how much I didn't want this, he doubled down.

My grandfather could not have chosen a better proxy for his mischief.

"Welcome to the fray," Paul says. He seems to have settled himself. "Paul Graves."

His handshake is firm, but he doesn't look me in the eye, either.

What are you hiding, Paul Graves?

"So," he says. "Where do we stand?"

"You brought the marriage license with you, yes?" I ask him. Hanna always has couples apply online, then bring the license to the last big planning meeting. She says she's learned from past disasters.

"I—no," he says. "I'll, um, pick it up tomorrow."

I give him a sharp look. His eyes dart, settling everywhere in the room except on mine.

"Or I can," Eden says brightly. "I know you've been super busy with work."

"It's been a cluster," Paul says—to me. "Haven't had a minute to breathe. But the marriage license is obviously more important than any of that. I'll grab it on my way out of here. You have plenty on your plate, darling."

And now he gives her a fond look. Which should fill me —as reluctant wedding planner and Hanna's dutiful brother—with joy.

Instead it makes me feel like my scalp is too tight.

I turn away from them and make a show of digging for the two-week checklist I need to run through with them.

"Let's make sure we've got everything we need." Eden's wedding isn't the first one I've taken over, and Hanna has spent so much time training me, you'd think lives were at stake.

Seating—check, music—check, photos—check, video—check. Check, check, check.

"Honeymoon—everything booked and confirmed?"

Eden shifts in her seat, leaning forward. "We're delaying the honeymoon a month. I'm curating an exhibit of art quilts at Five Rivers Arts and Crafts."

"It's a big honor," Paul says. He's packed his voice full of pride, but I don't believe it. I don't believe anything about him, and there's fuck all I can do about it. I hate that I'm back here, powerless to protect her.

"Well done," I say, and it comes out like a shrug, like indifference, which is exactly what I was aiming for—and now I straight-up hate myself. But I didn't spend all those months in that conference room and that courtroom keeping an iron thumb on my self-control so I could blow it now. My job is to make sure that Paul marries Eden two weeks from Saturday, that the wedding comes off flawlessly, that Weggers can find no evidence that I haven't done my job to the best of my ability.

I can't fail. Not at the expense of my family's land and my sister's business. No fucking way.

Which means I can't let myself feel one goddamned thing about Eden Becker. Not about her shoulder-length yellow-blond hair or her big green eyes or her pretty plump lips. Not about her slim form and delicate curves. And definitely not about the way her mouth tips into a smile when Paul praises her.

I'm already good at this. I had months of practice. I'm a pro at ignoring Eden Becker.

Two weeks, Rhys. Get through two weeks, and you never have to see her again. You can forget she exists.

Fat fucking chance.

I look down at my checklist. There are checkmarks next to every item except the marriage license. I'm relieved...and also disappointed.

It's a familiar feeling. I felt it every time we reached the end of a meeting with Teller, Eden, and her lawyer, Sally. I felt it every time I walked out of the courtroom, leaving Eden behind. Like I couldn't get out of there fast enough and also like I wanted to run back in and say all the things I'd never be able to say because she was—for legal purposes—my enemy.

"Then we're good?" Paul asks.

"We're good," I say. "You just need to show up for your final fittings and make sure you pick up the marriage license and be here two weeks from Saturday."

"We can do that," he says. "I'd better get back to the office."

"Paul's an oral surgeon," Eden says.

"Ah."

"It's a lot of wisdom teeth," he says. It's self-effacing in a way that seems genuine but that I also don't believe.

"Rite of passage," I say, and Paul grins. He gets to his feet and holds out his hand; I take it and we shake. "Nice to meet you," I lie. And then, the words getting ahead of my judgment: "Eden, actually, if you could stay behind for a minute, I'll just have you fill out this one other form."

There's no other form, but luckily no one asks what it is.

Paul thanks me and leaves.

Eden watches him go.

I want to tell her *There's something wrong.*

But on top of the fact that I owe my siblings this wedding, unimpeded, she has absolutely no reason to believe a word I say. I'm Public Enemy Number One to her.

Instead I say, "You didn't tell him who I am."

"You're the wedding planner. That's all he needs to know." She shrugs. "No point in making him hate you, too." She scowls at me. "Where's the form?"

"No form," I say. "I just wanted to ask you if Paul knew that you and I know each other."

"We don't know each other," she says. "You don't know anything about me."

She picks up her purse and leaves.

I lean back in Hanna's chair and exhale for what feels like the first time in an hour.

It's good that Eden hates me. The worst thing in the world would be if Eden's mouth curved in a small, pleased smile *for me.*

Then I might—

I might—

I don't know what, exactly, I would do.

But luckily, she hates me, so there's no danger of that.

I want to pick up one of the pretty knickknacks on Hanna's desk and hurl it against the wall.

4

EDEN

My wedding day arrives after a night of little sleep and a morning of barely eaten breakfast.

It's normal to be so excited before your wedding you can't sleep or eat, everyone assures me.

And I am *so* excited. After the pain of my divorce, it's lovely to know that by the end of today, officially and for the rest of my life, I won't be alone again.

For a girl who's been left as often as I have, that's huge.

The space where I'm getting married is actually an enormous converted barn, and the hayloft has been split into a groom's room and a bride's room. The brightly lit, mostly white bride's room has skylights and big windows that look out onto the gorgeous Hott property—a former ranch.

The decor is ranch chic—wooden beams, a sliding barn door at the entry, cowboy hats and ropes hanging on the walls, leather touches and accents of cow-print upholstery. One wall is a continuous dressing table with mirrors.

My gown hangs from a beautiful carved-wood stand. It's a shimmering white mermaid dress with elaborate beading that I love as much today as I did when I first laid eyes on it.

"You ready to put it on?" Mari asks, following my gaze. She's not only my friend and maid of honor but also one of Hanna's many sisters-in-law.

I nod, feeling an unexpected sense of awe. The hairdresser and the makeup artist just left. The photographer has already snapped a thousand photos of me. It's go time.

Mari helps me into the dress. It has to slip on over my feet; I step into it carefully, and she shimmies it up around my body.

"Oh my God, Eden, you look amazing!" she cries.

She stands back, arranging the train of the dress for me as the photographer's flash goes wild.

"He's going to swallow his tongue when he sees you!" Mari tells me.

On the other side of that wall, Paul's getting dressed, too —just without as many mirrors. He and I spent the night separately, by agreement, so I can do a big reveal this morning.

He's been remote these last couple weeks—busy and distracted—but I've chalked it up to how awful his work has been. I wish we were going on our honeymoon right away, but maybe it's better that it's a couple months out because by then he'll be less stressed.

There's a knock at the door. "Do you think that's him?" I gasp.

Mari opens it a crack and peeks out. "It's Satan," she says over her shoulder.

She was furious when she heard that Rhys was going to

be my wedding planner, even for only a couple of weeks. She and Hanna had words over it, Mari going so far as to say that Hanna was damn lucky I hadn't bailed out to Hanna's number one competitor, Five Rivers Weddings, but afterward even Mari said there wasn't any other way.

The real mind fuck, she'd said when she finally delivered that verdict, *is that out of all the small towns in America, you and Paul decided to set up shop in your nemesis's hometown. From there, the rest feels almost fated. In a bad way.*

Rhys has barely been in evidence this morning, which is fine with me. I know he's been around, making sure the day runs smoothly, and to his credit, it seems like he's doing a great job. I haven't heard a peep from anyone about problems, and everything has flowed like expensive wine at a high-end steakhouse.

"I need to talk to Eden," Rhys's deep voice comes from behind the door. "Alone."

"Come on, Rhys, don't be a dick," Mari says. "It's her wedding day."

"Now," he says sharply.

Mari gives me a WTF face and mouths, *You okay with that?*

I nod, but she doesn't open the door any wider. She's still watching my face, and I can't read her expression.

Rhys's voice comes again. "Mari, I need you to do something for Eden. ASAP."

"What's going on?" she asks, shooting me another look. Now she looks nervous, which makes my lungs shrink. For some reason, I remember the last wedding meeting, when Paul arrived in a tizzy.

Why? Why had he been so flustered?

Why hadn't I wondered before now?

Instead of answering, Rhys says, "Arthur Weggers is sitting in the back row on the bride's side, wearing a ruffled shirt and a royal-blue suit jacket. Sit down next to him and distract him with your sparkling conversation. I don't care what you talk to him about. Anything."

"What the hell?" Mari asks.

There's a moment of silence, then: "Hanna will come find you and Arthur, and when she does, she'll explain."

Mari and I exchange glances.

"You sure you're okay alone?" she asks.

I nod.

She gives me one more look—almost pleading—but steps out the door, followed by the photographer, as Rhys steps in.

He closes the door behind himself and leans back against it, as if shutting out evil spirits. "I need to tell you something, and you need to be—"

He stops, his eyes finally settling on me. Taking me in, from my upswept hair to the dusky makeup and berry lips to my bare shoulders and exposed curves, down the flare of the dress over my hips. Back to my eyes, his a hundred times more intense now.

I've been looking forward for days to the look on Paul's face when he sees me for the first time in this dress, but I know in my heart and several other more-honest body parts that however Paul looks, it won't be this gratifying. It won't make my heart stutter and my core clench and my whole body flush. It won't make it impossible for me to look away from the eyes on me, devouring me, taking in every detail and reflecting it back to me.

All those times Rhys's gaze flicked past me like I was beneath contempt, and now he swallows hard, his Adam's apple bobbing almost painfully, and I feel a surge of absolute triumph.

Then he looks away, and the moment is over. In fact, I'm pretty sure it never happened.

"—sitting down," he finishes.

He pulls a cow-print upholstered chair out and arranges it behind me, and I sink into it as instructed.

But he doesn't have to tell me what he's going to say. I've already connected the dots. Paul's disheveled state at our meeting, his failure to bring the marriage license that day.

Did he ever pick it up?

I think I know the answer.

It feels like someone has punched me in the stomach but also like a hot flush of the deepest shame. Somewhere in my body, I already know that I will *never* be able to face the people waiting out there in the audience again.

"Paul isn't going to marry me," I say. Not a question.

Rhys nods, not looking at me. Looking at some point off in the distance. It's cold, his not looking, and I want the earlier moment back, before I got gut-punched, when Rhys's gaze told me that no matter what anyone else could do or say, I was perfect.

Except I'd imagined that, and the truth is that I'm not perfect.

I'm *jilted*.

Oh, God, I'm *jilted*.

"He left a note," Rhys says, "for his brother to give to you."

"So why didn't Charlie bring me the note?"

"Because he never showed up this morning. He's a coward. Like his asswipe of a brother."

His voice is low and dark and hard, his jaw tight. If I didn't know better, I'd think he was angry on my behalf.

"But you're not."

Rhys laughs—a short, dark, unhappy laugh. "No," he says. "I'm not." And he hands me the envelope he's been clutching behind his back.

5

RHYS

She stands there, reading the note, and I try not to stare.

But it's impossible.

She's a shimmering goddess, and I don't only mean the sparkle of the beads on her dress. I mean the glitter on her eyes and cheekbones, the shine of her smooth blond hair, the gloss of her bitable lower lip. She's slim, almost willowy, but in this dress, she's all dramatic dips and slopes, and tearing my eyes away from the creamy curves that threaten to spill over the neckline of the dress is the second hardest thing I've had to do today.

Her hand, the one holding the note, drops to her side, like it's too limp to support the weight of the paper.

"I need to get out of here," she says, her voice lifeless. "Get me out of here."

My eyes find her face—I can't help it—and I see *her* again. The woman I saw that first day in my firm's conference room. Scared and alone and putting on a brave face like it was her job to hold the whole world together. She's

frightened and lost, and it isn't my fucking job to save her—
it will *never* be my job to save her—but for the first time,
and just this once, I can do what she needs.

"Take off the dress," I command. "There's no way to
sneak you out of here while you're wearing that."

The look on her face might be panic. "Someone has to
unzip it. Get Mari."

"There's no time," I say. "Turn around."

There's a long moment of hesitation. She has no reason
to trust me and every reason to hate me, and the whole
world teeters in the balance, waiting. Then she obeys,
giving me the low-cut back of the dress and acres more
creamy skin. This woman has never gone outside without
half a bottle of sunscreen on. When I reach for the zipper,
my fingers brush her back, and her skin is as soft as it looks,
as soft as satin.

Shut your eyes, I tell myself. *Shut your eyes.*

But I don't. I watch the zipper and my fingers all the way
down as the sides of the dress part, past the band of her
strapless bra, until I brush the curve of her ass above the
thin, barely there strip of her pale blue lace thong.

Before the dress can fall to the floor, she clutches it to
her chest and steps away from me. A moment later I've
forced myself to turn and stare out the window, and by the
time I let myself look back at her, she's slipped into navy
sweatpants and a Michigan T-shirt, thrust her feet into a
pair of sturdy sandals, and looped a leather handbag over
her shoulder.

I know that pale blue lace thong is still under there.

There's a cowboy hat hanging on the wall, and I grab it
and clap it onto her head. It's too big for her, which is

perfect; it covers her updo and puts her face in deep shadow. Without another word to each other, we're slipping out of the bridal prep room and down the back stairs of the venue, out the door, and to the parking lot. There are a few people still making their way from their cars to their seats, but if they recognize incognito Eden, they don't call out.

"Where's your car?" I ask.

"It's—I didn't come in my car. Paul drove our car here. Or was supposed to. Mari gave me a ride."

I tug her down the row of cars to mine. It's a BMW 740i, a rental. I don't drive in New York City, so when I get the chance, I like to drive something gorgeous and powerful. "Get in," I say, and she does.

I peel out of the parking lot and head toward town, which I know from her paperwork is where her condo is. But she's shaking her head. "I don't want to go ho—there," she says.

The fact that she can't call it "home" anymore cracks something in my chest. "Where do you want me to take you?"

"Just—drive," she says.

I need to go back to the venue and figure out how to handle the guests. I need to do everything in my power to keep Arthur Weggers from seeing the whole picture of what just happened. I need—

I need to do whatever she needs me to do.

She takes my silence as hesitation. She thinks I'm going to refuse her. "I can't go back there," she pleads. "Please. Just drive." And then, when I hesitate again, for a second, thinking of Hanna, "You owe me!"

I think of Eden in that courtroom on that last day, of the

slump of her shoulders and the way her head hung. Because of what I'd caused or at least allowed.

I had fiduciary responsibilities to Teller. Duties of loyalty and care. I couldn't ethically negotiate for what was less optimal for him. But also, I helped him hurt her.

I wiped her brave face off.

When that was the last thing I'd *ever* wanted.

I'll own that—for her, and also for my mom and Aunt Meryl and every other woman who's ever been wronged by an asshole man.

So I drive.

6

EDEN

ear Eden,

> *I know it's the biggest cliché in the book, but it's not you, it's me. I've always thought that when you know, you know...and I just didn't <u>know</u> for sure. And I thought you deserved better than that. I'm so sorry. I know this is the worst way to do things... I'll pay for everything.*

—Paul

It's quiet in the car. And quiet inside me. Perfectly numb.

The first question Rhys asks me is "Where are we going?"

"I don't know." And then, "Just drive."

He does.

I grapple with the ring on my finger, a solitaire circle-cut diamond. It catches on my knuckle and jams. Panic grips me, tight around my chest. Then the ring slips free and into my palm. I drop it into an interior pocket of my purse and zip it shut.

Scowling, I take the cowboy hat off my head and toss it into the back seat.

I hold my phone in my hand, balancing it on my palm, weighing my options. And then I remember.

The quilts for the exhibit are in the back of our car. The car Paul absconded with.

He has my quilts.

That cuts straight through the numbness. I don't know what to feel about my wedding, my marriage—

But I know *exactly* how I feel about that exhibit. I've poured myself into it. I've reached out to so many talented fiber artists. I've coordinated so many moving pieces. I've called in every favor, marketed like my life depended on it, drawn on strengths I didn't know I had.

I love my shop, but this exhibit is my *baby*.

My pride wants to curl up and die at the thought of texting Paul...but I don't have any other choice.

> Where are you? You have my quilts in the car. For the exhibit. I need you to come back with the quilts.

I make it as clear as possible that I'm not asking him to come back for me. I didn't go to two years of therapy to beg a guy who ditched me at the altar to change his mind.

I didn't go to two years of therapy to beg an asshole to love me.

I paid a lot of money for all that counseling.

Sent.

I wait for it to say *Delivered.*

And wait. And wait.

I go into Find My.

Paul Graves. Rush Creek, OR. Four hours ago.

His phone must be off.

I growl my frustration, startling Rhys, who glances at me.

"What? Where are we going?"

"Take 22 to 5."

Part of my brain is urging me to stop and reconsider this situation. *You're in a car with a man you* loathe. *That can't be a good idea.*

But right now? What happened in New York was a million years ago. There's only Paul and those quilts and my exhibit.

I text Charlie.

> Where is he?

CHARLIE

> I'm so sorry but I can't tell you that.

> He has seventeen quilts in his car and they're supposed to be hung in a world-class art quilt exhibit and if you don't tell me where he is I'll tell your fiancée you hooked up with that waitress in Vegas at the bachelor party.

Charlie's going to know Paul told me about the waitress in Vegas. He's probably going to be pissed at Paul. The thought gives me a thrill of delight. Maybe Charlie will beat Paul up.

There's a long pause. I question my hard-ball tactics, not for Paul's safety but because I'm not sure they'll work. Then the three dots appear.

CHARLIE

> He said he was going to the beach house
> to think about things.

> I think his phone is off.

> Yeah. He said he might do that, to get
> some mental space.

Code for: He didn't want to deal with me or any of the other fallout from the wedding he just torpedoed. I growl again.

"Are you texting Paul?"

I glare at Rhys. It feels great. "It's none of your fucking business who I'm texting." It's like a breath of fresh air through the desert of my heart. Who knew that anger was so cleansing?

A muscle ticks in Rhys's jaw. "I'm driving you to an unknown destination," he points out. "Plus, I'm your wedding planner and your wedding has just...unhappened. So technically, at the moment, it *is* my business."

"Do you even care about my wedding at all? Do you even *believe* in marriage?" I demand. "Given that you spend your life destroying them?"

I know I'm ragey and unhinged at the moment. I just can't...stop.

Am I hallucinating, or does the corner of Rhys's mouth tick up? "It's not a question of whether I *believe* in marriage. Of course I believe marriage *exists*. It exists like rattlesnakes and jumping spiders exist, whether we want them to or not."

"Oh, there's a romantic view."

"I definitely don't have a romantic view of marriage."

"Shocker."

"And for the record, I don't destroy marriages. I facilitate the unwinding of people's marital mistakes."

I raise my eyebrows. "That sounds like a convenient personal fiction."

He casts a quick glance my way. "Did I destroy your marriage?"

"No," I say. "Just my life."

He gets quiet, and for a split second, I feel a tiny bit bad. Then I quit that, because he doesn't deserve my sympathy.

"He has my quilts," I say. "Paul. He has seventeen quilts in his car—formerly *our* car—and I need them back."

Rhys's big hands, on the steering wheel, clutch tight enough that his knuckles whiten. "Is that where we're going? We're chasing Paul—to get quilts back?"

The way he says *quilts* is like the way most people say *liver*. Or *eggplant*. Or *cottage cheese*.

"They're supposed to be hung—preferably tomorrow, but as soon as possible—and go on display starting *in five days* for the entire world of quilt enthusiasts to fawn over." My voice cracks, and I'm pissed, because he doesn't deserve to know how much this matters to me. Or anything else about me. He already knows far, far too much.

He's scowling as hard as I've ever seen him scowl.

"Look," I say, biting the words out sharply, "the people who will come to this show buy tens of thousands of dollars from my shop online every year. Because I have a reputation in the quilting world as being someone who cares about the craft and supports it—who cares about and supports women artists. And right now, seeing as my romantic life has gone up in flames, my reputation in my industry, my ability to make a living, and my passion for my work are all I've got. I need this exhibit to go flawlessly. So you can either keep driving the direction I tell you or let me out so I can find another way to get there."

Rhys makes a soft huffing sound. He's quiet for a moment.

Then he says, "Well. It sounds like we're going wherever Paul is going."

I guess you could call that my first win over Rhys Hott. I only wish it felt like something worth fighting for.

"When we get to I-5, go north."

"I need to stop and call Hanna," I say once we're on I-5 and heading for Paul's destination, which is, according to Eden, his family's beach house.

Because let's review.

I'm supposed to make sure that Eden and Paul get married...and he just jilted her.

If Arthur Weggers finds out, Hanna will lose her business and we'll lose our family's land.

The bride in my car is understandably wounded and furious and determined to track down her (ex?) fiancé.

It's unclear whether this situation is salvageable at all, and if so, how I'd salvage it—but I have to try.

"Fine," she says.

When I pull over, there are twenty-seven missed calls from Hanna and another eighteen or so from my other siblings—she must have called them.

There are, however, no calls from Arthur Weggers. I'm going to take that as a good sign since I'm pretty sure he would lose no time in lording it over me if he had evidence I'd shat the bed.

I don't listen to my voicemails. I can guess what they say.

Hanna answers right away. "What the fuck, Rhys? Where are you?"

I quickly fill her in on everything that has happened since I got Paul's note and texted her, and she curses and moans for a while—as well she should, given the stakes.

But she's Hanna—ever practical—so in a few minutes she rallies and says, "You have to get them back together."

I've already thought about whether I can reunite Eden and Paul and rescue this situation for Hanna. In fact, at first, I thought that's where Eden was going. To chase down Paul, to plead with him. And as much as I didn't want that to happen, I also knew it might be the best possible outcome. For Hanna, definitely. And maybe even for Eden.

"Look," Hanna says. "I know she says she wants those quilts. But maybe that's an excuse. A way she can chase him down without looking pathetic."

"Why would she want to do that? He *jilted* her."

Hanna makes a scoffing sound. "People get cold feet!" she says. "I can't tell you how many times I've had to drag a groom out of a bar, pour water over his head and coffee down his throat, and prop him up at the altar."

"Jesus!" I say. "No wonder I have a job."

"It's not real ambivalence," she says. "They *want* to get married. They're just freaking the fuck out, because that's what people about to get married *do*. The worst case I've ever seen was two brides, both with cold feet. They're really happy now, though. I get a Christmas card every year from them thanking me for sorting them out. So that's what this is—cold feet. He just got 'em worse than average. So track him down, sober him up, and let's get this show back on the road. I told Weggers we were postponing the wedding because of a family emergency. Prove me right."

"And he bought the family-emergency thing?"

"Who knows what goes on in that man's head?" she says.

Can't argue with that. "What if I can't get them back together?"

"We can't go there," Hanna says. "We have to believe for now. Family emergency. Cold feet. Postponed wedding. Find him."

Her dogged certainty is contagious. "Okay."

"In the meantime, Arthur Weggers says you have to do all the rebooking and rescheduling yourself. Apparently you can delegate individual tasks to me, but I can't start doing damage control according to my own preferences, or you're not doing your job."

I groan. Mr. Letter of the Law. "Okay. Got it. On it. I'll contact the vendors—"

"And the guests, obviously. Tell them what we're telling Weggers."

"I can't tell Paul's parents it's a family emergency."

"Tell them it's *her* family's emergency."

"She doesn't have much family," I say, thinking, *See, I do know you.*

"And tell *her* family it's *his* family's emergency. Throw something in about everyone needing some privacy right now, so they don't compare notes."

"You're diabolical," I tell her.

"I'm good at crisis management and herding cats. You have to be, in my line of work. And in case this wasn't clear, I think you should *actually* rebook the wedding for next month so we can point to that if Weggers starts sniffing around."

"Are we available?"

"I did some scrambling and snuck her into a Sunday eleven-a.m. slot at the end of October. We'll do two that day."

"Can we pull that off?"

"We have to."

She names a date and time, and I write it down.

"Done," I say. "Or will be, as soon as I get back there."

"Which will be when?" she asks.

"Eden said he's at his family's beach house on the Washington coast, which is another...four and a half hours? We get her quilts—"

"Definitely get the quilts, but the main thing is you sit them down and make them talk it out until he realizes he was just freaking out and begs her for forgiveness and another chance. He's head over heels for her, and his ambivalence was temporary insanity caused by cold feet."

I can, unfortunately, picture the scenario Hanna is describing, and I straight-up hate it. I hate the image of Paul pleading for forgiveness, but even more than that, I hate the idea of Eden granting it. Of her slinking back into his squirrelly commitment-phobe arms and telling him that she understands his cold feet are nothing but that.

Still, there are two things I hate *almost* as much as that scenario: Hanna losing her business, and Blue Iron Mining getting my family's land.

And in the end, it doesn't matter how much I hate the idea of Eden and Paul getting back together, because even if they don't, I'm still the man who destroyed her life.

"Do you really think it's just cold feet?"

"Yes," Hanna says.

Sometimes I really appreciate my sister's clear-cut view of the world.

"I'll fix it," I tell her again and hang up.

WHEN I GET BACK into the car, Eden's on the phone.

"I know this is asking a lot, but can you take over running In Stitches till I get back?" she says to whoever it is. "Honestly, taking care of the store is the best thing you can do for me. I swear. I don't want company. I want to lick my wounds."

Silence.

"Rhys can drive me. Despite his other flaws, he seems like a safe driver."

"Thanks," I mutter, and she rolls her eyes in my direction.

I start the car again.

"He doesn't count as company," she tells the phone.

"Jesus," I say. "Tell us how you really feel."

"I love you, too, sweetie. And I'm going to be fine. I've been through worse." She's silent for a bit, then says, "I know. But I've done it before, and I can do it again... Yeah. Love you. Bye." She drops her phone into her lap, taps to hang up. "Mari," she tells me.

We both stare at the road for several miles without

speaking. I'm thinking about how to broach the million-dollar question.

"Hanna says," I begin, "that cold feet are really comm—"

"Don't," she says.

"Don't what?"

"Don't try to convince me that everything's going to be okay."

I close my mouth. Because despite Hanna's outsized optimism about Eden and Paul getting back together, I don't actually think everything's going to be okay. Even if they somehow patch up this episode of "cold feet," Paul will always be the guy who left her at the altar and humiliated her.

Under the best of circumstances, marriages are a shit show. To start one like this...

I can't wish it for her.

And yet I have to.

Fuuuuuuck me.

"I don't deserve what he did to me," she says.

"No," I agree, before I can stop myself. "You don't."

I'm sorry, Hanna.

"I'm not chasing Paul so I can talk him out of his cold feet or whatever made him jilt me."

Okay, look, I tell imaginary Hanna. *Even if it turns out Paul does just have cold feet, I'm not going to be able to convince Eden to take him back. He has to do that. I need to get them face-to-face so he can realize he's being a complete idiot.*

Because let's face it: Only a complete and total idiot would walk away from Eden Becker.

"You know what?" she says. "Let's not talk. You don't

really want to talk to me anyway. When we get to the beach house, we'll get the quilts and then get back in the car and drive again. That way we won't have to force a conversation."

"That's very...mercenary."

"Yeah, well, that's me right now. Mercenary. It's a put-one-foot-in-front-of-the-other situation, and so that's what I'm doing."

"If not-talking is what you need, then that's fine—"

"It's what you want, too," she says. "You don't want to talk to me and I don't want to talk to you, so we'd better find music we can agree on."

"I've got a driving playlist on my phone." I grab it from the door's map pocket and toss it to her. "Route 66."

"Original," she mutters.

A moment later the strains of Elliott Smith's "Waltz #2" slide from the speakers.

A couple of songs later, she bursts out, "What the *hell* is this music? You *drive* to this? I would fall asleep and swerve off the road. Or sink into despair, U-turn, and go back to wherever I came from."

"It's broody indie."

"Yeah. I get that. But how the hell is that *driving music*?"

I glance over at her. "You know," I say. "I got the impression from your divorce proceedings that you were—"

"A doormat?" she asks, and this time when I sneak a glimpse, she's glaring. "Meek? Weak? Pathetic?"

"I didn't say any of that."

"You thought it."

"Actually," I say, "I didn't."

I don't say, *I thought you were brave and beautiful.* I don't say, *That last day, when you left the courtroom, I didn't mean to follow you, but I did, and I saw you buy lunch for that homeless woman, even though we'd just taken all your money and you had every right to be selfish and keep every remaining penny to yourself.*

"I thought you were in a shitty place and needed a better advocate than Sally DeSantis," I say.

Goddamn. It turns out Eden was right—not talking would have been way better. There is no version of the universe where it's okay for me to discuss the details of her divorce with her.

"Sally did fine."

I clamp my jaw shut. Sally had traded half of Eden's time with her dog for her budding business, and she didn't have to. If she'd understood the intersection of divorce law and corporate structures better, she could have held out and gotten Eden both the business and full-time custody. And I'd hated Teller Austin, and it had just about killed me when I saw the grief on Eden's face about her dog.

"I would have done better by you," I say, because it's the only thing I *can* say.

"Yeah, well," she says, "instead you fucked me." And then, "Extremely poor choice of words."

A laugh rucks out of me.

"I really hate you," she admits.

"I'm used to it," I say, although I'm not. I'll never get used to her hating me. "Someone always hates me. Someone loves me and someone hates me, and I have to find a way to live with it."

"Boohoo-hoo," she says. "You chose to do it. You chose

to be a shark. You could have chosen to do those, what do you call 'em? Nicey-nice divorces."

"Collaborative." I bite back a smile. *Nicey-nice.* Maybe I could have at one point. But I have a reputation now. You don't ask a shark to help you figure out how to swim in the same pool as your goldfish ex.

I don't say that. I say, "Yeah."

She goes quiet, listening to Jeff Buckley's "Last Good-bye." "I do like this song," she says. "I just think your taste in music is funereal. And grossly wrong for driving."

"Well," I say. "The playlist is only ninety-seven minutes long."

8

EDEN

Five hours, two dubious sandwiches, a playlist of dreary songs, and several innings of a baseball game on the radio later, we arrive at the beach house, still not having said more than a few words to each other.

Which doesn't mean I wasn't hyperconscious of his presence. Of my decision to put myself in a car with a man I hate.

Of the sharp, electric sensation of my hatred, buzzing through my body.

There are no cars here, and the house is locked up tight.

"Jesus," Rhys says, surveying our surroundings as we unfold our stiff bodies from the seats. I put extra distance between us, grateful to be out of the car and away from him. "You said beach house. I was picturing a cabin."

The house in front of us is definitely not a cabin. It's a multistory wood-and-glass contemporary palace.

"Yeah," I say. "My in-laws-not-to-be have a lot of money."

Neither of us says anything to that.

I survey the Graves family beach castle—weathered cedar, windows facing the Pacific, carefully groomed gardens tucked around its foundation. "I really love this house. I'm going to miss it."

Right now, I'm sadder about the house than about Paul. I'm a stew of humiliation, wounded pride, and a burning desire to find my quilts. When I think about not marrying Paul, I mostly think about things I won't have: this beach house, financial security, bio-kids raised by married monogamous parents.

A question has been tickling my brain during the ride: Did I care more about what Paul could give me than Paul himself?

If Rhys has questions, he doesn't ask them. Instead he says, "He's not here. Where is he?"

He looks at me like this is a serious question. "I don't know," I tell him.

"What do you mean you don't know? Look on Find My."

"His phone's off. His last reported location was Rush Creek."

His eyebrows draw together. "Wait a second. I thought we were following him here on Find My."

I shake my head.

"We came all the way here with no idea where he is?"

"Charlie said he was here."

His look of disgust deepens. "Charlie is his *brother*. Why would he tell you the truth about where he is?"

"Because I threatened him?" I hazard.

Rhys scowls, shaking his head. "I thought you *knew* he

was here. I assumed we were following his dot on Find My. I wouldn't have driven five hours on Charlie's say-so."

I'm tired and hungry, and Rhys makes me want to dig in my heels. "Well, I don't know where he is, but Charlie said he was coming here."

"Maybe he went into town for dinner?" he suggests.

I duck my head and one arm into the cobwebby underside of the porch to extract the house key.

"Seriously?" he says. "They leave the key to their mansion under the *porch*? There's probably someone in there cooking meth."

"You're *grim*."

"I live in the real world," he says. "It's grim."

"You live in a grim corner of the real world. Everyone you meet is angry and hurting. It gives you a skewed view."

He rolls his eyes. "Thank you for the free therapy."

I climb the side steps and slide the key into the lock.

"Are you sure you should be doing that?" he asks.

"Doing what?"

"Breaking into a house that's not yours?"

I give it about three seconds of thought and conclude that Paul's decision to jilt me gives me all kinds of legal rights I wouldn't have otherwise had. "They should be glad I didn't smash a window and climb in," I tell him.

He arches an eyebrow but mounts the steps behind me.

The house is two stories, with the entrance on the bottom floor and the bulk of the house upstairs. It smells faintly of disinfectant when we enter; Paul's family has it professionally cleaned every three weeks regardless of whether they're here or not. When I learned that, I thought about my grandmother, meticulously scrubbing every corner of the house where I mostly grew up, almost completely by hand. Of course, even if she'd had enough money to hire someone to clean it, she might have insisted on doing it anyway, teeth gritted and shoulders squared, determined not to enjoy herself at any cost.

He follows me up the stairs, and I turn on the lights, flooding the big open great room. It's built out of ash-light wood, with a soaring cathedral interior and floor-to-ceiling windows that offer an unobstructed view of the Pacific. The kitchen is all pale neutrals, Scandinavian design—the expensive kind, not the Ikea version—and granite countertops.

"Nice," Rhys says.

The lights are off, the air in the house still in a way that suggests it's been days since anyone set foot inside. "It definitely doesn't look like Paul's been here." I cross to the couch and collapse onto it. "Where is he?"

"We should go back to Rush Creek," Rhys says. "We can't keep driving without knowing where we're going. He could be anywhere."

My shoulders slump. He's right. Without knowing where Paul is, we could easily have driven entirely the wrong direction. He could be halfway to the Grand Canyon by now.

I pull out my phone. Tap into Find My, and—

Paul Graves. Spokane, WA. Sixteen minutes ago.

I make a small, gleeful noise.

"What?" Rhys demands.

"Find My updated. He's in Spokane. At...a Holiday Inn Express."

Rhys groans. "That's more than six hours from here."

"But he's not moving," I say, watching the dot that is Paul. "He's probably checked in for the night, right?"

Rhys considers. "Makes sense."

"So we could catch him. Tonight."

He's shaking his head before all the words are out of my mouth. "Eden, it's after seven already—"

"I want my quilts."

"I know you're frustrated, and you need a win, but taking risks with our safety isn't—"

"You don't have to come with me," I say. "You can drop me at a rental car place, and I'll drive myself." I tap in a search for the nearest rental place, which looks like it's in Aberdeen, a half hour away—and basically on the way to Spokane. It won't take Rhys too far out of his way back to Rush Creek, either. I hold up the phone. "Drop me here."

"No."

His voice is flat. Hard. Nonnegotiable. The voice that won Teller's arguments.

"Then I'll get an Uber to take me to the nearest rental car place."

"Absolutely not. You are not driving all night. You probably slept like crap last night, you woke up at the crack of dawn to get ready for a wedding, you got your heart broken, we spent something like seven hours on the road if you count those disgusting sandwiches, you probably now have food poisoning—"

"I don't have food poisoning."

"—it's not safe for you to get back on the road and drive six hours in the middle of the night. And he's not *worth* it."

I cross my arms. "I need those quilts."

He stares at me, eyes like truth X-rays, until I look away.

And when I look back at him, something has changed in his expression. The stubbornness has gone out of it, replaced with something almost...soft.

I'm probably imagining it.

"Eden," he says. His voice has softened, too. I've never heard this version of him, but I imagine it's the voice he uses when he's trying to talk his own clients into a more reasonable position. And I don't want to wait for what he's about to say, maybe because I'm the tiniest bit afraid that he'll actually convince me. And I don't want to be convinced. I want to fly through the dark night in a fast car, fueled by righteous anger. I want cheesy pop music and the promise of my quilts and a purpose that will hold all the humiliation and sadness at bay.

I tilt my phone open and tap on the Uber app.

"Eden," he says. "What are you doing?"

"Ordering an Uber," I say. "Getting a rental car. Making sure Mari can cover the shop as long as needed. Going to get my quilts."

He closes his eyes. There's a beat of silence while I pause with my finger suspended over my car options, and I can hear both of us breathing, a little hard. Then he opens his eyes.

"Don't order the fucking Uber." His voice is both gentle and resigned. "I'll drive." His eyes narrow on me. "But we're eating dinner first, and you're sleeping in the car."

9

———————

RHYS

"**W**hat are you doing?" Eden asks a few minutes later.

This is a ridiculous question, because I'm visibly ransacking the beach house's cabinets and the refrigerator, but I answer seriously anyway: "I'm cooking dinner."

I line up my discoveries on the countertop—not exactly a woolly mammoth I've hunted, shot, and skinned, but pretty damn satisfying: One box of rigatoni, one jar of tomato-and-basil sauce, a bag of frozen green beans dated only three months ago, and a half-empty, non-moldy plastic container of grated Romano cheese. A veritable feast.

I can't undo any of the shitty things that have happened to Eden on my watch, but I can feed her.

She's staring at me.

"What?" I demand.

"I guess I wasn't expecting you to cook."

"It's not exactly gourmet. Boxed pasta, jarred sauce, frozen veg."

"I just didn't picture you cooking...anything."

"What do you think a single guy in New York City does for food?"

"Takeout."

"Your faith is touching."

"Can I—help?" she asks. She unfolds herself from the couch, stretching out long legs and pushing a strand of blond hair behind one ear. She steps toward the kitchen, lithe and fluid in motion.

Yes, I think. *You can stop being confusing and beautiful. You can stop getting divorced and married and jilted, you can stop needing to be rescued, you can hold still somewhere far away from me where I can't see or touch you.*

Somewhere along the line, maybe around the time I unzipped her dress, I stopped being strong enough to make her hate me. I started needing for her to see someone other than the asshole who'd stolen her money and her time with her dog and her *life*.

But I don't say any of that. I say, "You probably have a lot of texts and emails to reply to."

"God. I do."

"Go," I say, pointing to the couch.

She gives me an eyebrow that says, *Really? You get to boss me around?* But then she heads back to the couch and settles herself there, and I putter in the kitchen. Through the big wall of windows, as I set two pots boiling and a third with tomato sauce heating, I watch as the sun deepens toward orange. Near the horizon, where clouds have massed, the sky turns shades of pink and purple and wild blues—even green. My gaze strays back to her, curled up on the couch, long lean limbs and hair tinged gold by the dusky light.

I make myself look back at the sky.

"Sunset," I say, inclining my head toward it.

She looks up from her phone. "It's so beautiful here."

Yes, I think, admiring the way the light touches her face, licking the gleaming porcelain of her cheek. *It is.*

"Did you come here a lot with Paul?"

The words are out of my mouth before I can consider if they're a good idea, but she doesn't flinch.

"A few times," she says. "But I used to come to the beach with my dad when I was really little. When I came with Paul the first time, all these memories came flooding back. Sandcastles and kites and dipping my toes in the water and then crying because it was so cold it hurt. My dad would rub my feet to get the feeling back in them and then take me to the doughnut shop and let me pick out one doughnut for each hand."

"That's sweet."

"He was great," she says, eyes far away and sad.

I know—from the divorce and the wedding—the basics of Eden's parental situation. I'd even seen the *No* checked next to Eden's mom's name on the guest list, but I hadn't let myself think about how that might have affected Eden. Because in general, thinking about Eden was a terrible idea.

Still is, it's just that now I don't seem to be able to stop.

"He died when I was six," she says. "My mom is Caryn Simmons—"

I'd registered the fact of Eden's mom's fame, but with

the same self-imposed distance. Now I let it sink in, what that would have meant for her. "You're the child of pop royalty."

"Yeah, well, Caryn Simmons is fun for the rest of the world. Not so much for me. She was always recording or on tour. I was raised by my grandmother."

I think of her saying to Mari *I've been through worse* and *I've done it before, and I can do it again.* I've seen her put that brave face on so many times, and I wonder if each time she puts it on, it's harder to take off.

Also, there's a missing piece in there—the whole story of her relationship with her mom—but if she's not going to volunteer more, I'm not going to press.

"How's the guest situation?" I gesture at her phone.

She sighs. "Kind of a hot mess. Why did Hanna tell people the wedding is being rescheduled?"

I hesitate, but I might as well level with her. "She wanted to leave all our options open."

"I don't want my options open," she says. "I'm not taking Paul back."

I open my mouth, but she gives me a sharp warning look and I close it again. Not only because of the warning look. Because there is no bone in my body that believes taking Paul back is a good idea.

"Short term," I say instead, "it means you don't have to say you were jilted."

She ponders that. "It is kind of nice not to have to tell people the whole story," she says. "'Family emergency' is kind of great."

"Later on, you can tell them the truth if you want," I

suggest. "That your fiancé is a giant douchebag who doesn't know his ass from his elbow."

Fuck.

Sorry, Hanna! But he is!

She raises her eyebrows, amused. "That doesn't say much for my taste in men."

I stare at her.

She winces. "Yeah," she says. "Well. I'm swearing off them permanently, so you don't need to worry about me doing *that* again. I'm adopting your take on love and marriage."

She goes back to her phone, and I pull out mine.

> She's swearing off men permanently.

HANNA

> She's just saying that. When he grovels, she'll change her mind.

I don't want him to grovel.

I don't want her to change her mind.

> What do we do if she really doesn't want to marry him anymore?

There's a long pause, and then Hanna sends back:

> I'm going to pretend I didn't see that.

WE HIT the road as soon as we clean up dinner. My first act is to pull into a gas station. Eden jumps out of the car.

"Where are you going?"

"We need snacks," she says.

"We just ate."

"It's a road trip. We have to have snacks."

Eden's buoyancy is back. I'm not sure if that's a good or a bad thing. It's clear she needs to keep moving, and for now my job is to keep moving with her. Hanna obviously still believes Eden and Paul could get back together. I have my doubts—but I also know I'm not a reliable narrator. What I believe about and want from Eden doesn't live in the real world. It lives in a fantasy world where I never had to sit across a courtroom from her. Where we met under completely different circumstances, where there was no Teller Austin or Paul Graves.

That world doesn't exist, and therefore, Eden and I will keep moving. And for now, at least, I'll live in Hanna's world, the one where we're pretending we don't have a problem...yet.

I finish filling the tank while Eden's still inside. I head into the mini mart to hurry her up and discover that she's piled a basket nearly full of shiny, bright-colored snack bags.

"What's all that for?" I demand.

"To *eat*," she says, like I'm the dullest knife in the drawer.

"You're going to be sleeping, not eating," I remind her. "That was our agreement."

"I'm not sleepy," she says. "In fact, I can drive if you need me to."

I shake my head.

"Don't trust me?"

"It's not that. I'm a terrible passenger. I don't even like rideshares, but I tolerate them as long as I'm not sitting in the front seat, watching the driver's every move and awaiting my doom."

"Wow," she says. "That's—"

"I know," I say. "Grim."

"Did something happen to you as a child, Hott?"

There's a tease in her voice. It's the first time I've ever heard it, and it feels so fucking good it takes my breath away. It makes me want to tease back, to play.

"No. I was just born to be in the driver's seat."

Only the corners of her mouth tip. But it's enough. My whole body warms.

She looks away, like she didn't mean to let me see that much. When she looks back, the tease and the not-quite-smile are gone. "Do you want to pick out some of the snacks?"

I shake my head. "That shit is super unhealthy."

She gives me a disbelieving look. "Seriously?"

"What? It's true." I dig in her basket. "Cheetos? Bugles? Oreos? Cool Ranch Doritos? Do any of those even contain actual food?" I pull out the Cool Ranch Doritos and start reading the ingredients out loud, but she snatches them out of my hands.

"You don't have to eat them," she says. "But I will not allow you to kill my joy."

I roll my eyes. "The number of additives in those products will kill you *and* your joy."

She shakes her head vehemently. "Nope," she says. "They may kill me, but they will not even dampen my joy."

And with that, she takes her basket of junk food up to the front counter. I watch her go, biting back my own smile.

10

EDEN

We get back into the car, and I install myself for the long haul.

First, I tuck a fleece blanket around myself.

"Where did you get that?" Rhys asks as he starts the car and heads us north on 105.

"I poached it from my in-laws," I say.

He whistles. "You're turning out to be quite the lawbreaker."

"I think Paul and his family owe me at least this much. Especially given that he's still not responding to my texts."

"For sure," he agrees. "You probably should have taken the silver."

"I thought about it."

It turns out that it's challenging to keep hating Rhys. So far today he has rescued me from humiliation, driven me to the beach, cooked me dinner, called my ex a giant douchebag, and revealed that he has a sense of humor. It's a lot.

I open the center console, a fancy leather two-door thing. I set a bag of Sour Patch Kids, a bag of peanut butter M&M's, and the bag of Cool Ranch Doritos in the storage area.

"Easily accessible snacks," I tell him.

Rhys eyes the open console, then scowls at me. "That's my armrest."

"What do you need an armrest for?"

"To drive six hours without my right shoulder falling off."

"What are you, eighty years old?"

"Six hours is a long time."

"I told you I'd drive."

"And I told you—"

"I know, I know. That you're a control freak."

"I think the proper term is 'a car dom.'"

I swallow the snicker that boils up in me. And leave my snacks where they are.

"That armrest is *heated*," he gripes.

"Suck it up, princess," I tell him. "It's not that cold out there." I reach for the sound system.

His hand snakes in and blocks mine. "Driver controls the radio."

"No, dude. Everyone knows the passenger controls the radio. Besides, if you won't let me drive at all, that's not fair. I had to listen to ninety-seven minutes of your dirge list and way too much sports ball. We need a mood change."

I cue up my playlist and set it on shuffle. "What I've Been Looking For" from *High School Musical* comes on. Rhys groans.

"What?" I demand.

"This is from a kid's movie."

"Which you must have seen, if you know that."

"It was one of Hanna's favorites. We watched it a thousand times. Which was a thousand times too many."

"What I've Been Looking For" is followed by "Surface Pressure" and "All You Wanna Do," and Rhys says, "Please tell me this isn't all from musicals and Disney movies."

"This isn't all from musicals and Disney movies," I say as Taylor Swift's "You Belong with Me" fills the car.

Rhys's jaw ticks. His eyes roll. His shoulders twitch.

"What's wrong with this one?" I demand.

He heaves a long-suffering sigh. "He obviously *doesn't* belong with her. Let's look at the facts: She's clearly *not* his type. He wants someone who wears short skirts and high heels, and she's not comfortable in those clothes. If she keeps trying to convince him he belongs with her, they're both going to end up miserable."

I stare at his way-too-good-looking profile in the dimly lit car, agog. "Are you *serious*?"

"Would you argue with anything I've said?"

"It's a friends-to-lovers song!" I cry. "They're obviously going to end up together and be super happy. Because she sees him! And understands him. He's happy when he's with her, and that isn't true with the short-skirts-and-high-heels girl."

"I thought you were swearing off love and marriage."

"Just because I'm personally swearing off love and marriage doesn't mean I wish ill on other people who have found their perfect matches."

"*This*," he says. "This is why so many marriages end in divorce. Because we hear what we want to hear. And two people can hear the same song and find completely different meaning in it. Imagine if you were with a guy and this was your song, and every time you heard it you thought about how cool it was that he'd finally seen you for the awesome bleachers girl you are, and he thought about his ex-girlfriend and her short skirts and high heels and how he wished you'd get some personal style."

"Grim!"

"Realistic," he corrects.

One of his hands leaves the wheel. Settles briefly near his knee. Creeps into my Cool Ranch Doritos bag.

"What are you *doing*?" I shriek.

"Stress eating," he says. "Your playlist has driven me to it."

I do everything in my power not to crack a smile. "You don't eat junk food," I point out.

"That was before I realized that despite being divorced by a sociopath and jilted by a personality potato, you still believe in true love."

I can't help it; I snort at *personality potato*. "*I'm* the one who has the stress. I'm the one who got jilted. And if I'd known I was going to have to share my precious Cool Ranch, I would have gotten a bigger bag."

I sneak a peek at him. He's definitely trying not to laugh. And unfortunately, it looks good on him. I let him have the Doritos.

"God, these are disgustingly tasty," he says.

"Right?"

We're both quiet for a moment, worshipping at the altar of fake food. He quietly licks Cool Ranch flavor off his fingers, and I absolutely, one hundred percent, do *not* wonder how his tongue feels licking up the inside of his finger and across the tip of his thumb. How it would feel rasping over my own fingertips, drawn into the heat of his mouth.

Oh, hell.

I've tumbled into a sexual fantasy about a man who disassembled me like a kid's discarded playset.

We make our way through Maroon 5's "Memories" ("Memories of how I cribbed this entire song from Pachelbel's Canon," Rhys says grumpily), past Lake Street Dive's "Hypotheticals" ("Now this is actually a great song; you're one for, what, a hundred?") to "Try Everything."

"That's shitty advice," he says. "'Try everything.' I mean, *no*. There are a lot of things that are straight-up bad ideas. Bull-riding. Free solo climbing. Base jumping. Heli-skiing. Recreational fentanyl."

"She doesn't mean literally *everything*," I say.

"See?" he says. "And there we have it. Two people, same song, totally different interpretations."

I roll my eyes. "I don't see how that's somehow a refutation of marriage. You're so—"

"Pessimistic? Cynical? Misanthropic?"

"All of the above. You ready to tell me what childhood wound made you this way?" I ask, half-teasing...half...not.

He shrugs.

"Yes, Eden," I say, pitching my voice low to roughly imitate his. "Since we have another five and a half uninterrupted hours of being stuck in this car together with absolutely nothing else to do, I would love to tell you all about my childhood."

Rhys is quiet for a moment. Then with a sigh, he says, "What do you want to know?"

"You have, like, five siblings, right?"

"I have, in fact, exactly five siblings. Hanna and four brothers."

"You're all sort of Rush Creek famous at this point. I can't remember all the stories, but there's a chemist, right?"

"Quinn."

"And a movie actor—Shane. His name I know. Everyone knows his name. And his—"

"Don't say it!"

"—*backside*," I conclude. "We should just acknowledge, since we are in this car together for five and a half more hours, that I have, in fact, watched your brother doing the d—"

"And then there's my brother Preston," Rhys interrupts decisively. "Preston used to be in finance, and now he's *finding himself* in Rush Creek. God only knows what he'll end up doing. Maybe bull-riding."

"You changed the subject."

"You noticed. And then there's Tucker. He's our big mystery. Broody and mostly absent, and if anyone tries to get him to talk about what's going on with him, he closes up like a Venus flytrap devouring its prey."

"So you all grew up together in Rush Creek."

He gets quiet. It's not only that he stops talking. He gets quiet all over, his big, leanly muscled body statue-still. "Yeah," he says.

I decide I'm going to wait him out. I sit in silence, too, staring straight ahead as he merges onto I-5 north, not sure if he'll say anything else but not willing to give up on the possibility yet.

Even though I don't know why I want to know. I don't know why, suddenly, after hating him, I want a glimpse of the man, not the lawyer.

We go three exits before he says, "We thought we were gonna run the ranch together when we grew up. We actually swore a blood oath." He laughs, but it's not a real laugh. It's bleak and humorless, and it hurts my chest. "Kids, right? They have no idea."

"Do you ever wish you did? Run the ranch?"

"Hell no," he says. "That's not me. I never loved that work. I just—" He bites down on whatever he'd been about to say.

I take a stab. "Love your siblings?"

He slides me a surprised glance. "Yeah."

"Do you ever think about practicing in Rush Creek or somewhere on the West Coast? Instead of New York?"

Rhys shakes his head. "No. New York is where I belong. It suits my cold, sharky soul."

I file this away. It's exactly the way I would have described him when we were adversaries—if I'd admitted that he had a soul at all. And yet now that he's cooked dinner for me and insisted on driving the next leg of this impulsive trip, I'm pretty sure he does have a soul. Which calls into question both "cold" and "sharky."

"What made you want to become a divorce attorney?"

"It's lucrative. And combative."

That's definitely the shark answer. I wait.

He gives a half shrug, shifting his hands uneasily on the

wheel. "And I wanted to keep more women from getting screwed."

My eyebrows practically hit Earth's orbit. "Yet you represent assholes like Teller Austin and steal money and dogs from women who didn't do anything to deserve it?"

Okay, it's all *true*, but as soon as the words are out of my mouth, I regret them. Not because they're not accurate, but because I know they'll shut down this conversation, and I don't want that. "Uh," I say. "That was...harsh. Can we strike that from the record?"

Rhys makes an amused sound. "Sure, I guess. I mean, I deserved it. But yeah."

He's silent again as the road rolls under us, and I figure I've probably killed the conversation anyway, but then he says, "I took on Teller's case because a colleague begged me to, and I made the mistake of thinking if Teller was Jacoby's cousin, he had to be a good guy. And even though I strongly suspected that he was full of shit in absolutely everything he said, and particularly what he said about you, I couldn't prove it, so I didn't have cause to fire him as a client. But I fucking hated every minute of it. And—" He hesitates. "I did everything I could to rein him in."

Oh.

"I'm sorry about what I did to you," he says, taking his eyes off the road again for a split second. But it's long enough for me to see his sincerity. "If I could take it back, I absolutely, one hundred percent would." He returns his gaze to the highway, jaw tight. "I'm not supposed to say that. You could totally use this against me in a court of law."

Oh.

I'm suddenly remembering something.

"Sally got an anonymous email," I say. "It said I should dig back through my emails and texts to see if maybe I'd talked about the quilt shop idea with someone else before I met Teller. If maybe I'd taken a step or two to try to get the business started, like doing some informational interviews with other quilt shop owners. Since that would mean that Teller's claim on the business would be far looser." My face is on fire, my hands so hot I want to shake them. "You didn't by any chance...?"

"Please don't ask me whatever you're about to ask me, Eden," he breaks in. He's staring straight ahead, through the windshield.

So I don't.

It feels like I've been carved open, like my insides have tumbled out and been rearranged. I have to start over and make sense out of everything that happened all over again, from the beginning.

Rhys isn't the guy who took my life apart. He's the man who made sure I kept my business so I could rebuild my life when I moved to Rush Creek.

He sighs. "I'm especially sorry about Milo. So fucking sorry."

Milo. He remembers my dog's name.

"If it helps at all, I tried—everything. Teller was determined. He got his teeth into the idea of taking your dog, and nothing I could say made the slightest difference. I talked him down from trying for full custody. For what it's worth."

I'm not sure what to say. Or what to feel. "Oh," I manage, out loud this time. Feebly.

We're both quiet for a while. Then I say, "I—appreciate that."

There's an unfamiliar warmth in my stomach.

"Milo's with Teller right now?"

"Yeah."

"And you haven't…" He hesitates. "Gotten another dog?"

"I've wanted to. But I worry it wouldn't understand why Milo has to leave for six months a year. You can't exactly say, 'Your buddy is going to be with his daddy, but he'll be back, so don't be sad!'"

It's the first time I've told anyone that, even Mari, and my eyes get damp.

"Shit," Rhys says. Just that one word. But it's loaded with so much misery and sympathy that it, oddly, makes me feel better. It makes me feel heard.

Now and again the headlights illuminate the land around us—an expanse of rolling swamp land, a river snaking through it, hills like mountains in training. A few minutes later, the scattered suggestion of a town and a casino. He passes a slow-moving truck, then clears his throat.

"You asked what got me into divorce law. It was more complicated than wanting to arm wrestle and get rich."

Nothing he says to me now will surprise me. "I figured."

"My mom's first marriage was to a guy whose money and power she mistook for love, and she got completely screwed in the divorce. My aunt Meryl's first and only marriage was, if possible, even more of a disaster, and she ended up with basically nothing—and no skills, either. By then I was old enough to actually see the whole thing play out, and I heard her and my mom talking a lot about it. And in my head, I was like, that's so fucking unfair. So when Preston didn't come back to run the ranch and it became clear that we weren't going to stick to the oath, I knew what I wanted to do."

I still don't understand, because representing guys with money and power while they screw over women with none doesn't feel like fighting back for his mom and aunt. And he must sense that, because there's a defensive edge in his voice when he speaks again.

"Fully ninety percent of my clients are women. You don't get to be the most loathed divorce attorney in New York City by representing rich and powerful men. You get there by sticking it to rich and powerful men." He sighs. "But then magazines like *The Newer York* and *MANhattan* want to do a profile, and they want to interview Teller Austin, who's talking about how I'm 'willing to do what has to be done.'"

And that makes a hell of a lot more sense. In fact, pretty much everything about Rhys suddenly makes a hell of a lot more sense.

Sharks don't drop everything and take on roles they're ill-suited for to make things right for their sisters. They don't drive six hours for a pile of someone else's quilts. They don't dig around in cabinets to cook dinner for someone who's had a shitty day. And they don't pull a second shift through the night to keep someone they barely know from doing something dangerous and impetuous on too little sleep.

Most of all, they don't violate their own sense of honor and justice to save David from Goliath.

Rhys is wearing a shark suit, but he's something else underneath.

I need to know what.

11

RHYS

I'm relieved when Eden finally nods off, her head tipped against a bit of the fleece blanket she's folded between her and the window.

I'm glad to see her eyes closed. To hear her breathing even out and deepen.

Partly because it gives me a minute to think.

I can't believe she guessed about the email. And I can't believe I confirmed it for her.

If anyone ever finds out, I'll be disbarred.

Still, I wouldn't take it back. If I had to do it over again, I'd do it the same way.

And I'm not sorry she knows.

We climb the mountains while she sleeps, a little rain falling as we pass through the Cascades' windward towns. This drive is better in the daytime, obviously, but at least there's no chance of freezing in early September.

The car's clock tips over past midnight.

We've just crossed the Columbia River, following the

freeway on its turn north, when the engine stutters the first time.

I tell myself I imagined it. Because that's the kind of thing you'd imagine. Driving a rented luxury car, jilted bride sleeping in the seat next to you. Chasing her fiancé across the state of Washington. And then: car trouble.

Seriously, that can't happen in real life.

Even so, I'm braced, listening, for miles.

I've just relaxed when it comes again. And this time it's not so much a stutter as a—pause. Like a broken heart.

Fuuuuck.

I take the next exit and find myself...in the middle of nowhere.

Eden rouses. "What?" she asks. "Where are we? What are you doing?"

"Shh," I say. "Go back to sleep. It's nothing."

The engine chooses that moment to jolt alarmingly.

"That didn't sound like nothing," she says, sitting fully upright. "And neither does *that*."

The engine's whining now, like a child about to tantrum, which is pretty apt. And I'm not the guy who changes his own oil or tinkers under the hood, but I did grow up on a ranch driving aging trucks, so I recognize the sound of a failing fuel pump.

"Can you GPS the nearest gas station for me?" I ask her.

She does and gives me directions.

We really are fucking nowhere. In the dark, the landscape is featureless. Part of me wonders if I should have stayed on the highway, called for a tow. The rental car company would have been on the hook to arrange it. Now we're here. Wherever here is.

When we reach it, several miles later, the gas station has two aging gas pumps and a single garage. Miraculously, blessedly, there's someone inside the tiny booth area. A twentysomething guy in a Cougars snapback, video from his phone throwing colored light back on his face. He puts the phone down and eyes Eden and me with curiosity.

"You have a repair shop?" I ask him.

"My aunt's," he says.

"We have a fuel pump issue."

"She's out of town till late tomorrow night."

Well, shit. I look over at Eden; she mouths, *Quilts.*

"We can't wait that long," I say. "Any chance you could tow us somewhere that can help us right away?"

He gives me a skeptical glance. "Tomorrow's Sunday, man. You're not going to find anyone around here who's going to take care of it on a Sunday. Your best bet's to leave it here and Aunt Jane will take care of it first thing Monday."

I turn to Eden. She can barely keep her eyes open, lashes fluttering against her cheekbones in long blinks as I watch. I want to pull her into my arms and let her rest against my chest.

She's not yours to comfort, I remind myself. *She's a client's ex. And if this wedding can still work out, you owe it to Hanna —and to all your siblings—to give that every chance to happen. And hugging the bride, touching your lips to her hair, breathing in her scent...does* not *support that goal.*

"We could leave it here, try to get another rental?" I murmur to her.

"Yeah." She sounds exhausted. "It's not like we can drive it, can we?"

I hate the defeat in her voice, but I shake my head. We could nurse it a little longer, but it's going to die on us at some point soon. She pulls out her phone, and I know she's looking at Find My again.

"He still in Spokane?"

"Yeah?"

"What do you think he's doing there?"

"I don't know," she says. "He grew up there. Maybe he still knows people?"

"In which case he might stick around a couple days."

"He might?"

I make an executive decision, based on how bushed she looks—and how tired I am. I was up early this morning, too, and it's almost 1:00 a.m. I *could* drive another few hours, but by the time we lay hands on another car and get going...

"We should stay the night." I look to Snapback Guy. "Where's the nearest hotel?" I figure I'll call an Uber to get us back here in the morning.

"My aunt rents the room over the garage," he says. "Hundred bucks a night, clean sheets, pullout couch, full bath, hair dryer, fridge, microwave, TV. I'll bring you takeout from the local diner at eight tomorrow morning, included."

I look at Eden. She's leaning against the wall, her face pale, circles under her eyes.

Normally I'm a chain-hotel kind of guy—and a luxury chain at that, but Eden's blinks are getting longer and longer, and I need to see her cozy in a bed.

"We'll take it," I say.

12

———————

EDEN

Rhys unlocks the flimsy door with an actual metal key and makes a weird deflating-balloon noise when he looks inside.

I peer past him.

It's not awful.

It looks clean.

There's a bed, a couch, a coffee table, a small dresser, and a nightstand. One of us will have to take the bed and the other the pullout. I normally hate pullouts—thin mattress, poky springs—but I'm so tired, I almost don't care.

It occurs to me, suddenly, that neither of us has pajamas with us.

What will we sleep in?

Does Rhys look as good out of his clothes as he does in them?

"Hey," he says, and I swim to the surface of this flustering line of thought to find him watching me with one eyebrow arched, amused. "I'll take the pullout."

"Don't be ridiculous," I say. "You drove the whole day. You need good rest way more than I do."

Also, he's about twice my size, which means his weight will sag a pullout even more than mine. He's way taller than I am. And—I eye him—broader.

Not hating Rhys has done something unfortunate to my brain. Because while I always knew, intellectually, that he was ridiculously attractive, now I *know*.

Broad shoulders. Muscles that strain the seams of his expensive dress shirt. At some point tonight, he rolled his sleeves, and his forearms are bare. They're strong and sinewy and end in thick wrists and tapered fingers, the ones he was licking earlier...

Do. Not. Lick. The. Lawyer.

It's just that I'm exhausted and my defenses are down. Impulse control is the first thing to go, right? And judgment?

Obviously, I don't actually *want* to lick the lawyer. I was jilted *this morning*.

"Eden," he says.

I pull my gaze away from his forearms and find him watching me, a question in his eyes.

Whoops.

"I'm really tired," I explain.

"Which is why you're taking the bed," he says.

"We don't even know if the couch is halfway comfortable."

"It's *fine*." He tugs it open—blessedly, it's already made up—and settles his body onto it.

It sags like a hammock in the middle.

"No way that will be comfortable all night. Get up."

He pounds a fist against the sorry excuse for a mattress. "No. I'm happy here."

"Get. Up."

The corner of his mouth turns up. "Whoa. Bossy. Nope."

I try to wrestle him off the pullout, grabbing his arm and tugging, then reaching for his shoulders and rolling, but he's utterly immovable, even stronger than he looks. Under my hands, his body is warm and hard, all muscle, and unwanted warmth washes through me. I drop my grip, suddenly hot all over.

"Look in my bag," he says.

"What?"

"My bag." He points to his laptop bag, leaning against the cheap pressboard dresser.

I eye him suspiciously.

"I did some petty larceny of my own," he says, corner of his mouth quirking again.

I open his messenger bag and find two unopened toothbrushes, a half-empty tube of toothpaste, and two Old Spice deodorants in plastic shrink wrap. "I figured Paul and his family owed *me* that much," he says. "And they apparently stock the beach house from Costco—good news for us."

I have never been so glad to see a toothbrush in my life.

Also, I have a plan for getting Rhys to sleep in the bed.

I take one of the toothbrushes and the toothpaste into the bathroom and brush my teeth. The bathroom is small and basic—a sink with a single vanity door, painted white, a stall shower—but like everything else, it's clean, and I sigh with relief as I scrub my teeth and then use the small bar of soap and provided washcloth to wash my face.

Then I shuck my sweatpants, remove my underwear, pull my sweats back on, and rinse my thong carefully in the sink, wringing it out in a hand towel and hanging it on the bathroom's least conspicuous hook. I cover it with the hand towel, hoping Rhys won't move the towel and see it.

I come out, past where Rhys is sitting on the pullout peering at his laptop, and slide under the bedcovers. They're cool and soft, and they smell clean, and for a moment, I question the sanity of my plan to give Rhys the bed.

But he drove me eight hours today without complaining. He fed me dinner.

He saved my business.

I mean, he didn't do that *today*. But he did do it.

It means the score between us is even, which means that after he spent today taking care of me, the least I can do is let him get a good night's sleep.

As soon as I'm settled, he gets up and goes to the bathroom, and I get out of the bed and hurry to the pullout.

In the bathroom, the shower turns on with a quiet groan of pipes and a rush of water.

Oh. He's taking a shower.

Which means he's stripping off his clothes in there. Unbuttoning the expensive dress shirt. Unbuckling his belt —probably supple Italian leather—and unfastening his pants. Letting his clothes fall to the floor... No. He's probably carefully folding his clothes—not letting them touch the floor—and setting them on the edge of the sink, after first checking to make sure the counter isn't damp.

Hopefully he's not peeking under the hand towel I hung over my thong.

I hear the cadence of the water change as he steps under it, and my palms get hot.

I will not picture him soaping himself in the shower.

I will not picture him soaping himself in the shower.

What is *wrong* with me? This morning—I guess technically yesterday morning, since it's God Knows What O'Clock—I was engaged to marry Paul Graves. By noon I'd been jilted, and now, a little over twelve hours later, I'm fantasizing about another man.

Or *not* fantasizing about him. But still.

The events of the day have destroyed my sanity. That's all.

The water shuts off.

There's a pause—him toweling himself off?—and I hear the water running in the sink. Brushing his teeth. The door opens, and he steps back in.

His eyes find me on the pullout. "No."

I look over at him. He's wearing a plain white T-shirt and boxer shorts, and I have to immediately look away because it feels way too intimate to see him like that. And because his legs are tree-trunk thick, with the perfect amount of dark curly hair.

He strides across the room, scoops me off the pullout like I weigh nothing, and carries me to the bed. His body is a wall of muscle, and he smells—God, he smells good. His T-shirt is soft and still scented with laundry soap but also musky with today's efforts, and under that, I can smell hotel soap and Old Spice, the clean scent of his skin, and I turn my head to get closer—

He deposits me unceremoniously, and I try not to want it back: his warmth and scent and strength.

I'm just feeling needy because I was dumped *this morning*.

He glares at me, then crosses back to the pullout and plops himself down.

"Go to sleep," he says.

13

RHYS

The 8:00 a.m. breakfast knock comes *way* too soon. Because of course Eden was right; the pullout is wretched, and I can't actually sleep a whole night in it. At some point while Eden is quietly snoring away, I roll myself between two halves of the blanket and sleep the rest of the night on my back on the floor. It's carpeted, but ouch. And still better than the pullout mattress.

I answer the door, accept the breakfast plates, and tip Snapback Guy—whose name is actually Joe.

"Thank you for saving our asses last night," I tell him. "We really needed a place to stay, and this was perfect."

He waves off my thanks. "My aunt's still on track to be back tonight, and she can look at the car first thing tomorrow."

"No chance anyone around here might be able to look at it today?"

"Give it a go," he says. "Call around. But I don't know of

anyone within an hour of here who works Sundays. If you find someone, I'll tow you there."

"Thanks, man. That's awesome."

He waves that off, too.

"I'll look into rental-car options, too. Any chance you'd be interested in returning mine once it's functional?"

He gives me a look I recognize as an inquiry about price. "Depends on how far you have to drive it," I say, "but I'll pay twice what you could make doing anything else with your time, for as long as it takes to get there and back. And obviously anything else, like gas, snacks."

He grins. "Sounds like a sweet gig. You're on. Just let me know where it needs to get back to."

When he leaves, I check out the plates he's left us. Breakfast is hot: pancakes, bacon, hashbrowns, scrambled eggs, fruit—plus coffee and OJ. Eden's still snoring, and I don't know if I should wake her for hot food or let her sleep, but while I'm trying to decide, she stirs and opens her eyes.

"That smells *amazing*," she says.

"Do you want it in bed?"

Her eyes get huge. "Do you know what's weird? I don't think I've ever eaten breakfast in bed."

I frown. That's not okay. "In case you were still in any doubt, you've been with assholes."

"Not gonna argue with *that*," she says.

"You know my feelings about serious relationships, but if I were *ever* to allow myself to be in one—" I pause, because I'm wondering whether to say *again*, to bring up Fay and my one failed long-term attempt at lifelong monogamy. I decide against it. "I'd definitely bring her breakfast in bed."

"Ah. You do have a romantic bone in your body. I was wondering."

"Does it count as a romantic bone if it's purely hypothetical? If I were foolish enough to get myself in a relationship, which I would never do, *then* I would do a thing? I don't think that's romantic. It's more just...analytical. The correct course of action in scenario X is Y."

"Uh-huh," she says, pressing her lips together like she's trying not to laugh.

We sit on opposite ends of the couch and eat our breakfasts. It feels like ten years since dinner last night, despite all the junk food we chowed in the car, and I'm ravenous. I plow through the entire plate of food, and then I look over and she's done the same. She looks at my plate, and then we look at each other and laugh.

"That was really fucking good," I say, and she says, "God, it so was."

"At home I eat an egg-white omelet with veggies and a bowl of steel-cut oats with raisins and nuts," I confess.

"Of course you do."

"And you eat a bag of Doritos and a bag of peanut butter M&M's."

Eden rolls her eyes at me. "I actually have granola with milk—thank you very much."

She checks her phone. "Paul's still in Spokane. Whew."

"Still in the hotel?"

"For now."

"You said the quilts were supposed to be hung today."

"That was the original plan. The show starts Thursday. I have a little grace period, but not much."

If we overtake Paul immediately, we'll be fine. If he leads us on a longer chase...

I don't let my mind go there. "I'm going to search for alternate rental options," I say.

She nods. "I'll shower."

I find a car pretty quickly on my phone—it looks like it would be about a twenty-minute ride to the rental car place, and it's in the right direction. Worst case we might be able to pay Joe or one of his buddies to drop us off.

But when I try to book the car, the site freezes.

I grab my laptop out of my messenger bag, which is leaning against the wall not far from the bathroom. There's a gap under the bathroom door, and the steam from Eden's shower, scented with strawberry from the shampoo and conditioner Joe's aunt provided, wafts to my nose.

Funny, it didn't smell nearly this good when I was the one washing in it. Something about the fact that I know Eden is running her fingers through her hair as fragrant lather spills over her naked body—

Rhys Hott, get your mind out of her shower.

It doesn't help that last night, when I went to shower, I accidentally dislodged a hand towel, which fell to the bathroom floor, revealing Eden's lacy pale blue thong. I quickly picked up the towel and replaced it, but the sight of those flimsy panties would not leave my mind. Plus, the presence of them in the bathroom meant that they weren't on her body. Which meant that she had nothing on under her sweatpants.

Fuck. Me.

Thankfully, the shower shuts off right then.

I open my laptop and try once more to book the local car, but the site freezes again.

I call the rental car company and get told I have a one-hour-and-twenty-seven-minute wait for customer service.

"Any luck?" Eden asks.

I turn and see her, standing in the door of the bathroom. She's wrapped in one of the room towels, another one twisted around her hair. Her skin glows a soft pink from the heat of the shower, dewy and fresh, and my eyes linger on the upper slope of her pretty tits. The towel touches her thighs, barely long enough to make her fit for public viewing, and it still feels indecent in a way that stirs my cock under the thin cloth of my boxers. If she shrugged, I'd see everything.

"Rhys?" she prompts. "Any luck with the rental car?"

I tear my eyes from her soft, pale thigh and meet hers. She raises her eyebrows, and I know I've been caught. But she doesn't look mad. She looks—amused. Her gaze tangles with mine, and it's teasing, until I look away. Heat swims through my veins and settles, heavy, in my cock.

Shit.

This. This is why it was easier when she hated me. When she thought I was the enemy. The last thing I need is an invitation to do what can only be disastrous for all of us —her, me, Hanna.

"Rhys?" Eden repeats, and the tease is gone. Maybe I imagined it. Maybe I wanted to hear it enough that I hallucinated it.

"Uh," I attempt. "Um. Not so far. I think we need to

show up at the desk. I can't book it online and I can't get customer service on the phone."

She nods at that. "I'll get dressed and see what I can do to get us a ride. Where are we going?"

"I'll text you the address."

And then I grab the pile of my clothes and lock myself in the bathroom, shutting the door behind me like there's a zombie outside instead of the most desirable almost-naked woman I've ever seen.

14

EDEN

Huh, I think.

Rhys's eyes have just been *all* over me. I'm still tingly from the experience.

Unless I imagined it? Maybe he was looking at me judgmentally, like, *Put some clothes on, woman! No one wants to see that!*

Regardless, I grab my dirty clothes from yesterday, and—

Shit.

My thong is still hanging in the bathroom.

I knock on the door.

"What?" comes back a rough voice.

"My, um—" I roll my eyes at myself. He has a sister. It's not like he's never seen women's underwear. "If you kind of ball up the towel that's hanging there, my panties are, um, inside, and you can toss me the whole thing—" *Without, you know,* touching *them.*

Although I don't *hate* the thought of him touching them.

I sort of like it…

Jilted! common sense reminds me. *You're supposed to be mourning Paul.*

Paul who? my brain sends back.

A moment later the door opens and my thong flies at me. It's air-dried nicely. Phew.

As I slip it on, I don't let myself dwell on the fact that he did, indeed, touch it.

No more washing the undies in the sink and sleeping commando. It causes *thoughts*. And *feelings*.

First stop today—undie shopping.

Rhys emerges from the bathroom a few minutes later, dressed, hair rumpled but damp and semi-styled. He doesn't meet my eyes. Which is fair. The thong thing was kind of awkward.

Or at least that's one word for it.

I can feel the thong between my legs. It's just so *thongy* today. I don't remember ever being as aware of it before.

I wonder if he's thinking about it, too.

Oh, my God, Eden, stop!

In an effort to reset my horny monkey brain, I check my phone, which opens to Find My.

For a second, I'd almost forgotten about Paul. The quilts. The broken-down car. The fact that Rhys and I aren't just two people having breakfast together on a slightly awkward, unintentional road trip.

"Oh, shit," I say as I take in what I'm seeing.

"What?"

"Paul's on the move again."

"Where is he?"

"He just entered Montana on 90."

His brow furrows. "Where do you think he's going?"

"I don't know," I admit. "He went to college in Bozeman, so—maybe he's on his way to see someone? Or..."

Something has occurred to me. I literally can't believe I didn't think of it sooner. I think it's testament to how whirlwind yesterday was and how much my attention was focused on the quilts, because once it jumps into my head, I can't unthink it.

I bite my lip.

"What?" he asks.

"Before Paul moved to Rush Creek, he lived in Sioux Falls. With his—"

My heart is pounding. I can't make myself finish the sentence. *With his previous girlfriend. Grace Vain.*

When I look up, Rhys is watching me. Like he knows exactly what I was going to say. His expression is wary and also pitying. "You're probably right about Bozeman," he says, but he can't make it sound convincing.

He thinks I might be right. About where Paul went.

I look down at my phone again.

"What are you doing?" His voice is alarmed.

"Looking at his social media."

"Don't do that."

"I just need to know."

His voice is gruff. Irritated. "You need to know what?"

"Where he's going."

"And how will you find that out?"

"Maybe he posted something."

He's shaking his head. "Eden—"

I ignore him, tapping open Facebook. Instagram. Threads. Bluesky.

Paul hasn't posted anything on social media.

But maybe his parents have?

"Eden," Rhys says, more sharply, but I ignore him.

There's nothing obvious on his mother's Instagram. Nothing that says *My son just called off his wedding to chase after his ex-girlfriend who is clearly the love of his life.*

But now that I've let myself think it, I can't let it go.

I pull up Grace's Insta feed, scroll back, and there it is.

Grace has posted a photo of herself, looking fabulous. Long shapely legs under a short, flared skirt, a blouse that nips in at her slim waist. Shiny dark hair to her shoulder blades, smoky eyes, berry-red lips. And beneath it, the caption: *Hey all. Doing this on social media to get it done all at once. Henry and I called off our engagement. It was a mutual decision, and we're both doing okay with it. Thanks for not asking too many questions for a little while.*

Posted less than twenty-four hours before Paul's disheveled appearance at our last pre-wedding meeting.

I'm going to be sick.

I sink down onto the bed for a moment until the sensation passes.

"Eden," Rhys says again, this time gently. And he takes the phone out of my hand and turns it so he can see what I was looking at. He makes a sound—a grunt of dismay.

I try to grab the phone back from him, but he holds it out of my reach.

"What difference does it make now?" he asks.

"I need to know."

"You should turn it off. Put it away."

"I need to know," I repeat. "Give me the fucking phone."

His eyes widen. He lets me have the phone.

I scroll back in Grace's feed. Days. Weeks. Months. It's a cascade of photos of her and her ex-fiancé, Henry. We sail back in time through a parade of beaming good times— posing at the Falls of the Big Sioux, paddleboarding, a Fourth of July barbecue with friends, rafting, kite-flying, a Memorial Day picnic with her family, an Easter egg hunt with his family, her making a birthday wish with eyes squeezed tightly shut as Henry looks on adoringly, and then, there it is, six months back: a candlelit dinner for two, Henry's hands extended with the ring box open.

Henry proposed to Grace ten days before Paul proposed to me.

Paul proposed to me *because* Henry proposed to Grace.

Because Grace said yes.

Because Grace was going to marry someone else, someone who wasn't Paul.

"Paul *revenge proposed* to me," I say to the quiet room.

"It might be coinci—" Rhys tries, but I cut him off.

"I knew he wasn't over her. I fucking *knew*, and he told me a million times he was, and I still knew, and I believed him anyway."

Rhys swivels toward me. The movement's abrupt, but his expression isn't angry. It's something else, something I could almost mistake for sympathy if I didn't know better. "Hey. Hey. If you knew how many women could say those exact words...it doesn't make you foolish or stupid or any of the things you're beating yourself up with—"

I cut him off, afraid that if he keeps being that nice to me, I'll cry. "You were right," I say. "You were totally fucking right."

"About what?" he says, and I can tell: He doesn't want to be right this time. Well, too bad.

"Relationships are a joke. Marriage is a disaster. And love is a fantasy."

He looks like he wants to say something, like he wants to argue with me.

Instead he says, voice steely, "We need to get those quilts."

15

RHYS

I couldn't keep Teller Austin from destroying Eden's life two years ago.

I couldn't keep Paul from being a pile of dog turd in the park. And I can't unsee how much it hurt her to discover the truth.

But I can definitely help her get those quilts back.

We just need a car.

Joe drops us at the rental place company in nearby Galilee, which—I learn—is a well-known central Washington tourist town.

The rental car desk is staffed by a solitary gray-haired woman wearing a Wonder Woman sweatshirt and a weary expression. When Eden and I step through the door, she says, "Please tell me you're not here because you want to rent a car."

"Bad news," I tell her.

"Not as bad as the news I have for you," she counters.

"No cars?"

"Worse than that. The platform that our software runs

on got hacked overnight. One of those…what do you call 'em? Denial-of-service attacks. Some kind of security vulnerability in the"—she gestures at the ceiling—"cloud."

Eden makes a soft sound of despair.

"How long is that going to be?" I ask.

She shrugs. "We've been told it should be up and running again by mid to late afternoon."

"Will you have a car for us then?"

She wrinkles her nose. "I *should*? But without being able to look at the computer I can't say for hundred percent sure."

"Look," I say, "this is pretty important to us." I dig in my wallet and come up with a hundred-dollar bill. "Could you call me on my cell as soon as the software is up and running again?"

Wrinkles appear in between her eyebrows. "I'm not allowed to take bribes—"

"It's not a bribe," I say. "It's a tip."

She looks at the money, then back at me. "Sure," she says, lifting one shoulder.

"And there's another hundred for you if a car's available when that happens."

She thinks about that for a moment, then says, "I'll call you. Regardless."

"Thanks," I say.

We step outside the rental car office, and Eden sighs heavily. Resigned.

"We could hire someone," I tell her. "We could pay someone to drive us—"

"All the way across Montana *and* South Dakota? That's got to be eighteen hours."

"Someone will do it for enough money. And we might catch Paul before he gets to Sioux Falls."

She closes her eyes. "We can't," she says.

"We—can't?"

"He blocked me."

"He *blocked* you?"

"Yeah, I got ragey about him chasing after his ex-girl-friend and sent a text that said, 'You need to turn that car around right now and bring me my quilts, or I'm going to call the cops and tell them you're in possession of stolen property.'"

I whistle admiringly. "You're a bona fide badass."

She blushes. "Thanks. But I was a hundred percent bluffing, and he called my bluff by blocking me, which kind of fucks us for finding him before he reaches Grace's place."

I can still picture the crushed look on Eden's face when she put two and two together about Paul's probable where-abouts. "If that's even where he's going."

"That's where he's going," she scoffs. "We both know that's where he's going."

For her sake, I want to believe it's not true...but the evidence, even circumstantial, is pretty damning.

"So what we *really* need to do is fly to Sioux Falls."

She ponders that for a moment. "Intercept him there, you mean."

"Probably the fastest way to retrieve the quilts, right?"

Because whatever her reasons are for wanting to reach Paul, I can get her that one win. And getting wins is—well, it's not just my job. It's my calling.

I want Eden to get this fucking win.

And *then* I'll figure out how I'm going to save my sister's business and my family's land.

After another hesitation, she says, "Right."

We sit down on the curb outside the rental car office and search up flights.

A few minutes later, after coming to terms with how long it takes to get from the middle of Washington to the middle of the country, we have morning flights into Sioux Falls and a promise from Joe to drive us to a Spokane hotel near the airport for the night. Even if the flight's not till tomorrow morning, and even if we have to fly hundreds of miles south to hit a point that's due east of here, it'll still get us to Sioux Falls more efficiently than driving, and then we just have to find Grace Vain...and Paul.

"Now what?" I ask her. "We have some time to kill."

She gives a wry laugh. "I need to go shopping."

16

RHYS

"Shopping?"

"I need some—underthings."

"Ah." Of course, I instantly picture the pale blue thong, the soft slip of its lace between my fingers, even though I tried not to savor—or even notice—the feel of it. It probably wouldn't go over too well if I suggested that she rinse and re-wear it every day because I like picturing it on her. And off her. "Right. Me, too. And another shirt. Guessing I'm not going to find my usual brands here."

"I believe you're what we call *shit out of luck*," she says, biting her lip to hold back a smile.

I force myself to look away from the way that soft flesh gives under her teeth.

She messes around on her phone. "Yup," she says, grinning. "Nearest Nordstrom is in downtown Seattle."

"Whoops."

But I'm not upset. I gave Eden a reason to smile, and that's its own win.

She tilts her head. "So generic box store it is."

"Generic box store it is," I agree.

The woman at the car rental desk, whose name turns out to be Gertie, confirms—with a shared eye roll in Eden's direction—that no, there aren't any boutique men's clothing stores in town, and that yes, there's a box store in walking distance—about three-quarters of a mile—on the other side of Galilee's small downtown.

"You game?" I look down at Eden's feet. She's still wearing that pair of chunky-looking sandals she slipped on when she shed her wedding dress. "Those comfy for walking?"

"They're not bad. I've done a few miles in them and not regretted my decisions. Are *those*?" She inclines her chin toward my Paul Evans Oxfords.

"Good enough." I'm more concerned with the fact that the shirt I'm wearing will become a life-form of its own shortly, but that's the problem we're about to solve. I wince at the thought of the cheap shirt that will shortly take the place of this one—which cost $285 and was custom fit— and once again curse my grandfather for being the switch that set this chain of events in motion.

If you wanted to humble us, you've succeeded, I tell him. *You fucker.*

"Hang on." I go back to the car and pluck the cowboy hat out of the back seat.

"What are you doing?"

"Keeping the sun off your face," I say and plop it onto her head. Which turns out to be a huge mistake. She's so fucking cute.

She bites her lip.

I look away.

We set out and about ten minutes later hit what is obviously Galilee's downtown area. Shops line both sides of a charming small-town street that widens at one end into a green park area, which is bustling with, of all things, a—

"Quilt festival!" Eden crows, delighted, eyes bright. "I had no idea there was one in Galilee!"

It's not huge, but tens of quilts hang from wooden racks and tall scaffolds, waving gently in the breeze, blazes of bright color and wild designs. Even from this distance, I can see a vivid giraffe, a patchwork in every shade of red, a cat with a Cheshire grin and slightly deranged eyes.

"Oh, wow, look at that log cabin with all the blues. Gorgeous." She edges closer to the quilt, and I bite back a smile. She's cute like this, all fired up. Not thinking about worthless Paul and his bad decisions.

"Do you want to check it out?"

"I mean, we've got flights now, so we basically just have to kill time till then, right?"

"Right."

Meanwhile, Eden has drifted another three feet toward the quilts, like she's being drawn with a magnet.

"Yeah, if you don't mind?" she calls over her shoulder.

"I don't mind."

What I mean is: *I want to see you smile again.*

I follow her toward the quilts and stand near as she examines them one by one.

"Look," she says, pointing to some faint stitching on the surface of the quilt. When I step closer, I can see that it's not random—the stitches follow the shapes of leaves. And the quilt itself is all autumn color—rich, saturated earth tones with splashes of deep red and yellow.

"What am I looking at?" I ask.

"Okay, so, I don't know how much you know about quilts…" She's practically quivering with excitement—that's how much she loves talking about this.

"Absolutely nothing," I admit.

She explains that a quilt is a sandwich, and that the woman who quilted this one used her own small home sewing machine. "It takes a ton of skill and patience. She literally made all these leaf shapes by moving the quilt around under the machine's needle. It would be like if I held a pen still and you had to move the paper to draw leaves. Except the quilt is shockingly heavy and bunches up while you work. Mad props to her."

Damn, she's right; that's amazing.

All of a sudden, I can see that this quilt isn't just a big fabric blanket. It's layers, and each one took loads of thought and planning and effort. It's not some old-fashioned hobby; it's an art form.

She's still talking, explaining something to me about *burying knots* and *one continuous thread* and *edge-to-edge design*. She's bouncing on her toes, and her voice sounds like a smile.

And I realize I'm not looking at the quilt anymore, not following her finger as it traces the stitching along the surface of the fabric. I'm watching her instead.

Her cheeks are pink and her eyes dance, and she's beaming, so fucking beautiful that it takes my breath away.

Eden's fingers sweep across the surface of the quilt, and I feel the caress like a brush over tightening flesh. I want to drink her excitement straight from her lips, lean into her and devour her energy from the source.

My phone, buzzing, startles me out of the moment, and I reach for it.

"Hey," I say into the phone, striding to the edge of the quilt display.

"We have a problem." Hanna's voice is tight.

Shit. "Okay. Lay it on me."

"I just listened to a voicemail on the office line from Leah Piper."

Leah's one of my weddings; she's supposed to marry Penelope Parsons next Saturday.

"Their photographer received an email canceling the gig."

"What?!"

"Right?" Hanna says. "She called Leah because something about it felt off, and of course Leah *hadn't* canceled. But then Leah had a bad feeling, so she called a few more vendors, and sure enough, they'd received cancellation calls, too."

"What the fuck?"

"I know. Leah called me, in tears, asking if we'd figure out what was going on and take care of it. I'd do it, but since it's one of your weddings, I don't want to mess around with it and risk having Weggers say that we didn't follow the rules. Or having Leah call Five Rivers Weddings up and ask them to take over."

Five Rivers is a relative newcomer, only a few years old, but they've been steadily gaining ground in the unspoken competition to be the premiere wedding site in Rush Creek.

"I'll take care of it," I say. "I'll figure out what's going on, and I'll fix it."

"Thank you." I can hear the relief in Hanna's voice but also lingering tightness. "I'm worried it might be—"

"Sabotage," I finish for her, quietly.

"Yeah."

Ever since Weggers unveiled our grandfather's will and its offbeat demands, weird shit has been happening. And I don't mean the fact that my brothers and I have been dropped into Opposite Land. There have also been these... events. Plans that have gone wrong, situations that have threatened to keep me and my brothers from fulfilling the terms of our letters. They range from plumbing failures to planting false evidence to shadowy figures in the night— but they all threaten to make it impossible to comply with Granddad's will.

Just like what's happening to Leah and Penelope.

"Tell Tucker about Leah and Penelope's wedding," I say. "It's probably time for us to get up in Blue Iron's face about this bullshit."

Blue Iron is the company that will get the Hott land if my brothers and I fail at our tasks. That makes them the only ones with enough at stake to actively undermine us— which makes them the obvious suspect for everything that's happened so far. That said, we're far from having proof.

"Any progress? Have you talked to Eden about Paul?"

No, I think, *but I almost kissed her a few minutes ago.*

Not gonna tell Hanna that.

I reset my determination not to screw this up—any more than it already is. "She doesn't want to talk about it," I say truthfully. "We haven't caught up with Paul. He's somewhere in Montana, and we're in Galilee, not too far past where 90 crosses the Columbia. Eden figured out he's on his way to Sioux Falls, so we're going to fly into Sioux Falls and intercept him."

Saying that Eden "figured out" where Paul is going is a bit of a white lie, technically. Eden *thinks* he's headed to Sioux Falls, and I *think* her hypothesis makes sense. But we don't know for sure.

"So you'll meet him in Sioux Falls and see if you can sort things out." It's a statement, not a question.

"Yeah."

Sort things out. Meaning watch Eden reconcile with Paul. The thought makes my stomach clench. "In the meantime, I'll call Leah and fix whatever's going on with the vendors. And hopefully Tucker will find some proof that Blue Iron is behind all this."

There's a pause. Then Hanna says, "Okay. Fly safe."

"I will." I end the call.

It's not the flying that feels dangerous. It's my traveling companion.

That shouldn't be the case. I've had plenty of experience with burying my feelings for Eden. This is no different.

Except back then, there was no occasion to scoop her up and carry her to bed. No chance to be so close to her that I could smell the strawberry of her hair. I hadn't felt the scrape of her lace panties on my fingertips, and, worst of all, I hadn't known the look on her face when she stood face-to-face with something that lit her up from the inside.

I have the distinct, unwelcome feeling that I've reached the end of a tether.

Like I said.

Dangerous.

17

EDEN

"You done?" Rhys says when he rejoins me, in front of a wonky pineapple block quilt.

His voice is brusque, his posture stiff. He's the Rhys of a few days ago, distant and removed.

"Everything okay?" I ask.

"Everything's fine."

I don't press. I know him better now, and I know that sometimes he climbs inside the remote shell. It's a disguise, or armor. The way he meets the world when he doesn't feel comfortable.

Knowing I've caught a rare glimpse of the real him does something to my insides.

Eden, I chastise myself. *You were just engaged. He's your ex-husband's lawyer. He lives in New York.*

There are tons of *really good* reasons why I shouldn't take any pleasure in cracking him open. In having spent a day with the softer, more carefree version of him.

"I've seen everything I need to see," I tell him.

The show was small, and while he talked on the phone, I finished admiring the last few quilts, soaking up what they had to teach and writing down the names of an artist or two I'll follow up with when I get home.

"Shopping time, then?"

I nod.

We start off in the direction we've been pointed, following the instructions we were given. I hurry my steps to keep up with his long stride. I can tell already that at this pace, my shoes *are* going to be a problem, but I don't ask him to slow down. I know he will—but I also think he needs to be moving.

We turn onto the main drag, where a chain-link fence parallels the road.

He switches sides with me, nudging my shoulder, edging me toward the fence with the wall of his body, putting himself between traffic and me.

It's another of his tiny acts of kindness, like cooking dinner, like making sure I have the bed, like stopping at the quilt show, and it—along with his body heat—melts me another few degrees.

We skirt a parking lot, and another. I'm breathless, maybe because of the speed we're walking, but maybe because of the graze now and again of his shoulder against mine. It feels like that side of me is alight. I put one foot in front of the other so I don't lean into the sensation. So I don't turn and step into it.

There's a long stretch of sketchy too-tall grass and weeds, and Rhys looks down at my feet. "I'll give you a piggyback."

"Why?"

"Because your feet are mostly bare and there could be glass or needles or who knows the fuck what in here."

"I'm fine," I say. "I'll keep an eye and pick carefully."

"Just take the piggyback," he says.

I have my reasons for thinking it's a bad idea, but when he crouches, I secure my hat, sling my purse cross body, jump, and let him catch me. And yeah, it's a bad idea. His hands are on my thighs, fingers spread wide and strong, and I have to squeeze my legs together to keep my seat. Something in my low belly likes the feel of all of that way too much. Then he strides forward, and I can feel the bunch and release of muscle.

Rhys smells so goddamn good, musky and spicy, the kind of good that makes me want to bury my face deep in the scent. I lean my cheek against his shoulder, the brim of my hat folding between us, and grip him tighter with both legs and hands. He lets out a sound that's somewhere between a sigh and a grunt.

I think that means he likes this, too.

Like maybe he's as aware of the grip of my thighs on his waist as I am. Like maybe he can feel my nipples getting stiffer every time they accidentally brush his back. Or the way the seam of my sweatpants is hotter and damper than it was when I climbed onto his back.

Suddenly I realize we're standing still.

"We're here," he says, and there's amusement in his voice. "You can, um, get down."

My cheeks flame. I slide off.

"Thanks for the ride." My words are pitched too high.

"It was my pleasure." His voice is rough—or maybe that's wishful thinking.

I'm not looking at him, but I can feel him staring at me. I point at the store's sliding doors. "I'll just go—in there—and buy some—clean underwear," I say.

Awesome, Eden. Awesome.

18

EDEN

My face is hot as we part ways, agreeing to text and meet up when we're both done with our shopping.

I grab a basket and start filling it. Clothes, toiletries, makeup, and a backpack to shove it all into. I find a pair of slip-on sneaks that look like they might be marginally better for my feet than the sandals. I have no idea how much longer this trip will last, but I want to be prepared.

Underwear is my last stop.

I should buy a six-pack of serviceable white cotton bikinis. Being practical will keep my head where it should be—not thinking about whether Rhys liked the look of my pale blue thong. Or whether he has imagined activities involving the thong. Twisting it to the side to make room for his tongue or, better yet, removing it wholesale with his teeth.

Clearly, I have imagined those things.

I set the Good Girl Undies back on their cardboard rack and turn toward a display of Bad Decision Panties.

These underthings are flimsy. Frothy.

They're cheaply made and probably won't last five washings.

They won't feel nearly as comfy as the Good Girl Undies on a plane ride.

They're pale pink and seafoam and bridal lace and fuck-me red. They're thongs and cheeky bikinis and barely there *I'm pretending to be practical but you can see everything through me* boy shorts.

I want to buy one of each color, but I restrain myself and pick out five pairs because there's a *five-for* sale and it would be foolish not to take advantage of it, right?

I'm not buying them for Rhys. I'm buying them because everyone knows that how you feel begins with what you wear next to your skin. I'm doing it because every woman deserves pretty things. I'm doing it because I was jilted yesterday, and I should feel beautiful.

Jilted yesterday.

Except I haven't been thinking about Paul. I haven't been sad or angry.

I've been enjoying myself too much.

You're on the rebound, a voice says.

But what if I'm not?

How could you not be?

There is an answer to that question. It's been shoving at the back of my brain for the last twenty-four hours. And I haven't wanted to look at it too closely, because I don't like what it implies about me and my choices.

If I was never in love with Paul, that might be why it doesn't hurt as much as it should.

I push it away again, and I resume choosing panties. I'm

buying them because when Mari asks if I'm practicing self-care, I want to be able to say yes.

I pick out a robe—this time a practical one—and toss that into the basket on top of the undies.

I head to the front where I said I'd meet Rhys. He's already at self-check, running his items through the scanner, and he says, "Bring that over here."

"I can pay for my own stuff."

"I owe you," he says.

"Not anymore."

We stare at each other for a moment. Then he says, "Thank you. But I'm still buying. It's Teller's money. I've been saving it for this moment. Wealth redistribution. I'm the Robin Hood of divorce attorneys."

That makes me laugh. Still, I hold my basket closer to me, because it's one thing to have bought Bad Decision Panties and to idly contemplate whether Rhys has an opinion about my underwear—and another to let him buy them for me.

"Come on. Let me at least pretend to make it up to you." He grabs for the basket. I yank it out of his reach, and the robe falls, dragging with it five pairs of Bad Decision Panties, all clinging lacily to the robe's terry surface. The whole collection is spread out on the floor like a cheap window display in a downtown adult-toy shop.

I crouch to retrieve my stuff, reaching for the red lace thong first—it's so bright and garish and *obvious*, my bad decisions visible to Rhys and God and all the other shoppers—but my hand collides with something warm and strong. His hand.

He's crouched, too, and both our fingers wrap around

the red lace thong. Where they touch, there's a fizz of heat energy so strong I can't help looking at his face to see if he feels it, too.

Rhys slowly raises his gaze to mine. His eyes are blazing, and I can't move for a second, because there's no mistaking the way he's looking at me. My whole body flares with need.

We're both still holding the thong. I let it go like a hot potato, which is definitely the wrong move, because then there we are, squatting across from each other on the floor, my underwear in Rhys's hand, that heat still in his eyes, and oh, God, whatever he's thinking, I want it, too, I want it now.

My mouth is so dry, I desperately want to lick my lips. *Don't do it, don't do it,* I chant to myself, but of course instinct wins and I do it anyway. His gaze drops from my eyes to my mouth, and his pupils darken even more.

Abruptly he gets to his feet, grabbing the robe as he goes and depositing both it and my panties back into the basket.

"You should probably scan these yourself," he says and thrusts the basket into my grasp.

19

RHYS

I'm so distracted by the red thong that it takes me a while to realize Eden's limping.

As we walk back toward town—we still have an hour or so to kill till Joe picks us up, and I figured she'll be happiest at the quilt show—I pull a few paces in front of her. We're walking on a narrow stretch, so it makes sense, and I want to make sure I see any hazard that might hurt her—even in her new, more enclosed shoes.

But also, it's self-preservation, because if I look at her, I'm going to do something we'll both regret.

I came pretty damn close at the checkout.

It has nothing to do with me, I told myself when her lace underwear spilled onto the floor. *For all I know she wears lace thongs all the time—it's none of my damn business.*

But I hoped she'd bought them because she wanted me to see them. On her.

The electricity and the hope stirred up a potent chemical cocktail, making me buzz with dangerous need, so when I looked up and she was looking, too, when I let her see what I wanted, and she let me see right back—

Then I recovered my senses.

Because *even if there were a way to save Hanna's business without saving the wedding*—which I don't know that there is—she *got dumped. Yesterday.*

Yesterday.

Not okay. Not okay to take advantage of her vulnerability.

Because Eden deserves better than swiping right. She deserves better than *one and done*. She deserves better than Teller and Paul, and she *definitely* deserves better than me.

There is nothing—*nothing*—in my story that would make me a good bet for Eden. My story is full of bad role models and my own failure to do better than they did.

Those are the thoughts that distract me from the moment, which is why it takes me way too long to realize Eden's limping.

"Jesus," I say when I finally size her up. "You okay?"

"It's nothing serious," she says. "Just...you were right. The sandals weren't great for walking, and these"—she gestures at the slip-on tennis shoes—"are kinda...so-so. My feet are sore."

"Blisters?"

"No. Just very tired and muscle-sore."

"You want another piggy—"

"No," she says quickly, and even though I feel a stab of disappointment, I definitely think that was the smart answer. Eden's inner thighs are strong and soft as fuck, and having them wrapped around my waist made me want to pull her around my body to face me. To line up my hardening cock against the seam of her sweatpants, to see if she'd be hotter there. It made me want to know what it would feel like to have those thighs wrapped around my face.

All things I don't need to be thinking about, if I want to do right by her, which is all I've ever wanted.

So we keep walking, now side by side. And it feels good. Nice. Her arm brushes mine occasionally, and I try not to notice the new surge of electricity each time, the way it goes straight to my cock.

There's nothing to do except walk and talk, so we do. I ask her about how she got started with quilting (she learned it from her grandmother; sewing was the only time her grandmother sat still).

I want to know more about her grandmother, so she tells me: That she was small-minded and bitter, not very likable. That Eden knew she was safe but not *cherished* or *adored*. She longed, a lot of the time, for someone who would hug her and curl up with her and stroke her hair.

Dead father.

Absent mom.

Withholding grandmother.

Jesus.

My hands fist at my sides.

"Teller was very demonstrative," she says. "So it was hard to resist that. That's part of how I ended up in that marriage."

She doesn't say anything about Paul, and I don't ask. I realize I don't want to know. I don't want to know if Paul gave her everything she didn't get in her childhood, if she misses it now, if thoughts of him are creeping into the cracks in our conversation.

I hope not, and I hate myself for hoping.

She tells me about when she opened the quilt store, not long after she married Teller. His money made it possible for her to go from running an online store to a bricks-and-mortar one, which she still feels weird about, but also, "Thank God something good came out of that marriage."

When she asks what it was like when my aunt got divorced, I tell her about how much time Aunt Meryl spent at our house crying and how I wasn't old enough to understand, but I knew I wanted to stick it to the guy who'd done it.

"You were a sensitive kid," she says.

"I guess," I say, shrugging. "Or a vicious one."

She's shaking her head. "I can't believe I thought you were cynical."

"I am cynical."

Eden gives me a sidelong, extremely dubious look. "You're a giant softie," she says. "Wearing some serious chain mail."

She's wrong. Maybe I was soft at one point, but life definitely kiln-fired it out of me.

"Whatever you want to believe," I say, secretly pleased by her characterization, wrong or right.

"Ditto. We can agree to disagree."

I cross my arms. "You know what I could use right now? Doritos."

She snickers. "You're in luck. I crammed the bag into my purse."

"Dorito dust?" I hazard.

"Better than no Doritos at all."

"Hit me."

She does, and we walk back to the quilt festival, munching Dorito tidbits and talking about nothing at all, and at some point she says, "Is it really weird that I'm not thinking about Paul at all?" and I say, "No," but what I'm thinking is, *Oh, God, I am so, so, so fucked.*

20

EDEN

Joe picks us up and drives us to the hotel in Spokane. In the car, he and Rhys spar about college football—Rhys is a Ducks fans and Joe is a Cougs fan—and I sternly tell myself that Nothing Happened in the big box store.

We arrive at the hotel. Joe and Rhys work out the details about returning Rhys's BMW, and then Joe pulls out, leaving Rhys and me at the sliding glass doors to the lobby.

We approach the desk, summoned forward by a clerk probably in his forties, dressed in a gray button-down and tie, with his hair in a man bun. "Two rooms for Hott," Rhys tells him.

There's a long pause while the clerk taps on his keyboard. And then taps again. And taps some more.

"We have *one* room for Hott," he says.

"I booked two," Rhys says.

"I'm so sorry," the clerk says. "We have just the one. Let me—" More tapping. "Unfortunately, we're all booked up—"

Rhys turns to me. I can't read his expression. "Do you want to go somewhere else?"

My feet hurt. My brain hurts. I just want to *land* somewhere. And it's not like we haven't done this before. We shared a room last night.

"Please tell me it at least has two beds?" I ask the clerk.

"Two queens," he confirms. "And I'll give you a twenty-percent discount for the error."

I look back at Rhys, who raises his eyebrows at me.

"I feel like if we didn't kill each other last night, we'll be okay?" I say.

Of course, last night was *before*. Before the piggyback and the Bad Decision Panties on the store floor. Killing each other might be the least of our issues.

Still. If Rhys had any interest in acting on the chemistry that flared between us earlier, wouldn't he have done it? He wasn't jilted yesterday.

He has his phone out. He's poking at the screen, and when I look over, I can see that he's messing around with other reservation systems.

"There's a big blues festival going on," the clerk says, wincing apologetically. "And some kind of rock-collecting convention. Oh, right, and the UFO people. I'm so sorry. Big week in Spokane."

Rhys takes a few more tentative stabs at his phone, then sighs heavily. "I don't think we're going to find anything else nearby. Unless you want to try to get a rental car and—"

"No. This is fine. We'll be fine."

Famous last words.

"We'll take it," he tells the clerk.

We don't talk in the elevator on the way up. When we

reach the room, Rhys calls dibs on first shower. "For the good of the collective," he says. "I can't believe Joe didn't throw me out of the car."

I don't tell him I love the way he smells or ask him if we can save water by showering together, though I do wonder what he'd say if I did.

Instead I offer to go throw in a load of laundry while he showers, saving myself from the (delicious) agony of picturing water sliding over golden skin.

When I come back to the room he's dressed in his new clothes—an Oxford and a pair of gray jeans that he somehow manages to make look expensive. I try not to gawk.

The clothes don't make the man, I think. *The man makes the clothes.*

He also smells delicious, like soap and shampoo and Old Spice. I thought I liked him dirty, but apparently I like him clean, too, and despite my best efforts, my body reacts to the scent, that tugging, twisting sensation deep in my lower belly.

I try to focus on something else, but it's basically just that or my screaming feet.

"Are you limping?" he asks. "You *are.*"

"I'm fine." I try not to limp as I head for the shower.

It's a great showerhead, because Rhys chose the poshest possible airport-adjacent hotel and it's a nice one. I stand under the water for a long time, until I have to stop because my feet are straight-up killing me on the hard tile floor. I change into a decently cute skirt and a striped T-shirt and step out into the room.

No Rhys.

For a brief, ridiculous moment, I'm afraid. Afraid he got tired of chasing Paul, afraid he got tired of *me*, afraid he decided to go back to Rush Creek to clean up my mess or back to New York to be rid of me entirely. Then I hear my therapist's voice in my head: *Part of your brain will probably always be afraid people will leave, but you don't have to let it rule the way you live and make decisions.*

I take a deep breath and use my big, smart forebrain to rationally assess: Fifty bucks says he went to get food.

Right then, the door beeps and *chunks* and Rhys appears, holding a plastic bag in one hand and a big paper bag in the other.

"I switched the laundry," he says.

I'd forgotten about that. "Thank you."

"Left you a note," he says, gesturing, and I see it then, on the table: *Getting food, switching laundry. —R.*

It's short and impersonal, and my face gets warm anyway, because it's a small thing that matters, which is Rhys's specialty.

I catch the scent of something absolutely delicious. "Is that *Indian* food?"

"Yup. Hope that's okay. I know you were supposed to have samosas as one of your appetizers at the wedding, and I remember you being super excited about them. Wasn't sure what else you'd like, so I got a bunch of stuff we can split and try."

I wish he would stop being so nice. It's going to kill me.

"What's in the plastic bag?"

He reaches in and pulls out a bottle of Advil and—

"Are those *frog* slippers?"

"Not just any frog slippers," he says. The corner of his

mouth turns up, a grin he can't quite fight. "Heatable frog slippers."

I think of him again in that conference room, dark-eyed, stern, scornful, icy.

And then I look at him with the frog slippers in his hands and that almost-grin, and I know it's basically hopeless. It's only a matter of time until I give in and do something I'll regret, probably devouring his mouth like an ice-cream cone on a summer's day.

He tugs the slippers apart, breaking the plastic tag, which he tosses into the hotel trash. Then he opens the microwave and slides the slippers in, hitting buttons until the motor hums.

This guy, who doesn't believe in happily-ever-afters, brought me *heatable frog slippers.*

"Thank you."

It's ridiculously inadequate to the moment, so I try again. "That's probably—no, that's definitely—the nicest thing anyone's ever done for me."

"Seriously?" He looks horrified, and yeah, when I think about it, that's a sign I've been hanging out with the wrong people. The wrong men, at least.

But apparently my judgment regarding "right" and "wrong" men is pretty suspect.

"I think my bar's been too low," I say. "I'm raising it right now."

"Don't set it at *frog slippers,*" he says. "It should be a fucking high jump. You deserve a goddamned pole vault."

His voice is rough.

"Rhys," I say helplessly.

He freezes, and our eyes meet. For a long time. Longer

than people are supposed to stare at each other, until all the molecules in the room hold still.

No, not all of them. The molecules in my own body—those go crazy, rioting everywhere, but especially at the pulse point in my throat and the tips of my nipples and in my molten core.

Then the microwave beeps, and he looks away, clearing his throat. He opens the door, pulls out the frog slippers, and hands them over. Then he starts pulling things out of the paper takeout bag like it's a task that requires a hundred percent of his attention.

21

RHYS

We sit at the hotel-room table—Eden in her frog slippers—and eat the Indian food, which kicks ass. I Googled the best Indian takeout in Spokane.

We don't talk much, which is okay. Actually, it's great. It's that kind of comfortable you don't get that often, when you've spent a lot of time with someone and it feels right to just *be*.

When we're done with dinner, I put the leftovers in the fridge and carry our trash down the hall to the big trash can near the ice maker.

I make a detour to retrieve our laundry, and when I come back, the frogs are in the microwave again. "Do your feet still hurt?"

"They're still sore," she admits, pulling them out as the microwave beeps and sliding them on.

Don't do it, I tell myself.

But apparently I suck at listening to my own advice, because I set the laundry on a chair and say, "Sit."

She gives me an arch look. "Like a dog?" she teases.

"Please," I amend. "Have a seat on the bed."

She furrows her brow, but I repeat the request—the nice version—and she does it, hoisting herself back against the stack of pillows. I sit beside her and lift one of her feet into my lap, warm frog and all.

"What are...?"

"Shh," I say.

I slide the slipper off and take her foot in both my hands.

At that moment, I know I've made a mistake.

It's just a foot, but it's full of her nerve endings and the pulse of her blood through her veins and all the things that make her alive to the touch. It's warm under my hands—extra warm from the frog. And as I dig my fingers and thumbs into her sore muscles, kneading and trying to ease the tightness, her eyelids get heavy, and her lower lip softens enough to tell me it feels good. Her breath hitches at first and then slows—and mine matches it, like we're tuned to the same frequency.

It would almost be easier if she were writhing and moaning, putting on a show of enjoying my touch. She's trying to keep her pleasure under wraps, but she can't hide it from me, which does something primal to my snake brain.

I want more. I want to glide my hand up the inside of her calf to the hem of her skirt, loose and summery, to where her thigh goes pale and soft. I want to follow my hand with my lips. My tongue. I want to push her skirt up around her waist and bury my face against the cloth covering her, and I want to nudge my nose against her clit and breathe her deeply. Then I want to push the fabric aside and—

"Mmm," she murmurs, and I feel it like a shot of adrenaline. My cock is hard, inches from her foot resting on my thigh.

I set that foot aside and switch to the other one. Eden sinks lower onto the pillows, and I force myself to stay in the moment. This is what I can do for her right now, this is to make up for everything that's gone wrong—Teller, and then me choosing to represent Teller, Milo the dog, her money, Paul jilting her.

She's had a shitty time, and I can do this in the most unselfish way possible.

Her eyes drift closed, and I stroke my thumb over the sore arch of her foot and try not to stare at her face. At the long lashes throwing shadows over the curve of her cheeks, at the softness of her mouth, relaxed and peaceful and so, so lush. At the strands of hair that I want to push behind her ears.

She inhales a breathy little snore, and I realize she's fallen asleep.

I keep stroking her foot, kneading the fine, elegant muscles, not wanting to disrupt her or wake her. Then I set her foot down gently, watching to see if she moves, but she doesn't. Crawling up the bed, I ease some of the pillows out from behind her so there's only one left. She stirs and makes a small whimpering sound.

"Shh. Lie down."

She obeys, not opening her eyes, and I cover her by folding the bedclothes in half over her. She curls down into the cocoon I've made for her, snuffling. My chest gets tight.

I'm about to extricate myself from her bed so I can cross to my own when her hand snakes out and grabs my arm.

"Eden," I whisper.

I try to unfurl her fingers, but she won't let go.

She settles more fully into her nest with a little humming sound.

I'll wait it out. She'll fall deeper asleep and let me go, and then I can get up. I lie down on the pillows I've liberated from her, prepared to be patient.

22

EDEN

I wake in the dark and for a long moment don't know where I am. I'm curled on my side, and there's something delightfully warm behind me and a heavy weight across my body.

It takes me a moment to realize that the warm object is Rhys and the weight is his arm wrapped over me. His hand is tucked near one of my breasts—not touching. My nipple tightens in recognition.

There are layers of blankets between our bodies, a sort of sleeping bag he made for me by folding the covers in half.

He's breathing evenly, sleeping.

I fell asleep to the bliss of his hands on my feet, the gorgeous sense of being cared for. I remember him adjusting my pillows and urging me to lie down, his voice reaching me from a distance, like we were underwater. Halfway between asleep and awake, I knew I didn't want him to leave, and I reached for him.

He stayed.

I should wake him up. I should kick him out of my bed.

Except that's the last thing I want to do. I want to curl closer, to ease back into his warmth, to tuck my backside against his hips. To wrap his arm tighter and nudge his hand around the curve of my breast.

I do none of those things, but I do get out of bed and slide back in under the quilt and sheet. I fold his half of the bedclothes over him, so we're both covered, under the bedding together. Then I settle myself into the big spoon of his body, close my eyes and drift, wrapped in his warmth.

LIGHT POURS through the crack in the blinds the next time I wake, and I jolt into full consciousness, checking the clock. Whew—plenty of time to make our flight.

Rhys is still behind me, but sometime in the night he edged closer. His arm is still over me, his chest against my back, all solid muscle. And like the answer to my middle-of-the-night fantasy, his hips have found my backside, and I can feel the entire length of him, morning hard, pressed against me.

Holy crap, he's thick.

I want that.

Inside me.

I don't move even though every cell in my body is screaming at me to rock my hips, tilt back against him.

I don't move, even though I really, really want to squeeze my thighs together to ease the clamoring need in my core and clit.

I don't move, but I'm so, so tempted to slide my hand

under the edge of the skirt I fell asleep in, up to the edge of the red thong I couldn't resist putting on.

I could tease myself, just a little. I could slick a finger and run it across my clit a few times.

But before I can do it—or decide it's a terrible idea—Rhys stirs behind me. Groans. Presses closer, erection perfectly lined up against my ass.

Oh, *God*.

He's really hard. And deliciously big. And making me think about how good that cock would feel everywhere I want it.

I should get up! Quick! Before he wakes up for—

But it's too late. Behind me, I feel the moment when he freezes, his breathing suddenly held.

And there's only one sensible thing for me to do.

I pretend to be asleep.

He slowly eases himself away from me. I try to breathe the way people do when they're sleeping, but I can't remember how that works. Is it slow? Even? Or...I shouldn't pretend to snore, right? That's how people get caught at fake sleeping.

He rolls away, and I hear the slight thump of his feet hitting the floor on the other side of the bed. I lie perfectly still and listen as his footsteps move toward the bathroom.

The door closes and the shower starts.

Is he...?

Will he...?

I strain to hear. Something, anything. Breath catching. A rough groan. I want to know.

I want to be in there with him.

I want to get out of bed and knock on the bathroom

door. Push it open. I want to see him through the glass shower door. Hand on the wall, head down slightly, body curved forward over the thick length of his erection, held tight in his fist. I want to watch his hand move over the head, his grip on himself deliciously, punishingly tight.

One of my hands has crept down between my legs again, cupped around the warmth of my mound through my panties. The pressure feels so, so good. I could—

"Hey. You awake?"

He's standing in the bathroom doorway, towel around his waist, dripping.

"I was a dope and got into the shower without my stuff. Can you grab me my shampoo out of that bag?"

I ease my hand quietly from between my legs, roll out of bed, and hurry to do as he's asked.

Shampoo in fist, he retreats into the bathroom and shuts the door behind him.

I bury my face in my hands, shaking my head at my own behavior. And then, before I can do anything else foolish and deluded, I reach for my phone and check my messages.

23

RHYS

We touch down in Sioux Falls late Monday morning.

Thankfully, Eden and I didn't have seats next to each other. I can't imagine what it would have felt like to spend several hours with her arm resting against mine. Breathing the scent of her shampoo. Trying not to look down the V of the pretty top she's wearing. After knowing what it feels like to wake up with my arms wrapped around her and my dick nestled against the lovely soft curve of her ass.

The thought makes me duck my head and silently groan.

I'm pretty sure she wasn't actually asleep. I felt that moment when she went from tense in my arms to limp, trying to fake it.

How do you make this situation okay, though? Because if I ask, *Hey, were you awake when my erection was throbbing against your ass...?*

How does that end anywhere good?

I mean, there's the version where she says, *Yes, and I liked it.*

I need to not think about that.

Because if she'd liked it, she wouldn't have pretended to be asleep, right?

Also, by tonight she's going to be retrieving her quilts from Paul. He could see her, realize his mistake—if he has even an iota of good sense—and try to get her back. There's no universe in which she would have turned over in bed and pressed her mouth to mine, rolled her hips to meet me.

No universe except the one in my brain.

Two days ago she hated you, and for good reason, I remind myself.

I should be glad that by this time tomorrow we won't be together anymore. I'll have flown back to Rush Creek, and she'll have her quilts in hand and be headed back there herself. Possibly with Paul at her side.

God, I hate that idea so fucking much.

But I can't discount it completely, despite his terrible behavior, because this morning after her shower (during which I managed, through sheer effort of will, not to think about her naked and gleaming wet), she spent a long time in the bathroom fixing her hair and doing her makeup.

I think she wants to look good for him.

And she's succeeded. She looks absolutely beautiful. I mean, she always looks beautiful. But right now, she looks well rested and glowing, bright eyed, pink cheeked, berry lipped, and completely...

Kissable.

If I were Paul, I would get down on one knee and beg

Eden's forgiveness. I would grovel for all I was worth. I would claim temporary insanity.

But I'm not Paul. And if he does grovel, I won't try to talk her out of taking him back. Not only because of Hanna, but also because it wouldn't be fair to Eden. I'm not what she needs. If I hadn't known that before, I proved it to myself when I let Fay down.

As I do a quick run-through of the rental car's mirrors, seat adjustments, and so on, I reach into my pocket and pull out the slip of paper I scribbled on this morning. Hand it to her.

"What's this?" she asks. She unfolds it.

Grace Vain 143 Beech St, Brandon, SD

"How did you find her address?" The wonder and admiration on her face are all the reward I need.

"I did some sleuthing this morning while you were in the shower."

"Do you always stalk people like this?"

"I usually pay other people to do my dirty work," I admit. "But I've learned a lot from my private investigator colleagues."

She clutches it to her chest. "Thank you."

I get my phone synced up with Car Play, and we drive the twenty minutes or so from Sioux Falls to Brandon, navigating to the address in question.

We're both quiet on the trip, and she's pale as a ghost as we approach the turn for Beech. "I'm going to throw up," she says.

"You're going to be great. You've got this."

We turn onto Beech.

"Shit," she whispers. "That's his car." She points to

where the blue sedan is parked next to the curb. "He must have driven straight through the night. God," she says. "I was still—" She stops. "I was still hoping it wasn't true."

Of course she was. She'd been hoping he just had cold feet, that once he settled down and took a few deep breaths, he'd realize he still wanted to get married.

My chest hurts. *Fuck.*

I want to jam on the brakes. I want to say, *It's not too late for us to turn around and go back to Rush Creek.* I want to say, *You don't need those quilts.*

But I know she needs to do this. And what will being selfish buy me? Do I think that if she doesn't go to him now, she'll come to me? And what would that mean? At best, one night. Eden on the rebound, trying to prove something to herself.

Right now, it could be enough. Right now, I'd take anything I could get. And that scares the shit out of me. Because in the end, I'd still be who I am—a guy who doesn't believe in marriage and failed at the one serious relationship he attempted. A guy who took advantage of her when she was tired and scared and lost, somewhere unfamiliar and alone, knowing he couldn't be what she deserved.

I won't be that guy.

I pull up behind the sedan. "Do you have the keys?"

Eden nods, grabbing her backpack and pulling a key ring out of a small pocket.

We get out of the car together. She unlocks the sedan's trunk, and we begin swapping the quilts from that car to our rental.

We've just transferred the last quilt when the door of Grace's house opens and a man steps out.

Paul. He takes in the scene, eyes scanning icily over me, then softening on her.

Goddamn it, he has no right to look like he's glad to see her.

"Eden," he says. "What are you...?"

"Getting my quilts," she says. Her voice is hard, and God, I want it to stay that way; I want her to keep her defenses up; I want her to take her quilts and run away from him as fast as she can.

I want her to run away from him, and I want her to run to me.

24

EDEN

Paul shuts the door to Grace's house behind him, descends the steps, and approaches us.

Rhys steps closer to me, crowding me with the strength and warmth of his body, and all I want is to lean into it.

He bends and murmurs, "I'll take the quilts and go find a cheapish bag I can check them in for the flight back. There was a box store back a couple of miles. Text me if you need me."

Don't go, I want to say. *Stay.*

But I don't. I don't have any right to ask more of him than he's already given, and the truth is I have some things to say to Paul.

Instead I tell Rhys "Thank you" and try to let him know with my eyes how much it means to me. That he brought me here and that he's going to help me get the quilts back to Rush Creek. That he still, after all this, has my back.

Then he's gone, taking the warmth of his body with him, leaving me standing on a sidewalk in a strange town, facing my ex-fiancé. The rental car starts and pulls away, and inside, I'm still calling out to Rhys in my mind, *Don't leave.*

Paul has paused on the path, his eyes on the departing car. "What—what was he doing here?"

Such a good question, and I don't think I know the answer anymore.

I give Paul my blankest expression. "He wanted to help me get my quilts back."

He blows out a sigh of relief. "Of course. I thought..."

But he doesn't say what he thought.

"Eden." This time my name sounds like a plea. And when I look up at his face, it's all guilt and apology.

"You stole my quilts."

"God, Eden, I'm so sorry. I didn't mean to."

"You knew you had them and you didn't turn back. I asked you to, and you blocked me."

"I needed time to think," he pleads.

"Well," I say. "You got it."

I remember my realization when Rhys and I were shopping for clothes. That there might be a reason I wasn't more heartbroken about what Paul had done. That it was possible that I'd never loved him. I survey him carefully—his sandy hair, his blue eyes, his trust-fund-baby bone structure. He's a good-looking guy. He treated me well—until he didn't—and I could imagine a life in which we were partners—great partners, even—but standing here, I realize that I've been hoping this was over. That I could take my quilts and go, that there would be nothing to talk about.

I had it backward, what I said earlier to Rhys. I don't hope I'm wrong about Paul and Grace.

I hope I'm right.

"I'm so, so sorry." Paul's voice is watery but sincere. "I don't know what I was thinking. I was scared. I was terrified. I got cold feet, and I did a terrible, terrible thing. Can you ever forgive me? Can you—will you—let me try again?"

I stare at him.

"We can elope this time. Just you and me. We can go somewhere beautiful, tropical, maybe bring a few friends, and we can—"

"Are you—are you asking if I'll still marry you?"

And suddenly it's absurd, him standing there, still wearing his dress shirt, now unbuttoned so his plain white T-shirt shows, his hair disheveled, having stepped out of his ex-girlfriend's house, *asking me to marry him.*

"Eden." He gets down on one knee as I watch, astounded. "You came all this way—I know you must still care."

I'm shaking my head. "Get up. You can't do that. We're outside your ex-girlfriend's house. The ex-girlfriend you drove fifteen hundred miles to see." The reality strikes me with full, lightning-strength force. "She said no, didn't she? You asked her to get back together, and she said *no.* That's why you still want to marry me. Because she said no, and I'm your—*fallback plan.*" I shake my head, astounded by his gall. "Get. Up."

To his credit, he does.

"You jilted me more or less at the altar," I remind him. "You canceled a five-figure wedding at the last possible minute. You made all our friends and family travel to Rush Creek and then home again, for nothing. You humiliated me. You treated me like a consolation prize. And you think I'm going to *marry* you?"

"Please," he says. "Please tell me I haven't ruined everything."

I stare at him, at the wrecked expression on his blandly handsome face, at his tall, well-built frame. At the man I thought I would spend the rest of my life with.

It would be so, so easy to let him talk me into going back. Into marching forward with the life I planned. Two-point-five kids and a picket fence, winter vacations to San Diego, summer vacations in the San Juan Islands. Pretty good sex, a shared love of Marvel movies, the ability to plan a whole wedding without getting on each other's nerves.

And what's the alternative?

The unknown.

Which might be a lot like getting into a car with a near stranger, someone I thought I hated, emerging two days later *different*. Stronger. More sure of, at least, *what I* don't *want*. And maybe, just maybe, more sure of what I *do*.

"You haven't ruined everything," I say.

His chest inflates, like he's taking a full breath for the first time in our conversation. "Thank God," he says. "Thank you."

"You haven't ruined anything for me," I say. "If anything, you've made me see the truth a lot more clearly. I'm the one who should be thanking you. For saving me from making a huge mistake."

I open my purse, unzip the inner pocket, and pull out the ring, extending it to him.

Paul hesitates a moment.

"Take it," I say.

His jaw works. I think he's weighing the value of the ring against whether he can make one more attempt to win me back.

In the end, he takes the ring without meeting my eyes.

I'm not surprised.

I pull out my phone and text Rhys.

> Could use a pickup.

25

RHYS

Could use a pickup.

The text comes in while I'm standing in front of a display of luggage, trying to decide between a hard-shell suitcase and a—much cheaper—cloth duffel.

Okay, I tell myself when I see her message. *That's good, right? She didn't get into the car with him. They're not about to start a road trip home together.*

Except that's *bad.* Bad for Hanna, bad for Hott Springs Eternal, bad for my family.

And yet I can't stop the Christmas-morning feeling bubbling up inside me.

She didn't get into the car with him.

She's not with him.

She's probably torn up and grieving, though. She's probably finally dealing with the feelings she's been suppressing for the last few days.

I squash the kernel of hope that wants to form around the other possibility. The possibility that Eden told him to go to hell.

Even if she did, that doesn't mean...

It doesn't fucking mean anything. She got jilted two days ago. On top of which, she's had two serious relationships blow up, hard, in two years. She's doesn't want—

What? What would you be offering her anyway?

What can you offer her?

She owns a quilt shop in Rush Creek. She sees the best in everything and everyone.

You're New York City's sharkiest divorce attorney. You don't believe relationships stand a chance.

It's not like you've changed your mind about that. Especially not after what you saw her fiancé do to her.

You don't want to do that to her.

I grab the hard-shell suitcase—more protection for the quilts she loves, less chance of them getting wet or of something leaking onto them in the cargo bay—and check out as fast as I can.

When I get back to Grace's house, it's just her on the sidewalk. Paul and the blue sedan are gone. Eden is wearing her backpack on one shoulder. She looks exhausted. And she's still utterly, perfectly beautiful.

"Hi," she says and slides into the passenger seat.

"Hi."

"Can we go home?"

I don't ask what she means by *home* or what happened. She'll tell me when she's ready. "Yeah," I say instead. "We can go home."

"We'll need tickets."

I pull out my phone to oblige, but I haven't even typed our departure and arrival airports into Google when she says, "Why are you here? Still here. With me."

If I knew the answer to that...

But I *do* know the answer. In the beginning, it was because I owed it to her. Then it was because I owed it to Hanna.

But today? Now?

It's because I was hoping for this moment. The one where she walked away from Paul.

Her eyes rake over my face. They're vivid and green and curious, and they spare me nothing. The car feels tiny right now, my face heating under her scrutiny. My whole body heating. All those things I wanted to avoid—the scent of her shampoo, the warmth of her body, the lush curves of her tits, deliciously visible in the V of her shirt—they're all here, and I try not to but my gaze drops to the fullness of her lips, the corners sloping up in response, and when I look back at her eyes, they're on my mouth.

I don't know which of us moves first, but my hands find her face and hers tunnel into my hair, and when I set my mouth to hers it's like touching a match to autumn leaves; we both go up in flames.

She whimpers, and everything in me leaps in recognition. I did that to her, that sound is for *me*, she wants this. I kiss her hungrily, cupping the softness of her cheeks. I tease her lips until they open for me on another whimper, and her tongue sneaks out, finding mine, flirting and then stroking. It's my turn to make a sound. A grunt, then a groan as we angle our heads and the kiss deepens again, and she huffs out a breath in response and grips my hair tighter.

I need more of her, I need her now. I try to draw her closer, but everything's in the way—the shape of the seats, the gearshift between us, and bit by slow painful bit I'm pulled out of the moment and back to reality: We're in a car outside Paul's ex-girlfriend's house in Sioux Falls, South Dakota; Eden's a jilted bride, I'm her wedding planner who used to be her husband's divorce attorney; I'm Hanna's brother who was supposed to make this all okay—

I draw back abruptly.

"God, Eden, I'm sorry!"

Her lids are heavy, her eyes hazy, her pupils blown, but as soon as my words penetrate, her gaze focuses sharply on my face and color flares up in her cheeks. "You're—*sorry*?"

"You just got jilted, you're hurt and angry, and I'm taking advantage—"

She crosses her arms over her chest. "Is that what you think this is? You taking advantage? Because I'm pretty sure I'm the one who kissed you. And damn straight I'm angry. I'm angry at Paul for being an asshole, I'm angry at myself for playing my life safe after Teller..." She glares at me. "And now I'm angry at you, for treating me like I don't know my own mind. Because I do. I've been wanting that for—"

She stops.

We're both breathing hard, staring each other down. The pressure in my chest, the swirl of emotions I can't sort out makes it hard to catch my breath. It's not anger, not exactly, more like fear that I've blown this—whatever *this* is, that I've made things worse for her. That I'm like my dad or Aunt Meryl's ex-husband or Hanna's deadbeat father or Teller Austin or Paul Graves or *me*. Men who act on impulse, who take what—*who*—they need and discard women when they're done. When all I want is to be *better*. For her.

And I know what better looks like in this situation.

"We've only known each other two days," I say. "That's all. And I'm—I'm not a good bet, Eden. My own dad is a user. The other men in my life aren't good role models. And the only other relationship I've ever attempted—"

Her eyes move over my face. "A serious relationship?" she asks.

I nod.

"When?"

"A few years ago. Fay. She was someone I'd known in law school, and we ran into each other in the courthouse, grabbed a cup of coffee, and hit it off."

Eden nods. "Did she hurt you?" she asks.

She doesn't sound angry anymore. Her voice is soft. Her eyes are soft.

"No," I say. "I hurt her. Badly. I thought I could do it—marry her. Be with her. We'd even looked at rings. I thought I could overcome what I'd seen my dad and uncle do—but I couldn't. I broke it off, right when she thought I was going to propose. She was wrecked." I take a deep breath. "You were giving me shit the other day about not believing in marriage like it was Santa Claus or something, but the truth is I don't believe. Not for me, not long term. And I couldn't live that lie with her, knowing I could already see the ending."

She bites her lip.

"I'm not sorry I kissed you," I tell her. "Or that you kissed me. Hell no. Not even a little." I let her see the truth of that on my face, and her eyes darken. It makes me want to kiss her again, a need so fierce I almost give in to it. But I don't. Because being yet another man who hurt Eden would kill me.

"I'm not sorry I kissed you, but it can't happen again."

Her chest is still rising and falling fast, and I make myself look away, from the silky pale curve of her tits, from her peaked nipples, from all the evidence of what that kiss made her feel, but it's printed on my body. I'm hard as nails, and I want to kiss her again. I want to haul her into the back seat and bear her down into the upholstery. I want to be on her and over her and, fuck, yes, inside her.

Being *better* is shitty work sometimes.

She's quiet. Her breathing slows, gradually. Then she sighs. "You're right. That wasn't fair of me. Taking all those big feelings out on you. It doesn't mean—" She takes a deep breath. "I wanted to kiss you. I *still* want to kiss you. But I should probably...I know I need to..."

I wait, steeling myself, because whatever comes at the end of that sentence, it's not more kissing and it's definitely not fucking her in the back seat of this car.

"I need to give myself some time."

26

EDEN

In the end, we can't get on the same flight, so I fly home alone to Redmond, big suitcase full of quilts, AirTagged—thank you, Rhys—and checked.

When I arrive at baggage claim to retrieve it, Mari's standing there.

"What are you doing here?" I demand.

"Rhys texted me and asked me to meet you."

I roll my eyes. "Does he seriously think I can't get myself back to Rush Creek from Redmond?" But I'm only pretending to be mad. I'm actually adding it to the list of Rhys's small kindnesses.

Which only makes it a hundred thousand times harder that he doesn't want anything with me.

And I can't stop thinking about the kiss.

Mari throws her arms around me, knocking the cowboy hat off my head, squeezing and rocking me. "You've had a hell of a long weekend, and you need TLC."

"I'm *fine*," I insist—and then burst into tears.

"Oh, hon."

When she's done handing me tissues, giving me more hugs, and rescuing the hat from the floor, we claim my quilts and wheel them out to her SUV.

"If you feel like talking about it—tell me what happened," she says as she pulls out of the parking lot.

So I do. I tell her about my last three days, starting with Rhys bringing me Paul's note and ending with boarding the plane in Sioux Falls.

I leave a lot out, though. I leave out Rhys cooking me dinner. I leave out him tossing me my thong. Asking me if I wanted to check out the quilt festival.

I leave out him piggybacking me so I wouldn't get hurt. The two of us kneeling over my underwear, electricity live and dangerous between us. The frog slippers and the Advil. The foot massage. The two of us falling asleep in the same bed, waking tangled, his arousal thick and demanding against me. I leave out him going to buy a suitcase so I could bring my quilts home.

And most of all, I leave out the kiss.

I don't know why I omit those things. Maybe I feel like there's nothing to tell, like Rhys's rejection of me puts the whole story to bed.

Maybe I want to pretend the whole thing didn't happen.

I can do that.

Except for the kiss. I can't pretend that didn't happen.

I can still feel it, on my lips, on my tongue, between my legs.

The best I can do is accept that it was a one-time event and be glad Rhys stopped us before it could escalate.

I'm not sorry I kissed you. Or that you kissed me. Hell no. Not even a little.

That's the confusing part. Because it was clear he meant it. And if I hadn't believed the sincerity of his voice and expression, a quick glance downward had confirmed the truth of it.

But you could enjoy a kiss and not want the complications that might come with it.

I sigh aloud.

"I'm so sorry, Eden," Mari says softly, rubbing my shoulder. "Getting jilted—that sucks so much. And the thing with Grace, that had to really hurt."

"It stung. It hurt my pride so bad. But—" I take a breath, because this is the other thing I haven't told her yet, and I don't know how it's going to sound when it comes out of my mouth. "It didn't hurt *me*. Not the way it...*should have*."

"Ah," she says. "I—wondered."

"I kept waiting to care more about losing him than losing the quilts. I kept waiting to feel...heartbroken."

"It still might come," she says. "It's only been a couple of days."

"It might," I say. "But also maybe I liked the idea of Paul more than I liked Paul himself. And maybe..." I hesitate. "I've liked the idea of being loved more than I've...loved."

She's quiet for a moment. Then she says, "We're so much alike."

I nod. Mari never had a dad, and I lost mine when I was six. Both our moms abandoned us in various ways—mine for her singing career and hers because—well, she was flighty and irresponsible. We were both raised by family members who couldn't fill the void our moms had left behind.

We've talked about it a lot. Mari's mentioned how she

had trouble settling down and staying in Rush Creek with her husband, Kane, because she'd gotten in the habit of staying in motion so she could never want to belong somewhere and get rejected.

I thought I'd reached some peace with my own wounds because settling down in Rush Creek and letting myself be loved by Mari and her friends and Paul and his family had felt easy—

But maybe it had partly felt easy because—

"Maybe I wasn't scared of losing Paul because it wasn't *scary* to lose Paul."

She makes a soft humming sound. It's not agreement. But it's not argument, either.

"Damn," I say with a huge sigh. "Back into therapy."

She grins. "Never stops, does it?"

27

RHYS

That fucking kiss.

Every time I take my dick in my hand, every time I make myself come in the shower—muscles rigid, eyes slammed shut, hand slapped against the wall to keep myself upright—I feel like a complete hypocrite, because I said no and I want, want, want *yes*.

I want her in every possible way—next to me at a quilt show, curled up against me in bed, under me while I pound my frustration out in her.

I want to eat Doritos with her and tell her about my childhood, I want to hear more about her grandmother's mean love, I want to see her in every pair of those cheap panties, I want to buy her the expensive versions and tear them off her.

I can't stop thinking about her.

Over the next few days, my grandfather's legacy continues. I go back to my temporary job as a wedding planner. I dive into rescuing Leah and Penelope's disassembled wedding. Leah and I stay on top of the vendors to make sure nothing else goes awry, and the event comes off without a hitch.

I begin the process of unwinding the Eden-wedding disaster. I sit down with Hanna and update her on as much of the story as I can. I tell her about the drive, the car trouble, the rental-car issues, the walk along the side of the road, Eden's sore feet, the flight. I leave out the quilt show, the pretty underwear, the kiss, the way her round ass felt against my swollen cock.

For obvious reasons.

Even so, I think Hanna sees through my sketchy version of events. She gives me a long, curious look before saying, "I take it she wants to cancel the rescheduled wedding."

"Yeah."

It was one of the last questions I asked Eden before we left Sioux Falls. *Do you want me to cancel the wedding?*

I held my breath while she bit her lip, but finally she gave a short, tight nod.

I raised my eyebrows. *You can leave it a few days longer if you want to—just in case.*

She shook her head, and I felt a wild, stirred-up mixture of relief and the same hopelessness that had followed me around since I'd first met Eden in New York.

I hang my head, and Hanna sighs. "What's going to happen?"

"We're going to beg Weggers for mercy; that's what's going to happen. And if that doesn't work, I'm going to figure out what our legal recourse is. In the meantime, maybe we leave things the way they are. Just till we know what all our options are."

She nods.

A FEW DAYS pass before Weggers deigns to make time for Hanna and me to come to his office to discuss "the situation."

Neither of us knows what to expect. Weggers hasn't distinguished himself as flexible in the past. On the other hand, none of us has failed quite this dramatically yet, so we don't have any experience with the begging-for-mercy route.

Weggers sits behind his desk with his eyebrows arched like a short, bald, self-important supervillain while I confess my sins.

I give him a slightly more redacted version of the last few days than I gave Hanna—but it contains essentially the same information. And it makes me remember all the things I'm not saying. The moments between the moments —Doritos and Indian takeout and Eden's shy delight when I retrieved the laundry. (More evidence that she's only been with assholes.)

The feel of her hair between my fingers, her mouth hot under mine.

I shove down how much I miss her, because it's a fact that doesn't—can't—matter.

"I did everything I could," I tell him. "I followed her to Sioux Falls so she could try to reconcile with him—"

This is not an exact rendering of my motives, but give me a break; this is Weggers we're talking about.

"Remember when we talked about this, in the beginning. You said if the wedding got canceled for reasons that had nothing to do with me, you'd take it under advisement."

He makes a *Hmmm* sound.

"Please," I say. "Don't punish Hanna because this marriage wasn't meant to happen. I tried."

Weggers lets me suffer while he hems and haws, wrings his hands, then rises and paces. Hanna starts to speak, and I can tell she's filled with righteous rage, so I give her a pleading look and she shuts the fuck up, thankfully. Hanna is not a Weggers whisperer. She's not an anyone whisperer, although she does seem to know how to handle brides.

More pacing. A lot of throat-clearing and sighing. He consults a thick book on his bookshelf, which turns out to be the dictionary.

Then he says, "I *will* take it under advisement."

"Meaning we're off the hook for this one?"

"Meaning I'll investigate further and inform you of my decision."

A shudder passes through Hanna, and I give her another *Please don't make this worse* look.

"Thank you," I say.

As soon as we're out of his office, she lights into me.

"You let him— How can you let him be such an uptight little pretentious self—"

"He's impossible," I agree. "But getting into it with him is only going to make this worse for all of us."

"What if...?"

Her expression is anguished.

"I won't let you lose Hott Springs Eternal. I promise."

"You can't promise that. You don't know."

"I fucking know," I say.

What I mean is *I will fight for you with the last bone in my body*. She's right. I can't actually know that I'll win. But I'll go down swinging.

"I'll talk to Matias," I tell her.

"Matias—"

"My high school friend who's a lawyer in Bend now. Family and estate. If anyone knows Oregon estate and probate law, it's him. Between us, we'll come up with something. I won't let you down."

"What about when it's Tucker's turn?" she asks. "What if he doesn't—you know, come through?"

I know why she's worried. Tucker hasn't exactly been easy to pin down recently. And he's the only brother who hasn't gotten a letter from our grandfather, which means he's definitely up next. My grandfather had a fairness kink, so there's zero chance he'd let Tucker off the hook.

"He'll come through," I say.

Like my previous promise, it's not something I actually have the ability to commit to, but I'll do everything in my power to make it so. And no matter how miserable Tucker is, I can't imagine him letting us down. I can't imagine him letting *Hanna* down.

"Does *anyone* know what's up with Tucker?" she asks.

"He won't talk about it," I say.

"Have you tried? Like, really tried?"

I sigh. "The last time I tried was six months or so ago. I can give it another shot?"

"I think you should."

"I will."

"And in the meantime, you'll talk to Matias?"

"Yup."

I drop in on Matias, and we sit down in his office in Bend, which is in a white Victorian on the corner of two streets near downtown. His office furniture matches the Victorian vibe, which I bet the small-town clientele loves.

Matias shakes my hand, then pulls me into a hug. When I step away, he says, "I thought you were never coming back to Rush Creek."

"Yeah, me, too."

Matias and I have been in touch since we each found out the other had gone to law school. Every once in a while, he reaches out to me with questions, always ribbing me about how since I'm the "baddest-ass lawyer in New York City," he can trust I know my shit.

I spin out the whole story of the will and Eden's woes for Matias—the amended version, of course, and he listens carefully and takes notes.

"I'm not sure yet we want to go ahead with anything legal," I caution. "But I want to know what our options are."

"I know you know this, but since you didn't contest in the first four months, this is going to be way more of a long shot."

"I have some ideas," I say. "For one thing, we didn't get all the terms up front." I explain exactly how my grandfather has trickled the letters out via Weggers on a mysterious time frame.

"Interesting," he says. "That might be a possible loophole argument."

We talk more about the vulnerabilities of the will—and

of Weggers's execution of it—and Matias tells me he'll start preparing and let me know what he finds.

"You said you rescheduled the wedding for a month out. Have you canceled that yet?"

"Not yet, but we need to."

He nods. "Definitely call off all the wedding guests, return presents, all that jazz. But if I were you, I'd keep the vendors in place for now. Can't hurt, might help. I'm looking at this language here." He points. "*All of them must actually culminate with the planned ceremony. It's vague. Let me do some thinking. I'll work both angles—how to contest the will when we're outside the four-month window and whether there's room for interpretation in the wording of the stipulations."

"I can't fail my sibs," I tell him.

He gives me a sympathetic look. "Yeah," he says. "I know." He sighs. "Your best bet may *still* be kneeling and groveling for Weggers."

"You have no idea how shitty that sounds."

"Shittier than losing the land and your sister's business?"

My turn to sigh. "Fuck no."

"Well. Let's see how this plays out, but be prepared to try that route if I can't see a clear path out of this that won't cost you a fortune and lose you the land anyway."

I sigh again. "Will do." I run a hand through my hair. "How are things with you?"

"Fucking great," he says. "I love Bend, and the practice is kicking ass. We decided to shift the focus. Kind of the opposite of the way you went," he says, sounding faintly apologetic. "We were all burning out on hostile divorces, so we're only doing collaborative divorce now, and we're doing a lot of pro bono work advocating for kids who are getting screwed by the system." He eyes me. "We're looking for another partner." His voice is casual. "You wouldn't happen to know of anyone who's interested in leaving a big-city practice for a more peaceful existence, would you?"

"You mean me?" I ask, startled.

He shrugs one shoulder. "I mean, yeah, that would be the dream—someone like you. But I don't expect you to leave behind big-city money and glory for this. Just because I love it here doesn't mean you would, especially not if you're happy doing what you're doing there. That article in *MANhattan* sure made it sound like you are."

"Yeah, I am," I say without thinking, but then I remember the conversation with Eden. Her suggestion that I do *nicey-nice* divorces.

Matias grins. "My mom, she says divorce is a sacrament. Like marriage. Sacrament coming in, sacrament going out. Like baptism and death."

I laugh. "I take it she's divorced."

"Three times," he says. "The next time, she says she's going the collaborative route."

"Things bad with husband number four?"

He shakes his head. "Nah. Things are good. But she says everything has a shelf life."

I chuckle. "Shelf life. Yeah."

"She and her husband come over to my house for dinner every Sunday night. You should join us sometime. And feel free to bring a plus-one."

My mind jumps to Eden, to her scent and the drag of

her fingers through my hair, before I push the image away. "Not seeing anyone," I say.

He shrugs. "I can hook you up with a friend of a friend-with-bennies if you want. And Bend Tinder is not half bad."

I snort. "Thanks. I think I'm good."

"Well, text me if you want in on the Sunday-night festivities. And definitely let me know if you hear of any kickass lawyers with an eye on family practice partnership in Central Oregon."

I nod. "Will do."

On my drive back through town, my eye snags on In Stitches, Eden's store. The door opens and someone comes out, a form so familiar that my throat closes. Eden. She crosses the street toward Rush to Read Books and disappears inside.

I almost park my car and follow her. Every cell in my body wants to be in her presence again, to talk to her. To share a bag of junk food or split a samosa, to be headed somewhere with her in the seat next to mine.

I have to make myself put my foot back on the gas, because if I'm not careful, I'm going to be telling Matias I know a guy who wants that job.

Matias's mom has the right idea. Everything has an expiration date. And trying to hold on to something that's past its date just lands you with a whole lot of grief and a bad case of food poisoning.

28

EDEN

"I spent years wishing my brothers would come back to Rush Creek," Hanna says. "And now I want to send them all back where they came from."

Laughter ripples through the group of women gathered in Mari's living room.

I've been camping out in Mari and Kane's guest room for two weeks now, ever since they helped me set up the quilt exhibit and move my stuff out of Paul's condo and into storage. I found a new place to live, but I can't move in till October. Mari insisted I stay with them until then, and I took her up on her offer, temporarily moving in with her, Kane, and their two littles, four-year-old Zara and two-year-old Zayden.

I was thrilled when Mari roped me into tonight's activity. She and her friends—mostly her brothers-in-law's wives and girlfriends (Wilders and Wilders-to-be) and Hanna's brothers' wives and girlfriends (Hotts and Hotts-to-be)—get together to watch K-dramas once a week. They just started a new one—*Crash Course in Romance*—so it was the perfect time for me to join the fray.

We've just finished watching and discussing, and the conversation has turned to the Hott brothers.

"What are they doing to annoy you now?" Lucy inquires of Hanna. Lucy's a mom of two and the marketing genius behind Rush Creek's highly successful Wilder Adventures outdoors business. She's also one of those women who's so perfectly put together that you *could* hate her, until you realize that she's absolutely unjudgy and incredibly kind and generous.

"They have *opinions*," Hanna says darkly.

"It's a too-many-cooks problem," Sonya, Hanna's sister-in-law, says. "They all have ideas about what direction to grow the business in, according to their own passions. Quinn thinks we should take the Hott Spot–branded cosmetic lines national. Shane thinks—" She turns to her not-yet-but-almost sister-in-law, Ivy.

"Shane thinks we should hire out the whole ranch regularly as a movie set," Ivy says, rolling her eyes. "Because that's what Rush Creek needs—Hollywood descending en masse."

"Preston thinks we should turn some of the land back over to ranching and possibly run part of the resort dude-ranch style," Natalie supplies. Preston is the oldest Hott brother, and Natalie is his girlfriend. The will required them to work together to create a regular schedule of fun resort activities—which was Natalie's dream job but apparently a tough slog for driven, workaholic Preston. Seems like it's worked out okay for him, though, because he and

Natalie are now head over heels for each other and waiting to close on their new house in Rush Creek.

"And Rhys probably wants to open a Hott Springs Eternal divorce-consulting business," I say dryly. "End-to-end service."

All eyes turn to me. I bite my lip. *Way to go, Eden.* I basically just took the "girlfriend" role in this conversation, and that's the furthest thing from the truth.

Well. Not the *furthest*.

But one kiss followed by mutually deciding that it was a terrible idea does not a girlfriend make.

"Actually," Hanna says, her eyes on my face, "he suggested I add a marital-counseling element to the resort. He thinks all couples should have easy access to pre-marriage counseling during the planning phase." Her gaze sharpens. "What did you do to my brother?"

"Maybe he decided it would be a good idea to make sure no more grooms got last-minute ideas?" I hazard.

"I can't believe your ex-fiancé took off with your quilts!" Natalie says, a frown creasing her pretty round face. "What kind of asshole A) jilts someone and B) doesn't check to make sure that her stuff isn't in his car?!"

I'm not surprised they've heard the story. I wouldn't be surprised if all of Rush Creek knew it. This town is small, and gossip moves fast.

"Paul's a pretty big asshole," I affirm. "At the moment, I'm feeling like I dodged a bullet. And also? Like maybe I should have dodged it earlier. I definitely convinced myself I had some feelings for him that in retrospect I probably didn't."

"Don't beat yourself up," Sonya says. "We've all been there—staying too long when we should have called it."

I shoot her a grateful smile, then sigh. "I do still have to return all the gifts. Or," I say, rethinking, "make *him* do it."

"Yes!" Reggie—Sonya's bestie—fist pumps. "Make him do it."

There's a chorus of murmured agreement.

"What I can't believe," Natalie says, "is that you road tripped with *Rhys*. Wasn't he your husband's divorce lawyer? Talk about awkward."

"Yeah," I admit. "It was at first. But he's a good guy. Not every wedding planner would haul ass all the way to Sioux Falls to rescue stray quilts."

Hanna shakes her head. "Or he was desperately hoping he wouldn't be the brother who finally lost the land and the business."

I must be staring at her blankly, because she says, "You know. The will."

"I know about the will," I say. "But what about the land and the business?"

"Those were the terms," she says. "Rhys has to make every wedding he was assigned come off smoothly, or the Hott land will automatically pass to Blue Iron Mining, and obviously if that happens, they'll shut down my—"

"Hanna," Sonya murmurs, and she freezes.

The other women shift in their seats, giving off that contagious unease that happens when someone in the group has stepped in it.

"You didn't know." Sonya's voice is gentle as she takes in my expression. "He didn't tell you what the consequences were."

I shake my head. "I had...no idea."

"Shit," Hanna says.

"So if I didn't get back together with Paul—because I didn't get back together with Paul—you're going to lose the land and your business?"

"No," Hanna says forcefully. "That's *not* going to happen. Rhys won't let that happen. He's negotiating with Weggers. Talking to another lawyer friend. He'll get it sorted."

"God," I say. "I am *so, so* sorry. I ruined *everything* for you. For your family."

"No, you didn't," Hanna said. "My grandfather and Arthur Weggers and this goddamned will did. You didn't do anything wrong. You couldn't have acted any differently from how you did. None of us wanted for you to go through with a wedding that wasn't right for you. Not to a guy like that."

The rest of the women are nodding and humming and being unbelievably kind and generous considering most of their jobs—or husbands' or friends' jobs—depend on the continued survival of Hott Springs Eternal.

Meanwhile something else has become clear to me. Why Rhys was so nice to me, so solicitous. Why he followed me every last step of the journey, right to Grace's doorstep. Because he was still hoping I'd get back together with Paul, so he could save his family's land and his sister's business.

And I was so pathetically grateful.

I *kissed* him.

Oh, God, what an *idiot* I am.

"Where are you going?!" Hanna demands, but I'm

already grabbing my coat and shoving my feet into my shoes.

"There are a few things I need to say to your brother," I tell her.

29

___

RHYS

"Okay," Shane says, poking the firepit. We're sitting around it in the backyard of Quinn and Sonya's new house. We've finished the hot-dogs-and-sausages and brews portion of the program and moved on to s'mores and bourbon. "You've heard how the filming's been going, and I've heard about Quinn's new drug and Preston's endless soul searching—"

"Hey," Preston says, but it's good-natured. As a fellow driven New Yorker, I never minded Preston in his uptight mode, and I almost don't know what to make of his chill demeanor since he and Natalie got together and he moved back to Rush Creek. "I don't want to jump into something unless it's really what I want to be doing."

"He's doing that thing that most people do while they hike around Europe when they're twenty-two," Quinn says. "Finally discovering himself."

"I think what most people do when they hike around Europe when they're twenty-two is have a shit-ton of bad-idea sex," Shane says. "Preston has never done anything that's a bad idea."

Preston scowls. "That's not true. I've just never done anything impulsive. Well. Until recently. But they're not the same thing."

"What's the difference?" Shane asks.

"You can slowly wedge yourself into a life you hate," Preston says. "Which is a bad idea. Or you can impulsively finally let yourself be happy. Which is not."

"Huh," Shane muses. "That actually makes some sense."

We're all quiet for a bit, thinking about it. Or at least I'm thinking about it.

More exactly, I'm thinking about Matias and the job he more or less offered me, my life back in New York City, and how I feel about it. I don't hate it. But neither would I exactly call myself happy.

I'm not sure I've ever felt *happy*.

Yes you have, a voice responds. *You were happy on the road with Eden.*

But that wasn't real life, I tell the voice. *That was...a fluke. An anomaly. A glitch in the matrix.*

"I want to hear about this road trip of yours, Rhys," Shane says. "And where things stand with Weggers and the will."

Everyone turns to look at me, and I'm even more aware than I already was that I'm the first of four brothers to fail at his mission.

"He's *investigating*," I say. "And *taking the situation under advisement*. Fucking slowly."

"Do we think a financial contribution might help him think more quickly?"

"Jesus, no," Preston says. "It'll insult his pride and his ethics, and he'll fuck us on principle."

"Agreed," I say. "No, we have to give him time...and if he doesn't give in, I'm going to go all full-tilt legal on his ass. Matias Alfaro and I are working on angles."

"Anything we can do?" Quinn asks.

I shake my head. "I'll let you know as soon as I hear anything."

"Does anyone feel like Weggers is toying with us?" Shane demands. "Like he never had any intention of enforcing the will and he wants to see how far we'll take this?"

"No," Preston says. "I'm pretty sure he's not that clever or that manipulative."

"He's definitely manipulative."

"No. Granddad was manipulative. Weggers is...faithful, obedient, and rule-abiding."

"He's basically Granddad's dog in that scenario," Shane says.

Preston winces. "Well. Kind of."

We all ponder that for a moment.

Shane slaps a hand on his knee. "Well, at least tell us about the road trip. Let me get this right. You chased some runaway bride to Sioux Falls and hauled her back here so she wouldn't fuck up the terms of the will?"

I roll my eyes. "Who'd you hear that version from?"

"Nan at Rush Creek Bakery."

"Of course you did," Quinn groans. "And it didn't occur to you that she might have slightly twisted the story?"

"I like to give people the benefit of the doubt." Shane crosses his arms. "So if that's not what happened, what did?"

They all look at me.

"I'm sure she doesn't want the story repeated..." I say.

Three sets of Hott eyebrows rise, and damn, I've only made them *more* curious.

"This much is public knowledge," Quinn says. "The groom was the runaway. And he happened to have some of the bride's belongings, important stuff, in his car. She needed to go after him, and Rhys went with her, to see if maybe they'd reconcile—"

"—and they ended up with this whole *planes, trains, and automobiles* thing—" Preston adds.

"There were no trains," I correct.

"Still," Shane says. "You went all the way to Sioux Falls with her. That must have been kind of hellish for you."

It takes me a second to realize he's talking to me. "What?"

"You're, like, the king of divorce, and here you are, trapped in a car with a weepy bride, having to talk her into marrying this guy who ditched her—"

"It wasn't like that," I say sharply. "I wasn't trapped, and she wasn't weepy, and in the end, she realized she'd never wanted to marry him in the first place."

It's suddenly so quiet we can hear the crackle of the fire, the rhythmic croaking of what has to be a very cold frog, and the occasional hoot of an owl. They're all staring at me.

"What?" I demand.

"Holy shit," Shane says slowly, his voice almost a drawl. "You *like* her."

I want so badly to tell him he's being ridiculous...but I can't bring myself to sell out Eden like that. Because, fuck, I *do* like her. A hell of a lot.

"Yeah," I say. "Yeah, I like her."

Then they're all hooting and hollering and slapping my back and nudging my shoulder, calling out stuff about how the World's Biggest Cynic has finally fallen and the King of Divorce has met the Queen of Hearts and all this other bullshit, and finally the only way I can make them shut up is to yell "Stop!"

They all go silent again—this time joined by the frog and owl, who've obviously been scared into muteness.

"Rhys Hott," says a voice behind me, and even if the voice weren't as familiar as a recurrent dream, I'd know who it was from the way every cell in my body stirs in response to having her so close.

"You could have told me the truth. I could have handled it."

30

———————

RHYS

My brothers are pains in my ass, but I'll give them this: They know when to make themselves scarce. They introduce themselves as they're melting back toward the house—"Quinn, nice to meet you, sorry I have to go check on the dogs"; "Preston, Rhys's oldest brother, I need to call the carpeting guy back so he'll have what he needs in the morning"; "Shane, Rhys's movie-star brother, and I apologize heartily if you met my ass before my face—this is probably a letdown for you."

And then they're gone, and it's just Eden and me.

"You should have told me what was at stake," she says. "You should have trusted me. Instead you let me think you stayed all that time because you cared about *me*," she says. "You let me think you stayed with me all the way to Sioux Falls because you were a good guy. But you did all that shit —cooking dinner and stopping at the quilt show and buying the frog slippers and...all of it!—because you wanted to stay on my good side, so you could talk me into getting back together with Paul, so your sister wouldn't lose her business."

She's talking so fast, and her voice is so tight and tear-laced that it takes me a moment to understand what's happened. But then I get it. Someone filled her in on the whole big picture with the will.

"Eden," I start. Because she has it all wrong.

"You could have told me at any time during that whole trip that what you wanted was for me to marry Paul. That you *needed* me to marry Paul. We could have figured something out. Maybe I could even have—"

"No," I say flatly.

"You didn't let me finish the sentence."

"That's because I know what you were going to say, and the answer is no fucking way."

"We could have done some kind of fake wedding. Something."

"You still would have had to stand at an altar with that asshole."

"And maybe that wouldn't have been so bad. If your family's land and business are at stake—"

"No," I say again, and it sounds even harder, more brittle, and she flinches, takes a step back. We're both breathing hard again, like we've run a hundred miles to get to this point, which maybe we have.

"You're right that I should have told you. And you're right that it was selfish of me not to tell you. But you're dead fucking wrong about why I did it. It wasn't because I wanted to get you and Paul back together. The absolute dead fucking last thing I wanted was for you and Paul to get back together, because—"

My words have gone rough and gravelly, and it's not too late to hold them back, it's not too late to be a good man.

But I'm not a good man.

"—because I wanted you for myself. So, no, you're not going to marry Paul or fake marry Paul or anything even remotely in that ballpark."

She stares at me, wide eyed.

"I'm sorry," I say. "I'm sorry I didn't tell you what was at stake and I'm sorry I let you think I was a good guy doing a good thing when I'm actually a selfish bastard and I'm sorry—"

"Stop," she says.

"I couldn't do right by you and Hanna—"

"Rhys," she says more sharply. "Shut the fuck up."

I do.

Somehow, we've gotten closer, so close that I can see the gold-and-amber flecks in the green of her eyes, so I can see the small spray of freckles across the bridge of her nose. And somehow her hands have wrapped themselves around my forearms, and they're gripping me tight. Somehow, somehow, my hands are in her hair, twisting in the strands, so I can hold her head perfectly in place, so I can see her gaze settle hungrily on my mouth, so I can watch her lips part just before I claim her.

Mine, the kiss says.

From the first instant, it's not enough. I have her lips, but I want her tongue. I tease the seam of her mouth, and she opens to me, our tongues tangling and jousting. She moans into my mouth, and my cock hardens so fast that I get lightheaded.

I angle my head, chasing the silk of her tongue, trying

to tell her with this kiss—in case it's the only one, the last one—how much I need and want her.

Her body is slim and willowy but surprisingly strong. She presses herself to me like she's trying to get as close as she can, and her eagerness lights me on fire. I palm her—slender shoulders, the small of her back, the sweet, modest curve of her ass. She arches into me, seeking more, and when I raise my hand, she gives a soft moan of relief and presses her breast into my palm.

The gesture almost destroys me—it's so needy and so trusting at the same time. All I can do is give her what she wants, cupping my hand around the small but perfect curve of her breast, finding the needy tip with finger and thumb and teasing until she's half-riding my thigh, while I keep kissing her, the kisses getting deeper and messier, broken up with moans and nips and soft curses.

I can tell that if I keep going, I'll make her come, right here in—

I freeze. And slowly draw back. I close off the kiss. I gently peel us apart, setting her back from my overheated body, putting space between us.

Her eyes comb over my face, fearful and hopeful.

"I'm staying in Quinn and Sonya's guesthouse," I say. "Want to come inside for a drink?"

Her sudden grin is a spark in the dark, and in the firelight, she is disheveled and hazy eyed and unbelievably beautiful.

"Thought you'd never ask," she says.

31

EDEN

After making sure the campfire's out, we go inside. Rhys pours me a glass of red wine and himself a tumbler of whiskey, and we sit together on the couch. The guesthouse at Sonya and Quinn's new house is lovely—cathedral-ceilinged great room, big stone fireplace, windows that right now are big black rectangles but I'm guessing, from the location and direction, look out on the three mountain peaks we affectionately call the Triplets.

"I should have told you sooner how I felt," he says. "But I didn't want it to be true. I didn't want it to be true when I was representing Teller, and I didn't want it to be true when you were marrying Paul. Then you weren't marrying Paul but I needed you to be marrying Paul, and—"

He closes his eyes and shakes his head. "It was a fucking mess, and it was easier to keep ignoring my feelings. It had worked for me up to that point, so why wouldn't it keep working?"

"Because we were stuck in a car together?" I hazard. My chest has filled with a light, buoyant feeling that I think might be happiness. "And in hotel rooms?" I take the glass out of his hand and set it on the coffee table, set mine beside it. I throw a leg across his thighs and straddle him, knees on either side of his thighs. It feels so good to have him there, between my legs.

"The piggyback ride almost killed me," I say.

"It almost killed *me*."

"Mutually assured destruction."

Rhys sighs. "That's about the shape of it."

I jack my hips closer to his, and he makes a rough sound deep in his chest. I feel it everywhere. My body is hungry, and the only way to ease the craving is to press myself closer to him.

"God. You have no idea how much I've wanted this," he grits out.

"Me, too."

"I wanted this the first time you walked into my law firm's conference room."

"You did not."

"I did. I swear it."

"You wanted to squash me like a bug." I hold a thumb and forefinger up to demonstrate.

"I wanted to squash you between my body and the wall." He tugs my hips closer.

"You looked at me like I was the gum on the bottom of someone's shoe."

"I looked at you like you were the one woman I couldn't have and therefore wouldn't let myself want."

I thought the kiss in the backyard was intense, but this is something else entirely. Fierce and primal. Rhys's mouth claims and devours, and I'm barely able to keep up with the pace he sets. He seals his mouth over mine, his tongue seeking entrance, and I open to him willingly. We kiss and kiss, until I can feel my heartbeat setting the pace for my hips to rock against the hard bulge in his jeans.

I reach for his hand and bring it back to my breast. He lets out a grunt of satisfaction, his thumb brushing over the tight peak of my nipple, sending silver threads of need straight to my clit.

I can't stop grinding into him. I can't pull away from the touch of his fingers.

"Rhys."

"What do you need?"

As soon as he asks, I know. "You, too. I want you to come, too."

He shakes his head. "Tonight's about you. Just you."

I still my hips, and he makes a raw, dark sound, like it hurts him that I stopped. "Don't stop," he pleads.

"You, too," I repeat.

He's still hesitating. I shift my position so I can rock over the thickest part of his thigh, a hot, hard tree trunk of muscle against my over-sensitized flesh. I reach for his zipper.

His fingers intercept mine, anchor them. And I know if I'm going to get what I want, I'm going to have to tell him why I want it. And I'm hot enough that the words come easily, the confession slipping through bruised, swollen lips into the safe space between us:

"You looked at me like you hated me. You were this big, broody, restrained, ultra-serious lawyer, and nothing got to you. You were going to do your job, and I was nothing. Just this...nuisance in the conference room and the courtroom, something to brush away like a mosquito buzzing around you. And I want—I want—I need—you to fall apart. I need you to make a mess of me."

He groans, a harsh sound yanked from deep in his chest, and his head falls to my shoulder, and he doesn't try again to stop me as I work his button free, his zipper down. As I reach into his jeans and free him from the constraints of his briefs. In my hand, his cock is gratifyingly big and thick and so, so hard, the skin pulled taut over the pretty head. He makes another rough, wrecked sound, and God, I hope he's close, because I'm so fucking close, knowing I can do that to him.

Then he's kissing me again, deep and thorough, hungry, one hand on my hip, guiding my movements, the other still teasing the taut bead of my nipple. Heat and need curl and flare through my belly and thighs, pulling all the pleasure into a twisting, winding spiral that gathers everything with it. My thighs tighten around his, my core clenches around its own hunger, the bright pleasure in my chest tightens harder and deeper down, and then I'm coming, licking my pleasure into his mouth as he kisses his name and my cries off my lips. And then he's shouting—*shouting!*—his body rigid under me, his face split with pleasure, as he falls apart under my touch.

32

———————

RHYS

When I come to my senses, Eden is collapsed against my chest, her cheek pressed to my shoulder, one hand wrapped around my arm, holding tight.

I don't want to move, but—"Jesus," I say. "I really did make a mess, huh?"

I can feel her smile. "Uh-huh. Thank you."

"Well. Thank you right back."

Her smile gets bigger.

"Let me clean us up."

She slowly loosens her iron grip on my bicep, and I gently lift her and set her down on the couch, where she leans back and closes her eyes. She's beautiful like this, boneless and wrecked, her face smooth and relaxed.

I go to the bathroom and come back with a washcloth, which I use to clean her hand—every finger gently in turn, while she purrs at the warmth and sensation—and then myself. Then I sit back down next to her and say, "You have a dirty streak I wasn't expecting. And obviously, I love the fuck out of it."

Eyes still closed, she says, "I've never said anything like that before. I've never *thought* anything like that before. But something about this"—she gestures at the two of us—"makes me really want to be honest with you. It makes no sense that I would trust you. But I do."

I want—I need—you to fall apart. I need you to make a mess of me.

She got what she wanted, and it was only half because of her small, warm hand fisted over the taut skin of my cock. The rest of it was because I wanted that, too. To fall apart for her. For us to fall apart for each other.

"God. Eden. You fucking destroy me."

Her mouth curves into a smile. "Good."

I'm glad her eyes are closed, because I'm pretty sure the expression on my face is way too intense. I get myself back under control just in time, but then she opens her eyes and smiles right at me and that wrecks me all over again—the sunshine of it.

"Eden," I say.

"What?"

"Your phone is absolutely blowing up."

She reaches for it, swipes it open and reads, laughs. Hands it to me.

MARI

Eden, everything okay?

LUCY

We all want to know. You left in such a hurry.

HANNA

He's offed her and hidden the body.

LUCY

Your faith in your brother is touching.

HANNA

They've all been pushed too far by this will thing.

REGGIE

I've been watching this "will thing" play out for a while, and my money is on them banging like bunnies right now.

SONYA

Gentle, Reggie. She's not ready.

NATALIE

I don't remember anyone being gentle with me, and I definitely wasn't ready.

SONYA

Natalie, my love, you were born ready. And you've never needed anyone to be gentle with you in your life.

LUCY

She's not answering.

REGGIE

That probably means I'm right.

HANNA

Or I am.

I set the phone down, laughing. "They're not far off."

"What's going to happen?" she asks quietly. "With Weggers and the will and the land and everything. Can I help? I wasn't kidding about the fake wedding."

I shake my head. "It's under control. We can't do anything till we hear back from Weggers, who's deciding whether he can cut us some slack. I still think he might cave. And regardless, no outcome of this situation involves you going anywhere near Paul Graves."

I almost growl it, and that makes her smile. Which makes me smile.

"Do you think—will it be okay for Hanna?"

"I won't let it be anything but okay," I tell her. I lean over and kiss her again. When we—finally—pull apart, she says, "I should—probably get back. I stole Mari's car keys and her car. I should get them back to her."

I snicker.

"Plus, I have to teach a ridiculously early class tomorrow and all my supplies are at home, so I think I should head out, but—I don't want you to feel like I'm running away."

Eden pushes herself off the couch, and I feel a thousand things at once. Strongest among them is the urge to pull her back down, to wrap her in my arms and keep her here with me. *Don't go,* I want to say.

When I came to Rush Creek, I couldn't believe I had to give up my New York City life for a month. Now the remaining few weeks don't feel like nearly enough time. And I have to fly back to New York this coming Tuesday for a couple of days to make an emergency court appearance for a case I thought was on ice.

"There's a Hott family dinner Sunday night at Hanna's. Come with me."

She freezes, and I know I've gone too far.

"'Family dinner.'" She makes the air quotes, her expression stiff.

"My siblings and their significant others—"

"Does that mean that I'm *significant?*"

It feels like there's no right answer to that question, like if I say yes I'm asking too much of her, and if I say no I'm pushing her away—and lying through my teeth. So I dodge the question. "It doesn't have to be a big deal. I want to see you tomorrow night, and that's where I'm going to be. At a family get-together. Easton's an amazing cook, one of Hanna's friends from high school is coming, too, and rumor has it that Tucker might actually show up. It doesn't have to mean anything unless you want it to."

Do you want it to? I'm tempted to ask, but I'm not sure it'll do any good to know the answer.

She bites her bottom lip, worries it between her teeth. "Do they all hate me because I didn't marry Paul and screwed everything up?"

"*No.*"

She smiles. "Are they all going to *assume things* about us if I show up with you?"

My turn to smile. "Unfortunately, yes. They're going to assume that, in Reggie's words, we're banging like bunnies."

That makes her smile, too, and the tension eases in her face and shoulders. "Okay," she says. "I can live with that. I just don't want them to start putting pressure on you to, like, move back to Rush Creek and make an honest woman out of me or anything."

"I'll set them straight if they do that," I tell her.

I walk her out to her car, which is parked on the street

outside the main house. She pauses before getting in and lifts her face to mine.

I only mean to give her a good-night kiss, but as soon as my lips get close to hers, I feel the way the charged particles between us align, and I know there's no such thing.

"God," I groan, when I finally manage to break the kiss.

She's breathless, too, her hands plucking at my clothes. "I know," she says. "This is—next level. I feel like I've heard people talk about chemistry like this, but it's never actually happened to me."

I heave a sigh of relief, and she laughs. "You neither?"

"Me neither," I admit.

Then we're kissing again, her body molding to mine, and I'm pretty sure I'm going to drag her back to the guest-house, except that just then the door of Quinn's house opens and disgorges two of my brothers. We break apart like we've been electrified.

"Glad the argument's over," Shane says, and I roll my eyes at him and open the door to the car Eden stole from Mari and watch her drive away.

"Don't. Say. Anything. Else," I command my brothers. "And for fuck's sake, when I bring her to family dinner, don't get into the whole Granddad-matchmaking-fantasy bullshit."

"We would *never*," Shane says, and Preston raises his eyebrows at me, grinning, and I roll my eyes again and stride back to the guesthouse before my brothers can be any more of their pain-in-the-ass selves.

33

EDEN

"If this family dinner is anything like the Wilder family dinners," Mari says, "you should wear jeans and a sweatshirt and expect to end up with dog hair —if not vomit—and spit-up and a good amount of dinner on you. And that's if they don't make you play flag football or wiffle ball or—knowing the Hotts, it would actually be Nerf-blaster tag and Jell-O wrestling."

I set my favorite sparkly shirt back on the bed. "I'm not sure I should be going to this."

"Why not?"

"Because it feels...presumptuous. I'm not family, and I'm not likely to become family."

"Did he say, 'I want you to come to family dinner so you can practice being my future wife'?"

"No," I say. "But I feel like it's...implied. And I already feel like I have a history of rushing into relationships—and then rushing toward the altar—and regretting it."

Mari shakes her head. "When a lot of stuff goes wrong, it's easy to start second-guessing yourself. But that's actually when it's super important to lean in to trusting your instincts. You *know* what you want. And just because you can't guarantee a perfect future doesn't mean you shouldn't let yourself enjoy what's happening now."

"You sound like the voice of experience."

"I may have a bit of that," she admits. "Hey, how's the quilt show going?"

"So well!" I say. "We got a piece in the *Oregonian* and one in the *Seattle Times* and Five Rivers Arts and Crafts has been flooded with visitors."

"That's amazing! I bet that makes you feel better about driving halfway across the country." She gives me a sideways smile. "Not that you have many regrets."

"No," I admit. "Not about the drive, anyway. Just about the chain of events that *caused* the drive."

"Speaking of which, what happened with getting Paul to take responsibility for returning the gifts?"

"I called him and said, 'I need you to return the gifts.' I was ready to say he owed me, but I didn't have to. He just agreed to do it."

She rolls her eyes. "It's too little, too late, but at the least the fucker said he'd do it."

I laugh at her vehemence. It's good to have a bestie. "I told him I wanted them all returned by the end of the month, and he promised me he was on it."

"Good work," she says, beaming. "Is he back in Rush Creek?"

"Yup. Packing up the condo. I saw him briefly yesterday. I'd left some books behind. He said he's selling the condo and moving to Bend. He thought that would be better for both of us, and I couldn't argue."

"How are you feeling about the whole thing? Seeing him?"

"It was honestly fine," I say. "I couldn't believe I'd ever thought he was a good idea, and that was about it. I'm definitely starting to think my pride was hurt worse than my heart by what Paul did."

"And you have a *great* distraction." She grins.

I'd come home and confessed everything that had happened with Rhys to Mari, who was sitting up waiting for me with a knowing look on her face.

"How are things with him?" she asks.

"I mean, there's no chance that it could actually go anywhere. I'm basically viewing it as a rebound."

Well. I'm *trying* to remind myself that I *should* view it that way. And not to float away on a kissy cloud.

Mari's eyebrows go way up.

"I *am*," I say. "And I'm sure he is, too, because he works in *New York City*."

"Have you *asked* him?" she says.

"No, but when I said something about his family making assumptions about us ending up together long term, he said, 'I'll set them straight if they do that.'"

"And how did you feel about that?"

"Relieved," I say. "It would be absurd for me to jump straight out of Paul's frying pan and into Rhys's fire."

Even if every time I think about what happened last night, my body goes white hot and I tingle from head to toe.

I *like* Rhys's fire—I'll say that.

"Just because the timing utterly sucks doesn't mean it's wrong," Mari says.

"Just because you're happily married to the perfect guy

doesn't mean I have to make another dumb mistake right after the last one," I say.

She grins at that. "Okay, okay, I'll shut up. But I think you can safely go to one family dinner without risking ruin."

"I don't want to get roped into the whole weird mystique about the will matchmaking people. Quinn and Sonya, Ivy and Shane, Natalie and Preston. It's a combination of coincidence and probably a lot of self-fulfilling prophecy. If you think something's fated, confirmation bias will make you lean into it."

"Hmm," Mari says. "Hadn't exactly thought of it that way. You know," she says, "when I was trying to figure out whether Zara and I should stay in Rush Creek with Kane, it was a little like that, too. Lucy was already with Gabe, Rachel with Brody, and Jessa with Clark. And there was this family lore that if Gabe's dog, Buck, chewed up a girlfriend's possessions, she was The One. I thought it was total bullshit...until Buck ate one of my shoes."

"And then confirmation bias set in and you determined that you and Zara should stay with Kane, and you lived happily ever after, because confirmation bias has a fifty-fifty success rate at happily ever after, just like chance, dating sites, and arranged marriages."

"Whoa," she says. "Now who's the cynic?"

"Maybe I've been spending too much time with Rhys."

Although Rhys, to be fair, hasn't said anything cynical about marriage since the beginning of our road trip. And I remember how Hanna said that he wanted to introduce premarital counseling to the wedding-planning business. Hanna had dismissed that as more cynicism...but what if it wasn't? What if Rhys and I have swapped perspectives on happily-ever-after?

It's a disturbing question.

"Just go to dinner and enjoy the good company and don't worry too much about what it means," Mari says. "You deserve some fun after everything you've been through."

34

RHYS

I pick Eden up at Mari's at six. She has her hair pulled back in a ponytail, and as she slides into the car, I say, "Have I ever mentioned that women in ponytails are my kink?"

She laughs, a perfect, bubbly sound. "You have not."

I wrap a hand gently around her hair and draw her close to me, lowering my mouth over hers. Her mouth is warm and inviting, and it's several minutes before either of us is inclined to surface.

"Hello to you, too," she says, smiling, when I finally break the kiss. "Oh, good, I didn't totally underdress." She runs her eyes over me in a way that has my whole body heating. "Anyone ever mention you look as good in jeans and a T-shirt as in a button-down and slacks?"

"No," I say.

"Mmm," she says, half turning in her seat to press a hand to my chest, then stroking my shoulder and wrapping her hand around my biceps. "I approve."

"You don't have to stop," I say. "There's lots more of me to grope."

She laughs. "We'll be late."

"They're probably expecting us to arrive fifteen minutes late and still putting our clothes back on," I remind her.

"In that case," she says, and puts her other hand on my jaw, turning my head so our mouths meet.

We manage to keep it to five minutes, clothes on, because Eden makes me an offer I can't refuse, her hand slipping down to cup my cock through my jeans: "I want you to save this for later so you can make a mess of me again."

"Done," I say and—breathing hard—manage to get both my hands back on the wheel.

"So is this a long-standing tradition? Family dinner?" she asks when both of us are breathing more or less normally again.

"Nope. Brand new. My sibs started it after Preston moved back to Rush Creek. For a long time, the six of us were scattered to the winds, so it couldn't happen, but Natalie's such a coordinator that once she and Preston were together there was no stopping it."

"And you're sure it's okay that you're bringing a guest?"

"Yup. Ivy brings her sister sometimes. Hanna brings random sisters-in-law when their husbands are away on trips. Everyone brings strays from time to time."

"That's me," she says, laughing. "A stray."

"I think I'm the stray. You picked me up on your way out of Rush Creek."

"You were driving the getaway car."

"Maybe we're both strays and that's why we like each other."

She strokes a hand over mine, and it takes all my self-control to continue gripping the wheel.

We arrive at Hanna's a few minutes after that and are ushered into the fray. Eloise, Hanna and Easton's daughter, toddles around the living room while the adults coo and babble at her like they're the ones who don't know how to string together full sentences. Sonya and Quinn's dogs, Gus and Frank, roam back and forth among their owners, their other favorite humans, and the kitchen, where Easton occasionally "accidentally" drops a treat onto the floor. Gus is a rescue with one straight ear and one floppy one, a tuft of white hair on his brown head, and an absurdly long tail. Frank is a Chihuahua/Great Dane/Labrador mix where the Great Dane seems to have won out over the Chihuahua, except for his slightly ratty face. Neither of them is much of a looker, but they're the sweetest dogs I know.

If the possibility of losing the land is on anyone's mind, I can't tell. The mood is buoyant.

Eden has already met almost everyone present, but I introduce her to Easton, Eloise, Gus, and Frank, then step away for a second to hand Hanna a check I'd collected from one of our wedding clients. When I come back, Eden is crouched, scritching Gus's tufted head, smiling up at something Quinn has said to her. She looks like she's always been here, like she belongs with my family.

Something shifts and settles, warm, in my gut. I'm about to poke and prod at it, to see if I'm okay with letting it stay, when Hanna, who's standing by the front window, says, "You guys! Tucker's here!"

"Seriously?" Preston asks. "I would have put money on him not showing up."

Hanna surveys us. "We probably shouldn't all be standing around staring at the door when he walks in, or we're going to scare him right back out again."

Everyone immediately makes themselves busy, chatting with their immediate neighbor, fussing over a drink, or grabbing food.

Hanna tucks herself behind the small window of the front door, where she can watch Tucker's progress without being so obvious.

"It's good that he's here, right?" Eden asks me.

"It's great." And it'll be a nice bonus if I don't have to hunt him down and make him talk, because I'm guessing I won't fix what's dogging him by getting in his face.

"Shiii—" Hanna looks down at Eloise, who is aggressively petting Frank's head. "Sugar!"

"What?" Natalie asks.

But it becomes obvious a second later when Tucker's truck's big engine roars back to life in the driveway. A moment later, wheels grind on gravel, and the truck sounds recede.

"He's gone," Hanna says, unnecessarily.

Confused and concerned glances circle the room.

"Damn," Preston says. "Should have laid that bet." But it's half-hearted. He's worried—I can see it.

Hanna scowls. "He stared at the house with this weird expression on his face. Then he put his head down on the steering wheel and stayed that way for a while. Then he started the truck and left."

"Do you think he saw you at the window?" Natalie asks.

She shakes her head. "I don't think it had anything to do with what he saw. Or that wasn't the impression I got, anyway."

"God," Natalie says. "Poor Tucker."

I exchange glances with Eden. She bites her lip and steps closer. "Hey," she murmurs. "Do you think you should maybe...you know, go after him?"

"And leave you here with my family?"

"I'll be okay. You said you've been thinking you should talk to him. And it seems like maybe he could use a friend. Or a brother."

I know it must be hard for her, being on the spot with my whole family, so for her to make this offer feels...huge. Generous. I'm suddenly absurdly, deeply grateful that someone this big-hearted wants to be with me, for however short a time, in however limited a way.

And I crave so, so much more of her.

But now's not the time to dwell on that. We've given Tucker space, but enough's enough.

"Yeah," I say. "I should go after him. I'll either come right back here or text you to let you know where I end up. And—thank you."

"Of course," she says, and she tilts her chin up.

I kiss her, in front of my whole nosy family, and then I go after my brother.

35

EDEN

Easton calls us into the kitchen for dinner, which is two lasagnas—one spinach and pesto, and one meat lover's. I take a spoonful of each.

"Why choose?" I say, lifting a shoulder as Sonya comes up on my left.

"Indeed," she says, laughing, and does the same. "Woman after my own heart."

We sit together on the couch.

"So," a voice says, and I look up to find Shane, eyes amused, watching me. "You and Rhys, huh?"

"Shane," Ivy warns from the doorway behind us. She comes in and edges up to her fiancé. "Behave."

"Don't I always?" he asks innocently.

"Almost never," she says, sighing, but she smiles up at him fondly, and it's clear she adores him.

"This is amazing." I indicate my plate full of lasagnas, salad, and hot, tender garlic bread. "I want a lifetime invite to family dinner."

The whole room goes silent.

"Shit! No! I didn't mean it like that!"

They're all staring at me.

"I swear I didn't mean it like that. I just meant, you know, for the food."

"Uh-huh," Shane says. He's smirking.

I sigh.

"I can't believe Rhys left you alone with this crew," Sonya whispers. "He must have a lot of faith in your ability to hold your own."

"I told him to go. Maybe Tucker will talk to him."

"Yeah," she says. "I'm worried about him."

"No secrets," Natalie says. "It gives me seventh-grade flashbacks."

"We were just saying we hope Rhys can get something out of Tucker," Sonya says.

"Amen to that," Natalie says.

It gets quiet for a second while we all privately agree.

Gus sniffs his way up to my knee, then paws it for attention.

"Hey, dude," I say, leaning down and giving him a nose kiss. He jumps up on the couch, turns once, and plops down, snuggled up against my thigh.

"Look at him!" Sonya says. "He doesn't usually do that with anyone except me."

I scritch Gus's goofy little tuft. "I'd almost forgotten how nice it feels. It's been almost four months since Milo went to New York—"

"Milo?" Ivy asks.

"My dog. My ex has joint custody."

Sonya makes a sympathetic face. "That sucks."

"It kinda does," I agree, as Gus sighs and settles his face

on my thigh, politely not interfering with my plate so I can go on eating my lasagna.

"Hey," Natalie says. "I don't know if you saw, but the Rush Creek firefighters are doing a benefit for the shelter, and there are some ovary-blasting photos of hot firefighters and cute dogs." She pulls out her phone and passes it around.

When it gets to me, I set my fork down and flip through the photos, not seriously shopping, but…my fingers stop on one. The guy's not half as hot as Rhys, but the dog is flipping adorable, a cocker spaniel–beagle mix with mismatched floppy ears going in opposite directions.

So. Tempting. But there's still the problem of Milo being around half the time and not the other half. Reluctantly, I pass the phone back to Natalie.

Ivy is the first to break the silence. "Sonya and I went to your show at Five Rivers. It was incredible!"

"Aw, thank you."

"It was mobbed, too. The woman who runs Five Rivers says they've never gotten this many people at a show before."

I smile. I've been hearing good things from all corners —including from the quilters, who've been getting commissions and curated show invitations by the bucketload. It makes me really happy.

"So you run a quilt store?" Ivy asks. "That's pretty freaking cool. What got you into that?"

"My grandmother was a quilter," I say. "She taught me."

"Was?" Sonya asks.

"She passed when I was in college."

"I'm sorry."

"No, it's okay. She was a…difficult woman."

She tilts her head. "Difficult how?"

Every face in the room is soft with attentive curiosity, and I find myself, strangely, wanting to tell them more. "Cold. Withholding. Her only love language was teaching me to sew. And I was a lonely kid. No siblings, father died when I was little, and my mom was—absent. I figured out pretty quickly that being good at sewing would get me the attention and the affection I wanted."

"Poor kid," Sonya says. I like the way she says it, acknowledging what I went through but also making it clear that we both know it was childhood pain, so I don't feel like she's pitying me. "I'm surprised you ended up liking it so much."

"Yeah," I say. "Even once I realized how messed up our dynamic was, it didn't kill my love of quilting. If anything, it made me want to hold on to it more. Because she did let me down—but also, it was all she knew how to give."

"That's very generous of you," Ivy says.

"Took a lot of therapy," I say, laughing.

"Therapy for the win," Shane says. I flash him a quick look, thinking he's messing with me, but he gives me a nod and a warm smile, and I realize: He means it.

For all his irreverence, there's a core of kindness in him. Maybe in all the Hotts.

"I don't know a ton about quilting," Sonya says. "Do you make, like, the big ones? Like to go on beds? Or small ones that are artsier? Or…?"

"My grandmother's style was very traditional. Lots of perfectly formed squares with exactly quarter-inch seams, but the older I got, the more I experimented. She didn't approve, of course. She called them messy quilts. But by then I realized she wasn't the last word on quilting—or on life in general—and I started sneaking into other quilting classes and soaking up everything I could learn. And as soon as I could get the loans to do it, I started my own shop."

"That's amazing," Natalie says. "I love how you made something beautiful out of a hard childhood."

And damn, now I like her, too. I like them all, and that's —awesome, and it also sucks, because I'm *not* getting a family dinner invitation for life, just for tonight, and when Rhys goes back to New York there won't be any reason for me to hang out with this crew.

And if Weggers decides *not* to cut the Hotts slack on the will, my wedding will be the reason why Hanna lost everything, and no one will want *that* reminder at family gatherings.

It makes me sad.

"No!" Eloise says suddenly, and we all turn to look at the toddler, who is standing over Frank, the other dog. "No!"

"Oh, shit," I say. "That's my sneaker."

Frank has pilfered my shoe from where I left it by the door. Now he's got it wedged between his paws and is snuffling into it curiously.

"Frank!" Sonya scolds, reaching for the shoe, but Frank growls and doubles down over his prize.

"I have *no* idea what's gotten into him," Sonya says. "He never does this!"

Mari's words echo in my head. *There was this family lore that if Gabe's dog, Buck, chewed up a girlfriend's possessions, she was The One. I thought it was total bullshit...until Buck ate one of my shoes.*

No. I don't believe in fate, signs, or—anymore—happily-ever-afters. And I definitely don't believe in prophesies delivered by dogs.

But when I look up, I discover Hanna and Easton staring at me. And they both look like they're trying really, really hard not to laugh.

36

RHYS

I've never been in Tucker's apartment. The building is pretty run-down, and I'm sure all of my brothers at one point or another have tried to give him money and he's turned it away. As far as I know, Tucker has actually done pretty well for himself. Until recently, he was a joint partner in running a small private-security firm. Around the time my grandfather died, he let his partners buy him out.

That definitely netted him a good chunk of cash, but here he is, living in a one-bedroom rental in a building that needs work.

It makes me wonder if he's punishing himself for something.

I pound on his door. No answer.

If I hadn't seen his truck parked outside, I'd probably give up. But I know he's in here. And I know something's eating at him.

I've been a shitty brother to let him keep it locked up so far.

I pound again.

"Tuck. I know you're in there."

Silence from within.

"I'm not leaving. You can open up and talk to me, or I'm going to camp out here until you have to come out to get food."

More silence.

"I'm going to be pissed about it, though. And I'm going to start asking people you know what the fuck is going on. I'm going to call your buddies at the old firm."

"They won't talk to you."

Tucker's voice from right behind the door is rough, like he hasn't spoken in days. It's testament to how good my brother is at his job that he crept up to the door without making a sound.

"They might talk to me if I tell them I'm fucking worried about you."

Long pause. "There's nothing to worry about."

"Then open the door and tell me that to my face."

The moments tick by, and I can hear the sounds of the tenants of other apartments going about their business—banging pots and pans, fighting, groaning in pleasure or pain—it's hard to tell.

The door slowly opens.

Tucker's the biggest of all of us, the physical type they call a brick shithouse. He's always had the look of a guy who works out—hard—on a daily basis.

But he never looked haunted until recently.

"You're a dick," he says, without heat in his voice.

"Can I come in?"

"If you have to." But he steps back and lets me in.

The apartment's no nicer inside than outside—banged-up walls, a kitchen that's seen better decades. "What's up with this shithole?"

"This shithole is where I live."

"You could afford a lot nicer."

"Yeah, well."

"You going to tell me what's going on?"

He shakes his head.

"We're all worried about you, you know."

"I'm fine."

"You're not fine."

"I'm fine enough."

This time, he meets my eye. Levels his gaze at me. It's fierce and stubborn, more like the brother I remember. Tucker was the toughest of all of us, physically and mentally, the one who could run longer and play harder, the one who once hiked seven miles out of the woods with me on his back after I broke a leg on the mountain. It surprised none of us when he chose private security for a career.

If he doesn't want to tell me what's going on, he won't, and it's not like I can beat it out of him. One of us would end up dead, and it isn't him.

"At least tell me why you turned around and left."

I figure there's about zero chance of that, so I'm surprised when he heaves a sigh and gestures me toward the couch. "You want a beer?"

"Sure," I say.

"Sit."

I do.

He goes to the fridge and comes back with two Rush

Creek Head Rushes—a hazy IPA brewed locally by some brewers who are friends with the Wilder brothers. He shoves one in my general direction. I crack it, take a slug, and wait.

"I wanted to come tonight." He lifts a shoulder, a helpless shrug. "Hanna asked me, and you know how it is. I feel like—" That shrug again. "I owe her, right? We all do. You know?"

I do know. It's how we all got ourselves into these messes, trying to make up to Hanna what we screwed up before. And I'd known Tucker felt it too, but it's still good to hear him say it, that whatever's making him lock himself down, he does still care.

I didn't really ever doubt it. I've been pretty sure this whole time that it's caring too much, not too little, that's at the bottom of whatever haunts my brother.

"Yeah," I say.

"And then, I don't know, I showed up there, and—" He blows out a breath. "I could see everyone moving around, and I could tell even from the truck that you all were having a good time, and I just didn't want to bring this"—he gestures at himself—"in there."

"We can handle it."

"It's not that," he says. "It's—people want to talk. They want to know how I'm doing, if I'm all right. They don't say, 'Tell us what happened, we want to hear the story,' but that's what they're saying, right? I couldn't face it."

"I get that." I want to say, *Tell me what happened.* Not out of some sick need to know, but because you don't have to be a therapist to figure it might make Tucker feel better to say some of it out loud. Some things don't bottle up well.

But I don't push, because for the first time, he's told one of us that something *did* happen. And that's huge. Everything about his body language right now says he's shut tighter than a crate packed with illegal cargo. I've gotten all I'm getting from him tonight, but for Tucker, it's a lot, and I decide to be glad he opened up that much.

All I say is, "Well. If you ever decide you need someone to talk to, attorney-client privilege has made me pretty good at keeping shit to myself."

He gives me a look. I think it might be relief that I'm not going to try to drag anything else out of him.

I hold up my glass to *cheers* him, and we finish our beers in companionable silence.

37

EDEN

Rhys texts to say he's finishing up a beer with his brother and he'll be back in a few, so I spend some quality time with Eloise, who has recently discovered hide and seek but doesn't yet understand that her body—not just her eyes—needs to be hidden. Her favorite "hiding place" is lying on the couch in full view with a pillow over her face. It's the cutest thing ever.

Eloise eventually has to go to bed, and she asks me to read her a bedtime story, which Hanna gives a nod to. We sit in the rocker-glider in her cute red-and-white gingham room ("No pink," Hanna says succinctly. "Not my thing."), and I read her Sandra Boynton's *Barnyard Dance!* and *The Going to Bed Book*. She insists I be the one to tuck her in, but when I kiss her good night, she panics and says, "Mommy."

Hanna, who's obviously been lurking right outside the door waiting for this moment, trades places with me, and I go back downstairs.

I'm still on the stairs when I hear the low rumble of Rhys's voice, and something shifts and settles in my chest.

He was gone less than an hour, but it still scares me, how glad I am that he's back. And it only gets more intense when I descend the last few stairs and see him—tall, dark, broad, sturdy, and absurdly, ridiculously beautiful.

His eyes find mine and the corner of his mouth turns up, and I swear my pulse clicks into the comfort gear. It's like stepping back into your own place after coming home from vacation, and that's—too soon and too much and all wrong.

But all I want is more of what happened last night. More of his hands and mouth on me, more of the two of us yielding to each other.

"You want to head out?" he asks.

"Probably makes sense." I drop the words as nonchalantly as I can, given the pictures in my head.

I swear he winks at me, but that can't be right; the broody, controlled lawyer doesn't *wink*.

We say goodbye to his family, one by one. I'm enfolded in hug after hug, whispered to, "Anytime, you hear?" and "No matter what that idiot does, don't be a stranger, right?" It's too soon and too much and all wrong again—and I love every minute of it.

We head out to his car, and it's silent between us, and even that feels right. Like we earned the privilege of not talking, all those hours in the car.

"Hey," I say as we pull away from Hanna's house. "I freaking love your family."

"They're not bad." Contentment is thick in his voice, and I think about how different he sounds now, basking in the afterglow of their affection, than he did when he talked about being a shark. Two different men. But not. The same guy, maybe just denying himself what he wants a lot of the time.

And I'm a luxury he's letting himself indulge in, and that feels unbelievably good.

"I want to show you something," he says. "If you'll let me."

"Yeah," I say.

We drive out of town and into the foothills. We get out of the car, and he pulls a couple of blankets from the trunk.

"You bring women up here often?" I tease him.

"Wouldn't be convenient from my New York apartment," he teases back. "But no. Never brought anyone here."

"And yet you have blankets in your trunk."

"Grabbed 'em from Hanna earlier," he says. "I knew I wanted to bring you here."

There's a wide-open area—a meadow by day, I think—and he throws a blanket onto the grass. "Lie down."

"Usually there's some foreplay," I tease, but I obey, and —"Holy shit, Rhys."

The sky is spread out above us, black and shimmering with stars.

"Not a lot of light pollution out here."

"It's—beautiful."

"I've always felt like if you lie still long enough, looking up, you can feel the earth spinning."

I do as instructed, and I know what he means. Maybe it's just dizziness from the hugeness of the dome above us —but it does feel like we're in motion, the earth turning on its axis, whirling around the sun, swirling as part of the galaxy. I feel incredibly small and also huge, part of everything.

He rolls onto his side, and I do the same. His mouth seeks mine, hot in the cool night. We kiss tentatively at first, tasting and exploring, until I bite his lip and he goes suddenly feral, clutching my head to delve into me, slick and hungry. He explores my mouth thoroughly, then moves his lips over the shell of my ear, sending shivers everywhere, down the sensitive line of my jaw, over my throat, to the throbbing pulse at the notch of my collarbones. I'm warm, too warm, and I pull away from him, tug my shirt over my head, and he groans and resumes his travels, his lips and tongue playing over the upper curve of my breast, teasing along the lace line of my bra.

Rhys tugs one cup down and finds my nipple with his tongue, flicks gently over it, traces circles around it. Then the other one, back and forth, while pleasure bites its own line inside me, right down to my core. I'm moaning now, my hips seeking friction, and he pins one hip with his hand so I can't move, and that's exactly what I need—I'm half desperate.

He plays at my breasts until I'm wild with hunger, then continues downward, finding the button and zipper of my jeans, easing them down with my panties, breathing my scent and groaning his approval. "Jesus, Eden, you're delicious. I can't wait to taste you."

After removing my jeans entirely, he grabs the other blanket and tugs it over both of us, disappearing from sight as his tongue finds my slit and I jerk against him. It feels so fucking good, the heat and slide of his tongue there, exploring everywhere at first, then homing in on my clit.

He experiments, listening for my moans and whimpers but also "listening" with his hands on my hips for the way I tilt up to get more of his mouth, "listening" with his tongue as my clit gets more swollen and I get wetter. He listens, reads, like he's known my body for years, and it responds with trust and pleasure, blooming wide open for him, so when he slides two fingers in, I'm all eager welcome.

I've pushed the blanket away again so I can watch him, so I can feel the hard bite of night cold on my nipples. The pinch of that cold and the sight of him working me and the feel of his talented mouth and his curled fingers all conspire to wind me up fast, and the orgasm catches me completely off guard, tossing me into the sparkling black sky, and I come whining and begging.

38

RHYS

I'm so hard and ready that when she comes, I have to stop myself from thrusting against the blanket, against the ground, and following her over the edge.

What stops me is knowing that she wants me to, that she wants me to lose control, and I both want to deny her and give her exactly what she wants.

I want to do both, and I want to do them deliberately so she can wring all the pleasure from them that she can.

"God," she says. "I can barely think."

"Good. Then I've done my job."

I roll to my side next to her, and we lie like that for a while. She shivers, and we both reach for her clothes at the same time, kneeling and then standing, helping her back into them. I'm sorry to see her cover up. She's extra pretty in the moonlight, her nipples hard peaks under pink lace, the neat triangle of curls at the apex of her thighs darker than her hair but still blondish. Some of her body's moisture gleams on her skin, and I slick my finger through it and lick the taste of her off myself, and she shudders again, like an aftershock.

When she's dressed, she reaches for the button of my jeans.

"You don't have to do that. None of this is tit for tat."

Even though I know what she wants. But I need to make her ask for it. I need to make her say the words.

"I want to," she says.

"What do you want?" I urge.

"I want to suck you."

Even though I was partly expecting them, her words still catch an unexpected edge of pleasure, and my cock surges so hard in my jeans that I clamp a hand to the base, holding the orgasm at bay.

"Do it," I order.

She kneels without hesitation, and her eagerness catches me off guard, too. Everything she does is more and better than anything that's ever happened to me.

She unfastens my jeans, pushes down the front of my briefs, and frees me. The cold takes me down a notch immediately, and that's good. I want to last longer in her mouth, to stay as long as she'll have me.

She slips her warm mouth over the head of my cock and works just that much of me, tongue strong and creative, fist closing around the base, holding me steady while she plays.

Licking down the shaft, she takes more of me, her tongue flattening out along my length. She's good at this, and I don't want to think about the other men she's had in her mouth or how she learned to use her tongue like that, to play with the textures inside her mouth, giving me the velvet of her cheek and the rasp of her tongue and the smooth, clenching back of her throat in turn. I take what I'm given and let my brain go quiet and dark while pleasure palms my balls and winds around the base of my cock.

Despite the cold, despite her tight grip on my base, despite how much I want this to last, I'm edging up fast. She's too good, every new touch a surprise that jacks me closer to release, and I know there's only a little more of this before it'll be over.

"Where do you want me?" I ask her. My voice is broken and raspy. "Do you want me to come down your throat or all over your pretty tits?"

She lets me go in a heartbeat, my wet cock bobbing back against my bare stomach below the hem of the T-shirt I've lifted to give her clearance. For a second I'm not sure what she's doing, and then it makes sense; she's lifting her shirt over her head, reaching behind herself to unfasten her bra.

Holy fuck, she's gorgeous—small, round perfect breasts, nipples peaked tight by the cold. It's impossible to tell the color in the dark, but it doesn't matter, it just matters that they're taut and needy when I reach my hands out to pinch them.

Eden makes a small, desperate whimper and sinks her mouth back to my cock. I tease and roll and flick her nipples while she takes me as deep as she can, all the way to the soft, snug back of her throat, her lips and tongue tightening fiercely around my shaft, and then, when I can't hold back and the pleasure has nowhere else to go, she knows and pulls off with a soft, wet pop, and I come in long bursts of relief, white pulses on her bare tits in the moon-light, so hard I nearly black out.

39

EDEN

Dropping to his knees, he kisses me, his hand finding the slick mess he's made of my chest. "God," he says.

"I don't suppose you have a warm washcloth with you," I say dryly.

He leans his forehead against mine and says, "No."

"I didn't think so."

"I do have a towel; hang on."

He gets it from the car and cleans me up, then tosses the towel aside and wraps his arms around me. I hug him back, and we cling to each other, rocking, for a moment. As intense as everything we've done physically has been, in a lot of ways, this is more intimate, and my eyes prickle with tears.

"Hey," he says, drawing back. "You okay?"

"Yeah," I say. "I'm, um, *really* okay."

That makes him laugh. "Yeah. Me, too."

He tucks himself back into his briefs, zips and buckles

his pants, then guides me back down to the blanket, pulling the other one over us. We lie there for a bit, hand in hand, spinning through the universe. And that's intimate, too. Funny that you can have someone's cock down your throat but the wrap of their fingers around yours feels even more personal. I squeeze his hand, and he squeezes back.

After a few minutes, he tells me about his conversation with Tucker earlier.

"That's a little—"

"Mysterious, right?" he says. "There's more to that story. But no way I was going to pry it out of him. He'll talk when he's ready."

"Tucker hasn't had his letter from the will yet, right?"

"Nope."

"What do you think it'll be?"

"Something like what the rest of us had to do. Some job that's all wrong for Tucker. He'll probably have to guard a super-spoiled princess who's in line for the throne of Monaco or whatever."

I giggle. "And he has to protect her from evil forces."

"Evil fae warlords?"

He laughs. "Different will."

"I wouldn't put it past your grandfather."

"Me freaking neither."

After a while, he says, "I'm getting cold. You?"

"Freezing."

"You should have said."

"I didn't want to go."

He helps me to my feet, rubbing my arms to warm me up. "You want to come back to my place? We could, I don't know, watch a movie or binge bad TV. I could make hot chocolate. I have marshmallows left over from the s'mores. We could cut them up and make mini marshmallows."

"That sounds amazing."

We gather the blankets and get back into the car.

At his place, he hands me one of his sweatshirts and makes us both mugs of cocoa, and we settle onto his couch, sipping.

"When will you go back to New York?"

The words fall with more weight than I mean them to. I guess once you've traded bodily fluids, it's tough to keep things casual.

"I have to make a quick trip Tuesday to deal with some loose ends. Then I have two more weddings to get through. Friday and Saturday." He frowns, like something in what he's said bothers him.

"You okay?"

"Yeah—just..." But he doesn't finish.

"Do you think—" I hesitate, not sure whether to bring it up. But I know it's what he's thinking about. "Do you think Weggers *will* cut you slack?"

He cocks his head. "I don't know. I don't fully understand what motivates him. I think it might be one of those rare cases of *what you see is what you get*. My grandfather gave him a job, and he's determined to do it. In which case, the outcome depends on what he thinks my grandfather would want him to do. If I haven't gotten an answer from him by tomorrow, I'll check in with him. I don't know what's taking him so long. Maybe he's holding a seance."

I snicker but then sober. "And if he doesn't grant you an exception?"

"We'll cross that bridge when we come to it, but I'm not

going down without a fight." He shakes his head. "We can deal with that tomorrow." He holds up the remote. "What's your favorite TV show?"

I think about it a second. "I mean, probably *Outlander*."

"Would I like it?"

I grin at that. "No idea. It's all over the place. Time travel, romance, swashbuckling adventure."

"You mean, basically our road trip?"

"Maybe a little more violent."

Rhys's eyebrow goes up. "Like they actually come to blows over the music selection in their covered wagon?"

I snort.

He puts it on, and we watch, curled up together on the couch.

"How long is the show?" he asks after the pilot. "Like, how many seasons?"

"Eight. We won't get all the way through it before you have to leave."

We're both quiet. I can hear the hum of the guest-house's electric heat and the purr of the minifridge under the kitchen counter. I think I might be able to hear his heartbeat, too.

"We might not," he agrees finally, and I'm grateful he isn't trying to paper over that reality and also that he isn't offering solutions that will never work, like dating long distance. "But we could watch another one now."

It's not until he offers that consolation prize that I realize how much I want him to offer more. The whole season, the whole show, all the shows we could stream, me sitting next to him on the couch, head against his chest, feeling his heart beat against my cheek.

But I don't ask for it. He's not for me, and I'm tired of grasping for what isn't mine only to lose it in the end.

40

———————

RHYS

We fall asleep sometime during episode four, and when I wake up Netflix has auto-played several more episodes. I get the streaming and TV situation straightened out, and then I consider what to do about the woman sleeping on my couch.

I could leave her there. Cover her with a blanket.

But that's not what I want to do.

And I'm tired of resisting impulses where she's concerned, so I don't.

I scoop her up and carry her into the bedroom. I strip off her shoes and jeans while she protests sleepily but doesn't actively rebel, and I tuck her in under the covers. Then I climb in next to her, wrap my arms around her, and go back to sleep.

I WAKE to light streaming through the window and a heavy weight on my chest. It's Eden; she's draped herself over me so that her head rests in the crook of my shoulder and her arm pins me to the bed.

I tug her closer, and she stirs and snuggles her face into my chest. Then she lifts her head, gives me a sleepy smile, and says, "Good morning."

"Good morning. Want to come with me to Rush Creek Bakery for a stuffed croissant?"

"*Yes,*" she says, her eagerness making me laugh.

"You want first shower?"

She bites her lip. "We could *share.*"

"We could."

"You've seen everything already."

"I definitely have. And I'd happily see it again."

It feels early for a shared shower. I don't think I've ever showered with someone before the first time we fucked. But it also feels right with Eden, companionably shedding clothes, laughing about the fact that she's wearing panties from our road trip, her eyes stuttering and getting stuck on my cock for a long time, until I teasingly say, "Eyes up here," and even then, she keeps staring.

"You can touch, too," I say. By now my cock has responded to the admiration by standing up and saluting her, and when she reaches out and touches me, it twitches under her hand. Her exploration is curious and slow and lazy, not going anywhere, and it feels amazing.

We step in, and I can't remember the last time a shower felt so good—not only the hot water, but the heat and slip of her skin as we move to stand under the water together. I soap her body, admiring every curve and all the slick satin skin, and she does the same to me, her hand coming back to where she left off, stroking me, fisting. My fingers find their way between her folds, and we match each other's rhythm, my thumb on her clit, my fingers thrusting in and out of her as she works her fist tight around my shaft.

"Wait for me," she says breathlessly.

That makes me smile. "You're closer," I tell her.

"Am not."

"Let's make it a contest, then," I say. "I bet I can make you come before you can make me come. Loser buys breakfast."

"Mmm," she says, tilting against the tile wall, eyes half closed. "You're on." Her arm snakes out, and she reaches for a bottle.

"What are you doing?"

"Employing all the tools at my disposal," she says, dispensing conditioner into her palm and resuming her work. And holy shit, she has my number, her hand as tight as before but way slicker, sliding over my swollen flesh, working the base of the head with her thumb as her palm passes along the shaft.

"I didn't realize tools were fair game," I grit out, barely able to string the words together, my knees going weak as blood surges into my cock and energy coalesces at the base of my spine. I know the worst thing I can do is thrust into the tight grasp of her fist, but I'm having trouble helping myself.

"All's fair in love and war," she says, and the only thing that keeps me sane is that she sounds as close to the edge as I feel. I focus all my efforts on not coming, encircle her with my arm, and reach for the detachable showerhead.

"You said it, not me," I tell her. I part her labia with my fingers and let the spray from the nozzle fall right on her

most sensitive flesh; she gasps and arches and a flush
spreads up from her chest, and that's it for me—I'm gone,
coming all over her hand again, but if I'm going, she's
coming, too, and I lean to take one of her nipples into my
mouth, and she comes with a shout that's half pleasure,
half victory.

41

RHYS

We're both a little weak-kneed as we get dressed and ready to head into town.

"Where'd you learn the shower-nozzle trick?" she asks. And then, "Never mind. I probably don't want to know the answer to that, do I?"

"I had a girlfriend in college who informed me that she had an intense relationship with her shower nozzle," I tell her. "But I've never actually used one on anyone. I've never actually lived anywhere with a detachable nozzle before."

"I wouldn't have thought of it as a must-have," she says. "But if I were designing a bathroom from scratch, I would *definitely* install one."

"Having seen the results," I say, "me, too."

"I did still win," she says.

"You did," I concede. "Although I think, technically, we both won."

In the car, she says, "What are you doing in New York?"

"Just a quick court appearance to get closure for someone."

"Justice rolls on, huh?"

"Or something."

"I'll miss you," she says, smiling. "But I'll find a way to entertain myself in the meantime."

She'll miss me. I don't want to delight in that fact, but I can't help it. Because fuck it, I'll miss her, too, even if it's only a couple of days.

"I'll leave a key with you. You can come over and use my shower."

She gives a shiver of delight. "Totally taking you up on that."

"Totally picturing you doing so."

I seriously think about pulling the car over the side of the road. I could get both of us off before the cops showed up, right? "I can't get enough of you," I say, feeling like a sap but also like I want her to know.

For a second I wonder if I've overstepped, and then she says, her voice husky, "Yeah. Me neither."

Warmth spreads through me, and I think, *What would old Rhys have to say about this?*

He'd say you're treading with big boots on thin ice.

I don't fucking care.

We turn onto Main Street, and she says, "Rush Creek must have changed a lot since you were a kid."

"A ton. Some things haven't changed at all. I think those light standards and flower barrels have been around since cowboys met at noon for showdowns in the middle of the street."

We both eye Rush Creek's main drag. The buildings are low-slung, squat and Western, with long-plank siding. Dotted among them are cottages and a log cabin or two, plus an old-fashioned red train depot. In addition to our signature flower barrels and the tall wooden Ts of the lamp standards, there are lots of strategically placed benches, so wanderers can rest before being lured into the next shop.

Even today there are feed stores and tack shops and outdoor equippers tucked in among the gift and ice cream and bookshops. But the street is definitely dominated by establishments catering to the weddings and girls'-week-end-out crowd—gifts, beauty products, wedding dresses—and, more recently, Eden's store.

"Did cowboys really used to have shoot-outs at noon in the streets?" she asks.

"As far as I know, they were exceedingly rare."

"When you grew up, the rodeo was here, huh?"

"Yeah."

"Then what happened?"

"There were a bunch of protests around safety and animal welfare. There were other factors at work, too. Ranch land was being sold off because it was getting harder to make ranching pay. Cowboy culture was...changing. It was hard on everyone. People were afraid we'd become some Western ghost town. And then practically overnight, the hot springs appeared."

"Like magic?"

I laugh. "Like geology. Like moving plates and boiling magma and groundwater getting superheated."

"But it must have felt a little like magic to a struggling town."

"Yeah," I say.

"I mean, I don't think I'd be here running In Stitches if it weren't for those springs."

"I'm not sure any of us would be here if it weren't for those springs. Maybe Hanna. But she'd still be running adventures on the mountains. Which she enjoyed—but my sister is definitely meant to be in charge of her own business. I've got to give it to my grandfather. He may have stuck it to me and my brothers, but he definitely had a vision for what would be good for her. It's clear he loved her, even if he didn't have much patience for the rest of us."

"Do you think he didn't?" she asks. "I get the impression your brothers are pretty happy."

"But he couldn't have foreseen that. He didn't know what would happen when he called us all back here and set up the terms of the will."

"Maybe he had a better idea than you think," she says.

I toy with that idea for a while. She's right that my brothers—three of them anyway—are happy as clams right now in ways that none of them could have predicted.

And as I park the car in an unusual open spot in front of Rush Creek Bakery, I have to admit to myself that maybe *I'm* happy right now in a way I couldn't have predicted.

You're still an asshole, I tell my grandfather, and I can almost hear his rare, dry chuckle and his voice saying, *Tell it to the judge.*

42

RHYS

"If it isn't my lucky day! There's a Hott man in my shop!"

Rush Creek Bakery's owner, Nan, bustles out from behind the counter in her apron with her white cotton-candy hair wrestling for escape from a hairnet. Nan thinks our family name is hilarious and rarely misses an opportunity to tease us about it. And we all love her, even if she's a blabbing busybody, so we tolerate it.

She gives me a floury hug that leaves my T-shirt powdery, then holds me at arm's length for examination. "I won't tell you how much you've grown up since I saw you last," she says fondly, patting one of my cheeks.

We all grew up cramming our faces with Nan's breads and cookies, soaking up the comfort of the bakery, which is always warm and slightly steamy and smells like fresh-baked goods.

She registers the woman at my side and says, "Oh, Eden, I'm so sorry about your wedding. But you might have dodged a bullet. Better that he ran from the altar than from the first dirty diaper or toward the first short skirt."

It sounds like Nan now has her story straight, but I still wince on Eden's behalf. She bites her lip, smiling wryly. She seems to be taking Nan and her busted filter in stride. "Too true," she says.

"And you've gotten yourself a Hott man to replace that old-and-busted one!"

Nan jumps to conclusions like a jackrabbit on speed—but she's not wrong in this case. Eden does have herself a Hott man, and I'm happy to be had.

"I have him for as long as Rush Creek has him," Eden says, beaming. "He has to go back to New York City permanently in a couple weeks."

"Is that true?" Nan demands, turning back to me. "The other ones stayed!"

"It's true," I admit.

Nan crosses her arms and scowls. "That's a tragedy for this town. You can never have too many Hott men."

"Thanks, I think."

She bustles back behind the counter. "What can I get you two? Is this *breakfast*...?" She lards the word up with so much innuendo that it sounds like she's asking if we're planning to have sex on one of her tables.

"Yes. And we're *very hungry*," Eden says, winking at me when Nan's not looking.

"Two ham-and-cheese croissants. Warmed," I say.

"I don't have to warm them!" Nan says delightedly. "They're fresh out of the oven." She sets them on plates and pushes them across the counter to me. "On the house."

"You don't have to do that," I say.

"In fact, don't," Eden says. "Because breakfast is supposed to be on Rhys." She shoots me a teasing glance.

"Consider it a not-wedding gift," Nan says. "I like to celebrate close calls avoided."

We take a seat, and Eden releases a gust of nervous laughter. "She's—"

"A lot," I finish. "You okay? I know you've still got a ton of feelings about what happened—"

She bites her lip. "I mean, yes. Rejection *sucks*. He hurt me, my feelings, and my pride. But also, sometimes I'm really...okay." She gives me a wry smile. "It's hard to spend much time thinking about Paul being an asshole when..." She grins. "I'm thinking about that shower."

Her eyes hold mine, pupils flaring, and she slides her hand across the table, fingers slipping between my own.

Ah, jeez, nothing like getting hard in the bakery.

The door bell tinkles. I look up, grateful for the distraction...

Except it's Weggers.

Shit. This was *not* how I wanted this to go down.

"Well, well, well," he says, approaching our table as Eden, too late, pulls her hand away. "This is interesting."

Anything I say can and will be used against me, so I keep my mouth shut.

"Breakfast for two. Cozy. I believe you told me you did 'everything in your power' to make sure Eden and Paul's wedding went forward as planned. Did that include pursuing a romantic relationship with the bride?"

All my plans to be cautious and careful and diplomatic

fly out the window, along with the memory of Matias suggesting that kneeling and groveling might still be the best path to success.

"You—" I start, but before I can get out the rest of what I want to say, Nan swoops out from behind the bakery counter.

"You leave these people alone, Arthur Weggers. What kind of sick *turkey* picks on a woman who's just been jilted and a man who's come all the way from New York City to do everything he can to save his sister's land? You're high on your own power, and it's time someone took you down a notch."

Weggers pales.

"How do we even know you're for real? Maybe you forged the will and this is all your lunatic fantasy of revenge because you're Fox Hott's bastard teenage son he never acknowledged."

Wait, *what?* Eden and I stare at Weggers in disbelief.

"She made that up out of whole cloth!" he cries, pointing at Nan. "That's not even remotely true! How dare you malign my parents like that?"

We turn back to Nan.

"Well," she says. "It *could* have happened. It was a hypothetical."

"I've had enough of this," Weggers says, throwing up his arms. "You," he says to Nan, "need to more carefully consider your words, or someone is going to have you in court for slander. And as for you," he says to me, "I did exactly what you asked. I took the situation under advisement. And what I have concluded is that there is no way you could possibly have applied yourself to the task before you objectively when you clearly have feelings for the bride. So I'm not remotely inclined to let you off the hook."

And with that, Wegger sweeps out of the bakery with not even a backward glance of contempt.

"Huh," Eden says, biting her lip and looking like she's torn between laughing and crying. "That went well."

43

———

EDEN

Hanna buries her face in her hands.

"I'm sorry," Rhys says. "I should have thought about what would happen if he saw us together—"

"No," Hanna says. "It's not your fault. None of this is your fault. None of this is anyone's fault, except Granddad's, and there's nothing we can do about that." She addresses the distressed oak planks of Matias's law office floor. "If you weren't already dead, I'd..." She shakes her head, turns to Matias. "Okay, so now what?"

"The easiest thing," Matias says, "if you don't want to put the land at any risk or to involve yourself in what might be a protracted period of litigation, is to comply with the will."

"No," Rhys says.

He's wearing a linen dress shirt, rolled to the elbows, and he crosses his (beautiful, sculpted) forearms across his (I've seen it shirtless; it's Roman statue–worthy) chest.

"No one is putting Eden under any pressure to be anywhere near Paul Graves."

I get warm and tingly at both the dark alpha rage in his voice and the protective gesture, but also?

"I can take care of myself," I remind him.

He closes his eyes. "Fuck," he says. "I know you can."

When he opens his eyes, they're full of something. Heat. A dark intensity I like way more than I want to. "But I don't fucking want you to have to, okay? I don't want you anywhere near him and the idea of a wedding."

More warm tinglies. "Even if I'm happy to do it."

"No," he says. "No Paul Graves."

"Hear me out," Matias says, holding up a finger. "What if it's not Paul Graves?"

"That's what I was thinking, too," Hanna says.

Matias turns to Rhys. "What if it's you?"

Oh.

Ohhh.

It's not the worst idea ever.

"No," Rhys says.

If possible, his bitten off *no* is even harder edged than the last denial. Definite. Nonnegotiable.

The quick stab of a small sharp blade between the ribs.

But that's on me. A hundred percent. Because I let myself forget who Rhys is.

I take a deep breath.

It's good to be reminded of how hopeful I've let myself feel about this *thing* with Rhys. Hopeful enough that for a second there, I actually felt disappointed. And wounded.

Rhys believes in marriage like he believes in rattlesnakes and jumping spiders. He told me so himself.

And the one time he got within spitting distance of changing his mind, he couldn't go through with it. He didn't even want to kiss me until he made sure I knew exactly how much he would never, ever want something long term and serious again.

We're enjoying a few weeks of smoking-hot sex before Rhys goes back to being New York's favorite antihero. That's all.

And if I've caught a few feelings along the way?

That's my bad.

I tune back in to the present moment. Rhys is saying something to Matias. "...she's had a marriage and an engagement go south. She just got jilted. The last thing she needs is to be effectively *forced* to marry someone she doesn't want to marry, for reasons that have nothing to do with her."

I register that he's standing up for me, which is super nice. He's also right. I'm in no place to contemplate Matias's crazy-ass plan, either.

Right.

Reset.

"Seconded," I say firmly. "I've had enough marriage and almost-marriage for a lifetime."

Matias nods. "Yeah, I figured you'd both hate that idea. No way New York's favorite bachelor goes down that easy. I just thought I'd give it a stab."

"Try again." Rhys scowls.

"Isn't your brother Shane enga—"

Rhys is shaking his head. "They've got enough on their plates. Their public wedding is already planned, and their private wedding is well underway. There's no way I'm going to ask Ivy to alter her life again for this goddamned will."

"And there's no one else who can get married?" Matias glances down at his notes.

"No one's getting married who doesn't already want to get married," Rhys says.

Matias nods again, eyes flicking to his friend's face. "Noted."

Hanna sighs. "Rhys is right. No one should have to get married because my grandfather decided he knew what was right for me. I don't want to be the person who dictates someone else's future any more than I want mine dictated. And I'm not sacrificing what someone else wants so I can get what I want. That's not what this is about. I'm sure my grandfather didn't want that, either. *Did you, fucker?*" she inquires of the floor, which is silent in reply.

"Right, then," Matias says, collecting papers into a stack. "I'll start pulling together the will contest case."

"Do we—do we have a chance?" Hanna sounds scared.

Rhys's eyes snare on her face. His expression is as bleak as his sister's.

I reach my hand out and take his in mine. His is cold, mine is hot. I wrap my fingers tight, and he shoots me a grateful look. There's a small landslide in my chest before I remind myself of what I've just relearned: No matter how it feels, this can't last.

"There's always a chance," Matias says. "It's a pretty ridiculous setup. The only reason it's been enforceable so far is because you all complied, voluntarily. Which might make it harder to argue that all of a sudden, it's problematic. But...we'll give it a shot."

"Let us know what we can do to help," Hanna says.

Matias smiles. "Of course. There will be plenty for you to do if it comes down to court time. In the meantime..." He shrugs. "I'd suggest gathering any evidence you possibly can that your grandfather's decision-making was compromised at the end."

"Did you hear that?" Hanna demands of the floor. "My turn."

44

EDEN

Rhys leaves the next morning for his couple of days in New York, and I throw myself into work at the shop so I don't have to think about what happened yesterday in Matias's office.

Rhys's sharp, hard *no*.

After the meeting with Matias, we grabbed dinner with Hanna, then went back to Rhys's place and watched a few more *Outlander* episodes. We made out on the couch until things escalated and our clothes flew off and I came on Rhys's fingers.

Then I wanted to go down on him, and he reminded me that he was getting up at the crack of dawn for work. And I didn't push. Because...

Because it wouldn't have changed the essentials of the situation. The fact that he's already moving away from me, back toward his real life.

I'm standing at the front counter, cutting and folding fat quarters—eighteen-by-twenty-two-inch rectangles of fabric —when the door chimes and Paul steps in.

My stomach lurches and drops. As much as I told Mari that seeing him was a nonevent for me, the truth is more complicated. Even if my dreams about him were misguided, seeing him still reminds me that those dreams are over. It's a pin in a balloon.

A reminder of how easy it is for people to walk away from each other.

"Hi," he says quietly. He's holding a slim cardboard box in his hands.

"Hi."

"Uh, sorry to show up again. I know you probably want to be done with me—"

"You said it, I didn't," I say, and it manages to come out sounding not too angry and bitter, which pleases me. I don't want him to feel like I care, because, fundamentally, I don't.

"I sent all the gifts back, but—" He holds out the cardboard sleeve. "I was ninety-eight percent sure this one couldn't be returned, and I figured you'd maybe want to see it and decide what you wanted to do with it."

I take it from him; it's one of those sleeves they send books in, and this one is heavy, like it holds a coffee table book. "Thanks."

"I'm gonna..." He indicates the door.

"Yup." Politeness urges me to say something else, maybe *See you around* or *Have a great life*, but I can't actually force either one out, so I raise a hand in a half-hearted wave, and then he's gone.

The cardboard sleeve has been opened. I fold back the flap.

It's a printed glossy book, the high-quality kind you can order from a premium photo storage site.

Caryn and Eden, the book is titled.

My mom and me.

My stomach goes cold and heavy—way worse than when Paul walked in. It doesn't matter how much you tell yourself you don't care when someone walks out on you. If someone who should love you abandons you, it leaves a mark, one that doesn't get completely erased by time.

After a lot of therapy, soul searching, and conversations with Paul, I invited my mom to the wedding. I don't have much of a relationship with her, but not inviting her felt like it had more emotional weight than just including her. I was pretty sure she wouldn't come anyway and that if she did, she would at least not make things about her. She's good that way—if in no other.

She couldn't come. She was on tour. Her assistant, Luann, RSVP'd for her. *Caryn asked me to let you know that she so, so, so wishes she could be there, but she has a concert that night in Rome. She sends so much love—gift to follow.*

And here it is, that gift.

I open the book and turn the pages slowly.

It's photo after photo of me and my mom. There were lots of them when I was very little, until she left when I was four. Then there's a gap—nothing. She stayed away completely for more than four years, and the next time I saw her was when she visited me at my grandmother's. There are photos from that visit—me unwrapping the expensive gifts she's brought, me licking the ice-cream cone she indulged me with, me at the expensive kids' theater production she took me to.

At nine, I look happy with an edge of mania, like I've psyched myself up for the moment—and like I know it could be snatched away at any time.

Or maybe I'm just projecting back onto myself what I know now.

After the ice-cream-and-theater extravaganza, there was an average of one visit per year, the photos following the same pattern: age-appropriate indulgences and a few hours spent in her company—before she swept off again, back to her glamorous life.

In middle and high school, some of the photos are of me at her concerts or with her afterward, and I can still remember the mingled smells of her makeup and her sweat when she draped an arm briefly around me before she was called away—to sign an album or meet with a producer or because a rich-and-famous man invited her to have dinner with him.

By age fifteen or so I'd learned the pattern well enough not to let myself have feelings about her arrival or her departure: Seeing her was a thing I did to oblige her and my grandmother or because it benefitted me—the gifts were great, and I could take selfies with a famous pop star to impress my friends.

My mother was warm and effusive where my grandmother was not, and that sometimes made it hard to steel myself against her, but I did anyway.

It's just as hard to steel myself against this book. Against the thought that even though she couldn't come to the wedding, she bothered to pull this together for me. She sat with these photos and these memories, and they couldn't have meant *nothing* to her, could they have?

I don't want the tears to well up in my eyes; I don't want to want to call her to say thank you; I don't want to hope that maybe as adults we'll have a relationship.

I'm gripping the book too tightly, my hands shaking. The cardboard sleeve tumbles off my lap onto the floor, disgorging a sheet of paper—the packing slip, with its gift message:

Your mom asked me to put this together for you. We both wish you all the happiness in the world. Love, Luann.

45

RHYS

My court appearance in NYC is a nonevent, the final hearing in an uncontested divorce. I probably could have talked the judge into letting me Zoom in for it, but the client thanks me at least ten times for coming, so ultimately, I'm glad I did.

I think of Matias telling me that divorce is a sacrament, and I look at my client, who carries herself like I've personally lifted a thousand-pound weight from her shoulders, and I think, *I may be cynical, but that doesn't mean I'm wrong.*

It's my job, lifting that weight off people. Unburdening them.

This is my job. This is my life. New York is where I belong.

I haven't let myself think about where I'm going with Eden, but there has to be a reckoning at some point. Because this part of my life does exist. And because, fundamentally, I'm still afraid of hurting her.

I'm still the guy who, when it came down to a ring and a

wedding and the possibility of forever, walked away because my gut screamed *no* so loudly I couldn't ignore it.

If I try again with Eden, she'll be the one I'm hurting this time—and I can't stand the thought of that.

Eden walked into things with me with her eyes wide open. She knows who I am and what I'm capable of—and not. The other day she backed me up when I told Matias *no*.

I've had enough marriage and almost-marriage for a lifetime.

So it's not like she thinks I'm a good bet, either.

I pack up my messenger bag. I put on my coat—New York is having an early fall day—and sling my bag over my shoulder. I say goodbye to my client, shake opposing counsel's hand, and stride out of the courtroom.

And nearly crash into someone.

"Fay?"

"Ha," my ex-girlfriend says. "I wondered if I'd run into you."

Right. It's the courthouse where we first met.

"What are you here for?"

"Filing a motion in an upcoming case," she says. "You?"

"Final hearing."

"You won?"

"Of course," I say. Habit.

Fay smiles at that. She's tall and slim with dark hair neatly pulled into a bun and fingernails painted an elegant pale pink. I remember thinking she was beautiful, the way you can recall being feverishly sick without being able to summon up the sensory experience at all. "Ah, so you're ending another marriage. Always were cynical about that institution."

She says it wryly, without malice, but there's a sadness in her eyes.

"I'm so sorry, Fay. I was— I should never have let it go on as long as it did, knowing I couldn't—"

She's shaking her head. "I know you were—trying. I'm the one who should have known better. I knew how you felt, and I pushed and pushed. I was the one who kept hinting about ring shopping and a proposal, even knowing that I wasn't going to be the one who changed your mind."

"Still," I say.

"Apology accepted." Her smile widens. "Also, *thank you*. Because I'm engaged now, actually." She flashes a ring in my direction, and I catch a glimpse of a rainbow of semi-precious stones. "And if things had worked out between you and me, I wouldn't have met her, and that would have been a crime against humanity, because she's terrific."

My eyes widen.

"We met on a dating site," she says, grinning at my surprise. "On a whim I said *all genders*, even though I'd never thought I'd be into anyone except men. It turns out it pays to be open-minded."

"Wow," I say.

"Oh, yeah, so, belatedly: I'm bi." She beams.

I open my mouth and close it again. "Ah."

She rolls her eyes at my inability to utter more than one useless syllable at a time, but she's laughing. "And you? I assume you're still convinced marriage is a remediable evil?"

"I—"

That's as far as I get before words fail me.

Her eyebrows go up.

"You're not *married*," she says.

"No."

"Engaged, then."

"No."

"But thinking about it?"

An image pops into my mind. Eden. Crouching at the family dinner, hand on Gus's head, smiling up at Quinn.

"No..."

It comes out far less solid than the last two nos.

The corner of her mouth turns up. "But...?"

I shake my head.

She tilts hers.

"Who is she?" she asks.

I think of all the ways I could answer her question.

She's the ex-wife of a former client.

She's someone whose wedding I helped plan—long story.

She's someone I met when I went home to a town I thought I'd left behind forever.

She's a quilter and a shop owner.

She's feisty and joyful and stubborn and indomitable and sexy—

Fay is staring at me. And all at once, I'm pretty sure I know the answer. The only possible answer. It might be a cruel thing to say to a woman I was almost engaged to. I'm not sure. I only know that it's true.

"I think," I say carefully, "she's the one who's going to change my mind about marriage."

She grins. "I'm happy for you."

"I didn't think that person existed," I say. "The one who could change my mind."

"Yeah," she says, and her grin gets even bigger. "I guess we don't until we meet them."

46

RHYS

I slip my key into the lock of Quinn and Sonya's guesthouse, turn it, and push the door open.

It takes me a moment to register the sound I'm hearing, but the instant I get it, I go hot over all, my cock flushing thick with need.

It's been a long day of travel, and until a second or two ago I was mostly dreaming of a quick shower and some takeout, but now all my attention is on the soft rush of water in my bathroom—

She's in there, taking a shower.

Using the showerhead on herself.

I'd kept Eden updated on my travel progress, told her when I'd be back, and this was her idea of a greeting.

I'm a lucky, lucky man.

I knock on the bathroom door. "Honey," I call, "I'm home."

Her voice, when it comes, is husky. "I'm in here," she says. "Join me."

I'm already shucking my clothes.

She has the detachable nozzle in one hand when I step into the shower. I take it from her and hang it up. "I want to do that with my mouth," I tell her.

"You won't get an argument from me," she says, and she slides into my arms, warm and slippery and already soft and pliable with pleasure.

I hold her for a long time. It's only been two days, but it feels so good to have her back. We stand under the water together, and she tilts her mouth up and I take it (*mine, mine, mine*). I lick into the softness of her, imagining doing the same to her pussy a few minutes from now, and she kisses back, all yielding and needy whimpers. My cock bobs between us, hard, and she rubs her belly across it, and then, when I grunt, does it again, pushing harder.

"Let me just—"

I rush through shampooing my hair, and then she wants to soap me up, so I let her, loving her hands all over my skin, the care she takes with me, like I'm something precious. I do the same to her, being careful not to get soap anywhere it might sting, making sure my hands are clean before I slip two fingers inside her pussy to see where her playing has gotten her. Her muscles clench around my fingers, and oh, my God she's strong and wet and I curl my fingers to draw cries out of her, being careful to work her close to climax but not all the way there because I meant what I said. I want to lick her over the edge; I want to suck her clit until she can't help rubbing herself against my face.

I scoop her up, deposit her on the bathmat, towel us both dry, and then carry her to the bed, where I lay her out in front of me, like a feast. I kneel between her legs and kiss the insides of both thighs, and she shudders hello and lifts her hips, begging with her body.

She is so fucking soft against my tongue. Pure silk. For a while all I can do is worship there, tasting her, feeling that silk. Then I return to my senses and remember that this is for her, not me, and I tease around her opening with a single finger, watching as she tries to fuck herself onto it. I lick circles around her clit, lick her hard with the flat of my tongue, press my whole mouth against her and feel her push back. And then she's rubbing herself against my face, whimpering, trying to get more.

That's when I suck, and Eden's hips buck off the bed. She lets out a broken cry of pleasure, and she's coming, grabbing my hair, *hurting* me in the best possible way, telling me to please, please, please fuck her with my tongue, my fingers, my cock, please, please, *please.*

I don't.

It's not because I'm a masochist. It's because I know there are things I need to tell her, and if I let myself have what I want most, to be buried to the hilt inside her, I might not say them.

So I stroke her hair and kiss her cheeks until she comes down off her pleasure high. I bring her a warm washcloth and clean her up and let her protest that she wants me to get off, too, and even if I don't want to fuck her, I should still let her make me feel good, please let her, she wants to make me feel as good as I make her feel.

It's so fucking hot and I file it away for fantasy material for the rest of my life, but right now I have something else on my mind.

"In a little bit," I say. "I want to say something first."

"Okay," she says. She pushes herself up higher on the pillows.

"I've been thinking a lot these last two days, and I realized that I—"

I thought a lot about how I wanted to say this to her. Part of me wanted to go all in and tell her exactly what I realized when I was talking to Fay. *You're the woman who changed my mind about marriage.*

But it's too much too soon. She's also the woman who was jilted just weeks ago, she's also the woman who's been left so many times it hurts me to think about it. I need to be gentle.

So I say, "I want to try to make this work. Between us."

I'm not sure exactly what I'm expecting. A confession of love? A glitter canon?

What I get instead is a slightly blank look.

47

EDEN

I hate the feeling of hope that wells up in me.

I hate that I want to clutch his hands and beg him to mean it.

I hate that I already know how much it will hurt when he doesn't, when he changes his mind, when he takes back the ring, when he ends the marriage, when he leaves.

I hate that even though I'm standing on the edge of the highest, cruelest cliff, I can't stop myself from saying—my voice filled with hope, like an nine-year-old's asking her mom if this is the time she'll stay, "You want to do long distance?"

He shakes his head, and the wind rushes up at me from the edge of the cliff, the vast empty space beyond, but I don't fall, not yet. Because he's not saying *no*, he's saying something else: "I want to stay here. In Rush Creek. I have a friend who's partner in a firm in Bend that does collaborative divorce and a bunch of other family law stuff, and he wants me to join their firm."

He wants to stay.

He *wants* to stay.

But can he? Will he?

He said it himself—he's a shark. Sharks don't live in Rush Creek and do "a bunch of family law stuff."

How long would he be happy doing that?

How long would he be happy with *me*?

Before New York would draw him back?

It's my turn to shake my head. "You're not going to be happy doing that. When I brought up collaborative divorce on our road trip, you acted like I'd suggested you raise bunnies instead of doing law."

He winces. "That was before. You've helped me see other possibilities."

"No," I say. "You're setting yourself up—you're setting us both up—for failure. You take some job that's the antithesis of who you are, you try to yank the city boy out of New York and dump him in backwater Oregon, you take the cynic and try to turn him into the committed monogamist—and in the end, you can't make any of it work, because it's not you."

"It could be me," he says. "I want to try it."

Like Paul tried not to still be in love with his ex-girlfriend?

I shake my head. "I don't want to be something you try. I don't want to be the next woman you walk away from. And I don't want you to be the next person I care about who walks away from me."

I'm proud of myself. I feel strong. I feel safe. I'm making myself both those things. I don't need anyone else to do that for me.

"Hey," he says. "I don't want either of those things, either, and I wouldn't be telling you any of this if I thought either of those things would happen. I know you've been hurt, and I will *never* hurt you like that."

You won't, I agree in my head, *because I won't give you the power to.*

This is what I should have been able to do with Paul: push him away. This is what I should have said to Paul: *I won't give you the power to hurt me again.*

It's what I should have said to my mother at nine, at eleven, twelve, fifteen, sixteen, sixteen and a half, seventeen.

I can't go back and do that part over.

But I can refuse to be hurt again.

Rhys pushes a hand into his normally flawless hair. It's a little long right now, and it stands on end. "When I was in New York," he says, "I ran into my ex-girlfriend. And we started talking. She's with someone else now, and she's happy. She wanted to know if I still felt like marriage would never be for me. She said that she should have known that she wasn't the woman who would change my mind about marriage. And it made me realize. You're that woman for me, Eden. You're the woman who can change— who has *already changed*—my mind about marriage. I want to be with you. Not just now but for as long as you'll have me."

All I have to do is stay strong a little bit longer and this will be over. "That's what you thought about her, too."

"No," he says. A pleading note has crept into his voice, but I don't let it penetrate my shell. "I didn't. I knew it wasn't working for me. The mistake I made was trying to talk myself into it. I knew *she* was wrong for me. But you're different, Eden. You've been different from the beginning.

You made me want to break every rule I had for myself. You still do."

I cross my arms. Like I'm protecting myself—from him. "You shouldn't, though. You shouldn't break your own rules. Those rules exist for a reason. To protect yourself."

"I'm not scared, Eden. I know this can work. And I want to try."

I close my eyes. Open them again. "I know," I say. So strong, like steel, something that won't bend or break, that will be left standing when all the *trying* and the *this time is different* are done. "I'm the one who doesn't think it can."

48

———————

RHYS

Someone is knocking on the guesthouse door. I can't get up, because I'm weighted to the bed. This is the second morning in a row I've felt like I had the flu. Yesterday I stayed in bed so I wouldn't infect anyone else.

Today I'm pretty sure it's not the flu. It's just that my entire body has been turned to lead.

I pull the covers over my head and ignore the knocking. I can sleep through it.

"I'm coming in," says a voice. Preston's.

A moment later he's standing in the door of my bedroom, scowling at me.

"Hanna says you missed a wedding-planning meeting today. Are you trying to kill us all? You know what's at stake here." He looks hard at the expression on my face. "Jesus, dude, what's wrong with you?"

"Someone increased the gravity in my room to Jupiter levels, and I can't move."

He gives an experimental bounce on both feet. "I'm not feeling it," he says.

"Lift a foot," I say. "Does it feel like you're wearing an iron boot?"

He experiments. I appreciate his willingness to take my diagnosis seriously. "No," he says definitively. "Try again. What the fuck happened, Rhys? And don't bullshit me. I've known you for three decades."

I turn over and push my face into the pillow. I'm going back to sleep.

Except two strong hands flip me over and drag the pillow from under my head.

"Talk," Preston says.

He lasers his eyes into mine.

"I told Eden I want to stay in Rush Creek," I finally manage, unwillingly. "And she said she doesn't want me to."

Relief washes over his face. "Oh. Okay. We can fix that."

"What? No, we can't. She says she doesn't think it can work between us."

"Is she right?" he asks.

"No. But—"

"Then dude, what is *wrong* with you?" He crosses the room with single stride, throws open the blinds. Light rushes in, piercing my brain, even though I only helped myself to two whiskeys last night.

The covers are next; he rips them back and scowls when he finds me fully dressed.

"Up," he says, and then, when I don't move right away, he roars it.

Just like he used to in high school when I didn't get out of bed, and apparently my brain is still tuned to that frequency, because I'm on my feet.

He thrusts a finger toward my face. "What's your name?"

I give him a confused look. "Rhys."

"Rhys what?"

"Rhys Hott," I say, still confused.

"That's right," he says. "Rhys Hott. And what do you do for a living?"

"Break up marriages."

I'm still feeling extremely sorry for myself, thinking of the way Eden wouldn't look at me as she got dressed and slipped out two nights ago.

He rolls his eyes. "No," he says. "You convince people of things. People who don't have any particular reason to want to be convinced. You make compelling arguments, and you convince them to do what they didn't know they wanted to do."

"I don't want to convince her to do something she doesn't want to do."

"Something she doesn't *know* she wants to do," he corrects. "Did she tell you she doesn't want it? Or did she just tell you she doesn't think it will work? And did you believe her? Because you don't trust that you can be what she needs?"

I can feel my mouth hanging open.

He rolls his eyes again. "What do you think I've been doing these last couple of months?"

"Playing Nerf battle and banging Natalie?" I hazard.

He rolls his eyes. "That's insulting, dude," he says. "I've been working really fucking hard. And not only on inventing weird crap for resort visitors to do all day long, although that was a lot of work, too. I've been actually figuring out my own shit. Our upbringing did a number on all of us. You know how you can tell? Because we all left town and decided *never to come back*. That's a pretty big sign. Let me guess—you don't think you can be a good man, because none of the men in our lives were." He gives that a moment of thought. "Maybe Granddad, but only after he was dead, and I'm not sure that counts."

"You think he's a good dead man?" I demand. "Because I think he's a sadistic SOB."

Preston considers this. "I think he tried to do right by us in the end in his own fucked-up way. That's my story and I'm sticking to it. But my point is I know a thing or two about not feeling like you know how to be a good person. And when the woman you love tells you you're not what she needs, it can be way too easy to believe it. But she can be wrong, too. Especially if life has knocked her down a bunch recently." He gives me a sharp look. "Like, say, she's been *jilted at the fucking altar*."

Oh, Jesus, I'm an idiot. I feel like smashing my forehead into my palm.

But also, for the first time since Eden walked out, I feel hopeful.

"Okay," I say. "So what do I do?"

He gives me a dark look. "Well, first you take a hot shower and put on some less stinky clothes."

"And then?"

He shrugs. "How should I know? I'm just the fun-and-finance guy. You're the marriage expert. Figure it out."

I flip him the bird, but we both know it's *Fuck you, I love you, dude.*

RHYS

I do as Preston instructed. I shower.

Well, no: First I kick him out. Then I shower.

Then I call Matias.

Six hours later, Matias and his partners and I sit in the conference room, drinking pretty decent coffee, and they tell me about how they're running the firm.

"Work-life balance," Evelyn says. "Family comes first. And we turn down cases if they don't pass the sniff test."

"Only collaborative divorces. We'll only go into combat mode for people who need us on their side. We de-escalate everything we can, anytime we can," Chun says, pushing her silver-salted dark hair behind one ear.

"And we want the proportion of pro bono–to–paid cases to be as high as we can support and still all be comfortable with our salaries," Matias says.

He passes a binder across the table, open to a series of charts and graphs. I study them. No one is getting rich working here, but they're all getting paid enough to support a comfortable lifestyle. The rest of the money is being used to win cases for people who wouldn't otherwise be able to afford to fight.

I could do this, too. Instead of trying to strike down all the assholes of Manhattan, like that will somehow retroactively make up for my father and uncle being the worst kinds of humans.

Like that will somehow make *me* not like them.

How long have I been trying to prove I'm not one of them by fighting them?

Too long.

I decide I want this fucking job.

"I did some digging," Chun says. "Ninety-two percent of your clients are women. I talked to some lawyers who've worked with you, some of your clients, and a few members of opposing counsel, and the general consensus is that you're one, extremely reasonable and two, prone to taking on cases pro bono, which as you well know isn't a thing in divorce law."

"Damn," I say, impressed by her research skills. No one's ever called me out on either the percentage representation or the money stuff.

Evelyn's nodding. "You're *exactly* the guy we want. What we need to understand is whether you're serious about this. New York City to Bend, Oregon, is no joke of a change of heart. We don't want to invest in you and have you discover three months down the line that you can't deal with small-town life."

"I grew up here," I say. "I know everything there is to know about small-town life."

"And you left, and rumor has it you vowed to stay away forever."

Ah, Rush Creek. Thank you for never changing. "Not because of small-town life, though. Because my grandfather was—" I search for the right words.

"A dickish dick who dicked," Matias supplies.

"That does somewhat cover it," I admit.

Chun snorts. "Okay, but that still doesn't explain why a guy who lives in one of the biggest, liveliest cities in America would trade it in for Bend and far less money."

Here I am again, faced with a list of all the ways I could explain myself:

I'm super impressed by this firm, and I want to be a part of it.

I think there's a better, more peaceful way to end marriages.

I'm done trying to slay my father and my uncle by proxy.

But it still feels like there's an even truer answer, and I owe it to myself—and Eden—to give it.

"I met someone," I say. "A woman."

Chun snorts again and gives Evelyn a knowing look. "Told you," she says.

Matias stares at me. I've stunned him. "You told me you weren't seeing anyone."

"I wasn't, exactly, yet...at that point. I didn't think it was going to—happen."

"Does *MANhattan* magazine know that the mighty Rhys Hott has fallen?" Matias demands.

I laugh. "Not yet, but I'm sure I won't be able to keep it a secret for long."

Chun gives me a skeptical look. "And if things don't work out between you?"

I think of Preston, scowling and fierce. Of all three of my brothers: Quinn, grumpy and withdrawn; Shane, pretending not to give a shit about anyone or anything; Preston, working so fucking hard to atone for whatever it was he believed he'd done wrong.

I think of them now. Lighter. Brighter. Better.

Preston's words: *What do you do for a living?*

Sometimes you have to be reminded of who you are.

"Things will work out between us," I say.

"Awfully sure of yourself," she says.

Good thing they didn't see me earlier today with my face in the pillow. But I've been a lawyer a long time. There's no one who doesn't get knocked down from time to time. The question is always *What do you do when you get up again?*

"You've read the articles," I say. "You did the research. Anyone you talk to say I'm someone who gives up a fight before it's won?"

Grins and nods from—I hope—my future partners.

"And now, if you'll excuse me? There's somewhere I need to be."

I'm ordering fabric online when Rhys walks into the shop.

I haven't seen him since four nights ago, when I told him I didn't think we could work.

Since then, I've clung to the feeling I wrapped around myself. Strong. Safe. Like impenetrable armor. No one else can make me safe—not mother, not father, not grandmother, not husband, not fiancé, and definitely not...whatever Rhys is. *Only I can make myself safe.*

I can refuse to set myself up to be left again.

"Hey," he says.

I look up.

He's beautiful. In another era he would have been an actual warrior instead of a fighter for marital justice. He would have had a sword in a scabbard and a dagger at his calf, but he would have worn exactly that same expression —*Don't fuck with me.*

Despite myself, despite all my resolve, I shiver and my

body warms, and against all good sense, I want him to be my warrior. The man who'll fight *for me*.

And that's exactly what I can't want, it's exactly what I need to walk away from.

I realize I've reflexively picked up my rotary cutter, the blade winking in a shaft of morning sunlight, and I set it down again. He doesn't actually have a sword. I don't need to literally keep myself safe from him. I just need to not fall for whatever speech he's about to give me. He went to law school to learn how to get people to do what he wants them to.

That's okay. I went to the school of fucking hard knocks to learn how not to set myself up for pain.

Rhys scowls. "I don't like how we left things the other night." He crosses his arms. There's nothing soft in his expression, nothing soft in the set of his shoulders or the determination on his face. "You said you didn't think it could work between us, and I let you walk away. That's not the man I want to be. That's not the man I'm *going* to be."

My stupid, hopeful heart beats halfway out of my chest.

I want this. I want him. So much.

Somewhere along the way, I let myself fall in love with him. I don't know if it was when he cooked me dinner or suggested we stop at the quilt show or booked me plane tickets to Sioux Falls or bought me frog slippers—or when he let me take him apart.

It was probably way before that, actually. It was probably when he set the cowboy hat on my head on the morning of my wedding and led me out of the building with no questions asked, doing what I needed even though it was messy and inconvenient for him.

What if...?

What if that's exactly who he is?

What if it's not?

"There's someone I want you to see," he says. "Can I bring him in?"

My mind flashes to all sorts of possibilities, none of which make sense. One of his brothers. Paul. Teller—but that makes even less sense than the other options.

"Stay there." He points.

A moment later the door chimes, and then again, and then he's standing there, a leash in his hand—

A leash?

He drops the leash, and the creature on the other end of it bounds forward—medium-sized, with curly red blond–and–white–and–black splotches and spots and floppy ears and a snout that's blunt enough to suggest some bulldog or pug or boxer in his heritage.

"Milo!"

I fall to my knees, and the bundle of loving mutt-y energy, my baby boy, my darling Milo, jumps up, licking my face, panting his joy.

He licks tears off my face, and I look up at Rhys. "How...?"

He grins down at me. "I went back to New York yesterday. Had a long talk with Teller. I reminded him that sometimes in the heat of battle, we fight for things out of spite that we don't actually want as much as the other person does. And I told him that I'd gotten to know you a bit and it was clear to me that Milo meant a lot to you...and that I thought Milo might be a lot happier living in one place year-round and that Teller might be happier not pouring so much money into dog-walking and dog-sitting while he works and travels on his ridiculous schedule."

"You didn't!"

He nods. "And he agreed that perhaps Milo would be happier with some space to run around in the backyard of a little house in Rush Creek, Oregon, than cooped up in a New York apartment. So he signed custody back over to you."

"Rhys…" I can barely manage his name through my happy tears.

"Just so you know," he says sternly, "this isn't a grand gesture. I don't believe in grand gestures."

I snort. "Are they like jumping spiders or rattlesnakes?"

"More like cotton candy," he says. "Pretty but not very satisfying. But this isn't one."

"What is it, then?"

"It's just setting right something I wish I'd been able to do differently. Restoring order."

That makes me smile.

"I did *think* about grand gestures a lot. I can tell you all the ideas I considered and dismissed. Kidnapping you on a big road trip, buying the shop next door to yours so you can expand, strong-arming Paul into giving you the condo."

That makes me smile. "I don't hate any of those," I say, still kneeling beside Milo and soaking up his sloppy kisses and puppy breath, my hands buried in his fur, my heart beating nearly out of my chest with joy.

"They're all still on the table," Rhys says. "Just say the word. The reason I decided not to do any of those is because *I get it*. I get why you don't want to jump into this and why you can't trust it. You've been dealt a shit hand. No one you've ever cared about has stayed, and the one person who did wasn't exactly warm and loving to you. I wouldn't be able to trust me, either. And here's the thing: I want you to be safe, which means I don't *want* you to just trust whatever performative alpha male bullshit I dish up for you. I don't want to fly you to Paris and give you a huge rock and tell you I'll never leave you, because I don't want to seduce you. I want to *deserve* you."

I *almost* make a little helpless noise, because holy *shit*, he's good. Like, I had NO IDEA he was that good. I feel lucky he didn't use the closing-argument magic on me sooner because I would have folded like a fat quarter on display.

Instead I shorten up Milo's leash, stand up, take a deep breath, and wrap my armor tighter around myself.

"You don't have to say anything," he says. "I'm not asking you to say anything or promise anything. You don't even have to agree to see me ever again. I just wanted to tell you that I took a job at my friend Matias's law firm in Bend and I'll be working there as soon as I wrap things up in New York. The events of the last few weeks have made me realize I don't love who I've become, and I want to feel like I can look myself in the eye in the mirror. Plus, three thousand miles is a long way to come once a week for family dinners."

I snort at that.

"I guess what I'm saying is that I'm here and I'm not leaving."

I want so many things. I want to take off the armor and wrap him around me instead. I want to let him in, all the way in, and keep him there as long as he'll stay.

I want it to be like it was in the car, just us, moving forward together.

And on the other hand, I want never to have gotten in that car and discovered that it was possible to love so much more deeply than I'd ever loved before. That it was possible to want someone so fiercely that any loss I'd ever experienced would pale in comparison to how much it would hurt to lose him.

"If I tell you to leave, will you?" I ask.

I see the hit register, a sudden flash of pain behind his eyes, but he does an admirable job of shuttering them. "If you tell me to leave you alone, I'll stay away. But I'm in Rush Creek to stay, Eden. I'm here for the long haul."

Our eyes are locked on each other's faces. There's quiet resignation on his as he waits for my verdict.

I don't know what's on mine. I hope I'm not as transparent as I feel—terrified and hopeful at the same time.

EDEN

"What did you tell him?" Mari demands, crouching to love up Milo, who treats her to all the nose licking and face panting.

"I didn't tell him to leave me alone," I admit. "I couldn't. I opened my mouth and closed it. Like a fish. But I couldn't get the words out. After a while he said, 'Okay. I'm going to take that as good news for now. See you around?' and then he kind of laughed and said, 'I actually do have to leave the store. But just the store, okay? I'm still here.' And he went out."

"Aw," she says.

I don't admit how much I'd wanted to grab his arm and keep him here—in the store—a few minutes more. But also how much I wanted to tell him to take his certainty and his commitment and shove them, because I'd seen them before, and they hadn't done me any good at all.

"I wish I'd told him to leave me alone," I say.

Milo tilts his shaggy head, resting it against my leg.

"Do you really?"

I bite my lip. "No. But I wish I'd wanted to tell him to. I wish I didn't...*like* him so much."

I wish I didn't love him.

Mari tilts her head, considering. "This reminds me of how it was with Kane and me," she says. "I was pregnant with Zara, and I didn't know whether I should raise her, because I didn't feel like I had any idea how to be a good mom. My own mom had been such a disaster, and I was a hot mess. But I had good people in my life, and they were all telling me, basically, that I didn't have to figure out the rest of my life. I just had to figure out that day, and if I stayed that day, and the next day, at some point it would start to make more sense."

"And did it?"

She nods. "Yeah. One day I realized I'd stayed more than a year and that it had been months since I'd thought about leaving."

"But I'm not the one who needs to stay," I say. "He's the one—"

She nods. "But he's asking you to want him to, right? He's telling you he'll leave you alone if you want him to, but what he really wants is for you to want him to stay. So that's the question you get to ask each day. Do I want him to stay today? Should I tell him to leave me alone? Today it seems like you didn't want to tell him to. Maybe tomorrow you won't want to, either. Or maybe you will, and that's okay, too. But I think it's pretty cool that he recognizes that you've been hurt badly enough that the only thing that will help is seeing him stay and stay and stay."

"What if he can't stay...forever?" I ask.

Mari takes a deep breath and sighs it out. "Yeah, I don't

like that one, either," she says. "I mean, nothing is forever. We all leave this world eventually, and sometimes we leave people we don't want to leave behind. But that's not a good reason not to live, right? Being human is a giant *fuck you* to everything that can go wrong. Putting one foot in front of the other and just *showing up* is so hugely brave. And don't get me wrong. It's *hard* to be brave when shitty things have happened to you. When the people who were supposed to love you sucked at it. But the choice is, basically, shrink or grow. You can stay safe, but it will always make you smaller. Or you can be brave and get bigger. Let in more people and more light, and yeah, it'll hurt sometimes, but sometimes it'll be the best thing you ever did."

I stare at her. And then, unexpectedly, I start to cry.

She puts her arms around me and holds me until I manage to stop. Milo shoves his face between us.

"You want to talk about it?" Mari asks.

I tell her about the book my mom didn't make for me and the moment of stupid hope that I allowed myself before I figured it out.

"I've been there," she says. "My mom is still pretty useless. I let her see the kids from time to time because I want to model forgiveness and generosity for them—but she and I will never have a real relationship again. It never stops hurting, but it's a lot better now that I can be the kind of mom I wish I'd had."

"I like that," I say. "I'm not sure if I ever want to be a mom or not, but I could still try to be the kind of person I wish she was. The kind who would show up for her daughter's wedding and make her own damn book instead of having her assistant do it."

Mari smiles. "I definitely think you're that kind of person."

"So I just...what? I just don't tell him to leave me alone?"

"Yeah," she says. "And maybe someday you'll feel like you can tell him you want him to stay—but there's no rush."

"And in the meantime? What do I *do*?"

Mari tilts her head. "What do you want to do?"

"I don't know," I admit.

She smiles at that. "When I don't know what to do, I don't do anything at all."

"That sounds...hard."

"Yeah, it can be."

"Like you do literally nothing?"

"I let things happen."

"That sounds boring."

She shakes her head. "The amazing truth is...it never is."

The next day, Rhys brings me lunch.

The door of the shop chimes, and he's standing there, two paper bags from Spa Day Sandwiches in his hand.

He hands me mine. "I had to guess," he says. "I went with ham and brie, but—"

"That's perfect."

"You can tell me to leave you alone. I can go eat mine on a bench on the green. Or—anywhere else."

I shake my head. "You don't have to leave."

His eyes flash to mine.

"Today," I clarify and bite my lip.

The corner of his mouth twitches.

We eat our lunches standing up at the front counter, me on one side, him on the other. I'm the only one in the shop, and even though I could sit in the back and ask people to ring a bell for service, I don't like doing that. This is better.

It's comfortable. It's companionable. We talk about a

vision I have for redesigning the shop and the interview he had with Matias's law firm.

We don't talk about *us* or the future.

He brings me lunch every day after that. Every day, he says, "You can tell me to leave you alone."

Every day I say, "You don't have to leave," and he waits, and I add, "Today."

I look forward to those lunches more than anything else in my life.

One day, he asks if I can leave the shop for a little while. I say yes. He hustles me to the car and drives us toward Bend. I can't figure out where we're going until he pulls up in front of Five Rivers Arts and Crafts.

"I haven't seen your show yet," he says.

He sets the pace as we walk among the quilts and their admirers. He asks me questions about how they're put together. Good questions. Thoughtful questions. When we're done, he tells me that my show is *way* better than the one we saw on the road, and that every minute of our trip was worth it, just to make this show happen.

"And for a hell of a lot of other reasons." His eyes are steady on mine. "Happy to list them for you, when you're ready."

He drives me back to the store. At the door he says, "I've taken up a lot of your time already today. You probably don't want me to come in for lunch." He shows me the sandwiches in the cooler in his back seat.

"Don't leave," I say.

I almost forget to add, "Today."

Move-in day comes for my new apartment. Mari and Kane help me move. Rhys shows up at nine with a box of doughnuts and a flat of coffees in hand. "I heard a rumor that you were moving today," he says. "I came to see if I could help. You can tell me to leave you alone."

"Don't leave," I say.

He waits.

I don't say *Today*.

He fights back a smile. I do, too.

He's good at moving furniture. For one thing, he's extremely strong. But he's also excellent at figuring out how to maneuver big things through small doorways and stairwells. He can rotate objects in his mind. He also goes out and gets us sandwiches at lunch and pizza and beer for dinner.

Over dinner, Kane wants to know what's going to happen with Rhys's granddad's will.

Rhys sighs. "We've got till the end of the month. Most likely, we're going to end up contesting. Hanna gets a call almost every day from a bride who wants to get married 'as soon as possible' but 'not that soon.'"

"I guess that's not *super* surprising," Mari says. "No one wants to be rushed into marriage."

"And no one should be," Rhys says. "The last thing any of us wants is to give guys like me more work."

But his tone is teasing, and I love how relaxed he seems as he moves toward his less-sharky life.

After dinner, Mari and Kane leave, but Rhys stays. He helps me make the bed and unpack enough kitchen things that I can muddle through breakfast tomorrow morning.

When he says he should go, I say, "Hug?" and he hugs me. He's warm and muscular and I missed everything about him—the smell of soap and deodorant and his musky sweat, the hardness of every plane of his body, the small exhalation he permits himself when I'm in his arms, like finally, finally, he can relax. I remember how much I loved being the place he felt safe enough to lose control, and my whole body goes molten as those memories flood me.

I don't want him to leave, but he does, and I don't try to stop him.

He skips several days of lunch—he's warned me this will happen, because he has to go back to New York to take care of some things—and I miss him.

When he comes back to town, he tells me he'll pick me up at store-closing time and that I should have a change of clothes that can get dirty.

I try to figure out where we're going. A hike? Canoeing?

"And Milo's invited," he says.

I wear jeans and an old T-shirt and climb into his new rental. He drives me to the outskirts of the town, to a low building in an industrial park, with an incongruous patch of grass planted in front of it.

Rush Creek Animal Shelter.

My heartbeat picks up. "Rhys?"

"No pressure," he says. "But Natalie mentioned that there was a dog here she thought you were interested in adopting..."

I bite my lip.

"She's still here. I checked. She's a little older, so she's the last one who hasn't been adopted from the firefighter campaign. Now that Milo's with you year-round— Are you crying?"

He wipes a tear from each of my cheeks with his thumbs.

We go inside and meet Cressie. She's every bit as adorable in person as she is in her photos—a little smaller than Milo, ears akimbo, eager and panting as the woman working the shelter front desk lets her into one of the meet-and-greet rooms. She comes straight to me, puts her paws on my knees, and looks into my eyes with her big, soulful brown ones.

I'm smitten.

We bring Cressie outside to meet Milo. He comes cautiously out of the car and trots over to her. She preens a bit. He sniffs around her face, then all around her entire body, then comes back and licks her snout. She licks back, then ducks her head in the universal puppy sign for *Let's play*. And they do, on the grass outside the shelter, while Rhys keeps an eye on them and I finish up the adoption paperwork.

"Thank you," I say when we get back into the car, Milo and Cressie on the back seat in a puppy pile.

"Making the world right, one dog at a time," he says, grinning.

"Dissolving marriages and uniting dogs with their people since twenty-whatever."

"I mean, there are worse job descriptions."

A few nights later, he texts to asks how Cressie is settling in and if I think the dogs will be okay on their own for an evening. Cressie has spent most of the day trotting around after Milo while he introduces her to all his favorite things—the faintly peanut-butter laced Kong he willingly shares with her, the smelliest part of the apartment's small dog yard where the squirrels like to hang out, the spot in the fence where you can bark at the dog in the next complex's dog yard till someone makes you stop. When they tire themselves out, they plop down together on the rug and curl into nestling commas around each other.

I snap a photo and text it to him.

The dogs will be fine.

The phone rings a moment later. "Can I take you to dinner?" he asks.

"Is this a date?"

"Do you want it to be?"

"I think so," I tell him.

"Okay," he says. "Let's try it, then."

We go to Jane's Bistro, and he gets beef bourguignon and I get ahi tuna over jasmine rice and seaweed salad. Afterward he drives me back to my new place. He walks me to the door.

"You can come in," I say.

He says, "When you invite me in, I want you to mean it."

I can tell he reads my hesitation, and I read his disappointment, but it's okay. I think we both understand now about being patient. And this slow trickle of pleasure is not so terrible. It's delicious, especially when he leans down and kisses me good night. It's a first-date kiss—a good one—sure and confident but also respectful, his mouth slanted perfectly, certainly over mine, his lips sealing the kiss off with a greedy nip that makes me gasp before he draws back and strides away.

I watch him go and want to call, *Come back!*

I want to invite him inside, and inside me, and I want it to mean what we both need it to mean.

A week after that, Sonya and Quinn have a long-overdue afternoon housewarming barbecue, and I go. I don't know if Rhys'll be there, but I hope he will.

It's a great party. The house is packed to the gills—Hotts and their friends, Wilders and their friends. Nan the baker is there, but Arthur Weggers isn't, even though Sonya invited him. Food and drink cover every surface in the house, and children run amok in the best possible way. It's noisy and fun, and I have to go out on the back deck to catch my breath because it's so much.

"Hey," a deep voice says.

I know exactly who it is, not only because I'd know that voice anywhere but because the feel of my pulse picking up and my skin tightening all over is just as familiar.

"Hey," I say.

He comes up behind me. Close. Crowding me to the rail.

"You can tell me to leave," he murmurs.

"Please don't leave," I say.

Rhys sets a line of kisses down the side of my neck, and I shiver and back myself up against him. He's hard. Aroused. I wiggle against him. He turns me in his arms. Sets his mouth to mine. It's not a first-date kiss. It's hungry and needy. My whole body lights up; I'm completely here for it.

The door opens behind us, and we jump apart. "Cake time!" Hanna cries, and we follow her inside for dessert.

What I want is for *us* to leave, to leave this party and

maybe the whole world behind, to go where it's quiet and just us.

It hasn't been long, but I'm starting to see what Mari meant. That *forever* is actually a string of *today*s. That no one can promise forever, but one *today* after another is a start.

That trusting when you have no reason to isn't stupid—it's brave.

It might hurt again someday, but it might be worth it in the meantime.

53

RHYS

Acts of faith are funny. They're the opposite of that popular saying *The definition of insanity is doing the same thing repeatedly and expecting different results.*

Faith is about doing the same thing over and over again and expecting, finally, different results.

I don't expect anything after Sonya and Quinn's party. I haven't let myself expect anything this whole time. Because I meant what I said to her. I don't want her to be something I feel entitled to. I don't want her to come to me because she owes it to me or because I've somehow tricked her into it.

I only want her if I deserve her, and I only deserve her if she believes I'll never hurt her. And I can't tell her that. I can only show her.

I help Sonya and Quinn clean up, and then I retire to the guesthouse. I need a place of my own, and I'll get one soon, but I'm trying to get things straightened out with my old and new jobs first, and then I'll deal with housing questions. So for now, it's the guesthouse.

I've showered and pulled on a pair of sweats and a T-shirt when there's a knock. I'm so sure it's Sonya or Quinn that I don't even hesitate; I just open the door.

But it's Eden.

She's standing there, still wearing the clothes she had on at the party—a pair of tight black velvet leggings that turn her slim body into a paradise of curves. It was the cling of those leggings to the swerve of her hips and ass that made me lose control enough to press myself to her backside on the deck, even though I'd told myself I wouldn't touch her unless she asked me to.

I was too weak for that, and I have zero regrets; I can still feel the firm curve of her ass against the steel of my cock.

She's wearing a loose wine-colored top with a scoop neck that draws my eyes straight to her tits, which I've been trying not to stare at all night. I don't stare now, either, but only because I can't take my eyes off the other thing she's wearing.

The cowboy hat, tilted at a jaunty angle.

From under the hat, she's smiling at me. In her hands, she has a folded quilt. She opens it and holds it up, her face barely visible peeking over the sweep of it.

"Made this for you," she says. "It was almost done tonight. I just had to go home and finish sewing the binding. I was hoping you'd still be awake."

It's nine individual squares, and each square is a moment from our road trip, images pieced together from scraps of bright-colored fabric, just shapes and outlines but easily recognizable: her cowboy hat, the stack of quilts that sent us on our way, the view of the ocean from the beach house, the gas station where we spent the night, the quilt show, the piggyback ride, her lace underpants, the frog slippers, the airplane.

My heart pounds.

"I'm happy," she says. "I'm happy in a way I've never been happy. I want to be with you. All the way, in all the ways, for as long as it makes sense to both of us. And if it can't last forever, I think I'm okay with that, too."

In the low light of the guesthouse porch, her face is half-lit, but her eyes are bright, and her smile is big, and all I want to do is drag her inside and take her like the caveman she turns me into.

But I make myself be patient because she deserves that.

"I'm not," I say. "I want forever."

Her smile gets bigger.

"I mean," she says. "That's okay, too."

SHE'S BROUGHT the dogs with her, and she retrieves them from the car. They race each other into the guesthouse and begin sniffing all its corners before briefly tussling over right-of-ownership of my favorite corner of the couch.

Meanwhile, I tug Eden over the threshold and shut the door behind her. I take the hat off her head and sail it, Frisbee style, to the couch, where the dogs sniff it and then turn up their noses.

Then I kiss her.

Her mouth is cool and soft, and she tastes like the chocolate cake we ate at the party, and I can't get enough of her. I can't get enough of the silky feel of her or the way she whimpers every time our tongues touch or the way she clutches my hair like she'll do anything to make sure I don't stop kissing her.

I can't get enough of the fact that she came to me, that she's mine. I want to be so deep in her that there's no doubt in either of our minds.

We kiss and kiss, like we can't get enough, like we're willingly, happily drowning, gasping for breaths when we have to before going back for more. Her hands in my hair, mine at the small of her back until she wiggles herself against my erection. Without meaning to I pull her closer, cupping the delicious curve of her ass in the palm of my hand. Drawing her tight to me. Groaning at the feel of her, not only there but everywhere—the satin of her hair, the soft press of her tits against my chest, one of her hands wrapping hard around my bicep.

Eden pulls back, struggling with her top, and I help her, untangling her and tossing the shirt over her shoulder so I can take her in. The light in the room is low, and she's especially beautiful like this, in a black lace bra that pushes her small tits up like a feast for me. I accept the offering and draw a line of kisses across that lace edge, then push one cup down and circle her nipple with my tongue. She bucks against me, whining, and I decide *that's* my new favorite sound.

While I work both her nipples, she tips her hips hard against me, the vee of her thighs squeezing my cock between my body and hers. I bend my knees and thrust up against her, and she pushes herself harder into my mouth, into my palm. I can tell she's going to be easy for me tonight, that I could make her come without even trying. I pull back, put some space between our greedy thrusts, ease off her tits so I'm just playing lightly with them.

"More," she begs.

"I want to make you come while I'm inside you."

"Oh," she says. "Yeah. That. I want that."

Laughing, I scoop her up and carry her to the bed. I lay her down and finish undressing her, then do the same for myself. Then I dig in the nightstand drawer for a condom and roll it on.

I spend a long time on the next step. Because I want to enjoy every single second of it—of taking her and making her mine and being inside her. I brace myself over her, looking down at her face, her eyes hazy with pleasure that *I'm bringing her*, her mouth soft and hungry. I kiss her again, lowering myself over her so my cock grazes her mound, and she bucks into the touch, lifting her hips and grinding to get as much friction as she can.

"Patience," I say, and she growls.

I slip a hand between us, between her folds, finding her wet and slick. "I need you to tell me you want this," I say. "I need you to tell me you want me to fuck you. And I need you to say you'll tell me if you want me to stop."

"I can tell you to leave," she says, nodding. "I know I can. And I know that if I don't, you'll—" She hesitates, and her eyes fill up with tears.

"Oh, God," I say. "Eden."

"It's okay," she says brokenly. "Good tears. I know if I don't tell you to leave, you'll stay."

"That's right. I'll stay. As long as you want me to."

"I want you inside me," she says. "I want you to fill me up. I want you to fuck me."

"Just the tip," I say. "You can only have the tip."

"Bastard," she whispers as I slide the head of my cock between her lips, up over her clit, down to where her moisture pools, up again. Over and over, until she's whining again. Then I nudge myself inside her. Just the tip. Just the head. Breeching her. Parting her. Watching her eyes go hazier, her mouth go softer, her head fall back.

"More," she begs again.

It's taking every ounce of patience I have. I want to thrust into her. I want to fill her, to pound her. I want to show her how much I've held back and how much I want. But I just give her another inch, and another, while she tries to lift her hips and press me deeper.

She's so tight. So hot. She's a vise around my cock, and the sensation is just as intense around my balls, around the base of my spine.

Eden squeezes her inner muscles, and I try. I try so hard. But she's kneading me and begging with words and sounds, and I'm *not* superhuman. I'm just not.

I thrust, hard, all the way home, seating myself in her, and we groan together, because it's—

"So good," she moans.

"So fucking good," I agree. "You feel so good."

And it's true, the sensation of it is practically overwhelming, but that's not what matters right now—it's the way she's looking at me, her face so open and needy, so full of...

"I should have said this before," she says. "This is a terrible time to say it. You just have to know that I've been thinking it for weeks. Since you said you were staying. I love you."

"I don't think it's a terrible time," I say. It's a lot, though. So much. My chest full of her words and my cock full to bursting for her, my whole body on the edge of detonation, hot and wild and uncontrolled. "I love you, too," I say. "I have for a long time. I will forever."

I dip my head, find a nipple, still thrusting, looking for the angle and the depth that will make her lose her mind, and then I find it. I know because of the way she gets suddenly wetter, because she starts murmuring my name brokenly, and then I add a hitch of my hips up over hers, tugging her taut, grinding into her mound, and she comes apart under me, crying and whining and moaning, her muscles clenching and unclenching, her arms wrapped tight, her cheek pressed to mine, and I can't do anything except follow her over, to wherever we're going next.

EDEN

Rhys gets up to get rid of the condom. I lie in bed, wrapped in bliss, my whole body bathed in warmth.

"Eden," he calls from the hallway.

I don't think I'd call his tone *alarmed* exactly, but it's... something. Alert. It gets me out of bed and into the hallway, where I can see what he sees: Cressie and Milo lying side by side on the couch, tucked tight against each other, Cressie's snout resting on Milo's.

"Are they...always like this?" Rhys asks.

"Oh, yeah," I say, grinning. "It's definitely true love. They're completely inseparable. I have to keep them both on the same side of my body when I walk them. And Milo won't let me put Cressie in her own crate at night. He barks until I let her in with him."

I can't read the expression on Rhys's face. It looks like he's been smacked in the gut, but not entirely in a bad way.

"Eden," he says slowly. "I know how we're going to fix things with the will."

"What do you mean?" I ask warily.

"I mean," he says, a smile creeping over his face, lovely and mischievous, "Cressie and Milo are getting married."

LATE THE NEXT MORNING, around the conference table in Weggers's office, Matias, Rhys, Hanna, and I present Weggers with the plan.

"Look," Matias says. "The will doesn't say the bride and groom have to be human. It doesn't say the bride and groom have to be the same bride and groom as the original plans call for. It just says that the planned *ceremony* has to occur. The planned ceremony *will* occur."

Weggers sniffs. "You know that's not the *spirit* in which this was intended."

"True," Matias says. "I also know that you like to be true to the *letter* of the law. Plus, it will save us both so much time and trouble if I don't file the contest."

Weggers eyes him warily.

I wouldn't want to go up against Matias in a court of law, and apparently Weggers is thinking the same thing, because he straightens himself up like a cat trying to preserve its dignity and says, "It's true that I have a fondness for the letter of the law..."

He says it like it's a good thing, when I think the whole idea of the letter and spirit of the law is the opposite? Spirit is good, letter is bad? But obviously no one points that out.

Once the meeting with Weggers is done, Hanna confirms the vendors are all still available, and I reach out to as many local guests as I can to convince them to attend

Cressie and Milo's wedding. It's not a tough sell because I include a small album of the hundreds of photos I've taken of them since Cressie came home. Everyone agrees that they're the perfect couple.

We know we won't get quite as many guests to RSVP as Paul and I had originally, but—Matias points out—the will doesn't say that the ceremony must be attended by any particular number of guests.

"I like to operate in an 'if it doesn't say I can't, I can' mindset," he says, grinning.

Finally, by late afternoon, everything's set, and Rhys and I head back to the guesthouse and fall into bed together, exhausted.

"You must be so relieved," I say.

"I won't breathe completely easy till after it's over...but I'm pretty sure I'm off the hook. Talk about under the wire."

"It's the wackiest solution ever. You're a mad genius."

"And you love it."

"You know I do," I say, putting my palm to his cheek, a day of scruff rough and delicious against my fingers.

He makes a sound that's half sigh, half groan.

We make love again, and it's slow and sweet until it isn't, until it's wild and unhinged and I'm telling him to fuck me like he means it, and he lasts three seconds after that, which is so hot—Rhys out of control—that I come with his fingers on my clit and his roar in my ear.

Then we talk.

"I still need to take this slow-ish," I warn.

"I know," he says.

"I'm not moving in with you or anything."

"That's fine," he says. "I don't have anywhere for you to move in *to*."

"I do," I say. "But I'm not ready to issue an invitation."

He laughs. "I don't need one. I mean, maybe the occasional sleepover."

That makes me smile. Look at us, right? "Oh, God, Rhys, of *course*. More than occasional, probably. I'm not ready to let you leave—the bed or the room, I mean."

He grins at that. "Yeah," he says contentedly. "Why is sex like that?"

"Like...?"

"You know. Like with some people it's just sex. And with the right person, it's—"

"Like holiday lights coming on in the dark," I say.

"Ha. Yes. The old-fashioned, non-LED kind. With no bulbs missing."

"When you get them seated in the tree right, so they're distributed evenly and tucked back at different layers, so you get that all-over twinkle—"

"This is the worst metaphor *ever*," he says. "I'm trying to say that I didn't actually believe there was a whole other level, but what I feel with you is definitely a whole other level."

I'm quiet, because my feelings are too big for the moment. "Yeah," I say. "Me, too."

"So, okay, no cohabitation for a while. Just sleepovers. Lots of sleepovers."

"And maybe we never get married. We can be one of those couples that's been together fifty years—"

I realize what I've said.

He's smirking at me. "Fifty years, huh?"

"I'm just saying, we could be together and there doesn't have to be any lifetime commitment involved."

"What if I want lifetime commitment?"

"No marriage proposal for at least a year," I say sternly. "You don't believe in marriage anyway."

"I think we've been over this: I *believe* marriage exists. I just have never believed it was a good idea. Before."

"But now you do."

Rhys bites back a smile. "If I tell you I do, will it freak you out?"

"Probably." But I'm grinning.

"Slow-ish," he says. "We can revisit this question another time, on another day, with more perspective."

I hug him. Hard. "I love you."

"I love you, too."

"And you can be my boyfriend," I say. "We can be exclusive. And we can keep doing *this*."

I gesture at our boneless, pleasure-soaked selves, still curled together in the bed.

"That sounds good to me."

"And you should definitely stay. In Rush Creek. I—"

My voice gets choked. I have to stop. I realize that in all of this, I haven't said the one thing I've been thinking for days, as I pieced the squares of the quilt together, as I laid in the last few stitches through the layers of our time together.

I haven't said the words that matter most to him. Not yet, not exactly this way:

"I want you to stay."

RHYS

The bride wears white.

With guidance from the staff at Pawsitively Perfect, Rush Creek's dog-lover's boutique, Eden attached a ring of white roses flowers to Cressie's collar.

The groom is dapper in a black-and-white plaid bowtie collar that's too loose (I was in charge of tightening the collar. I have many skills, but it turns out I'm not great with slider buckles.).

Apparently—go figure—you can become ordained online in minutes, for free. It was not difficult to find a willing officiant in the person of my brother Shane, who has never missed an opportunity to be in the spotlight.

Hanna's favorite organist cues up for "Here Comes the Bride."

When Cressie appears at Eden's side at the end of the aisle in the Hott Springs Eternal wedding barn, Milo, who had been exercising great patience but straining at the end of his leash, slips his bow-tie collar and runs down the entire length of the aisle to lick Cressie all over her face.

"I didn't say, 'You may kiss the bride,'" Shane grouses, barely audible over the laughter of the attendees.

We get Milo dressed again and lead both the bride and groom to the altar.

"If anyone objects to this union, speak now or forever hold your peace," Shane intones.

"I'm *still* not sure this is legal," I hear Weggers mutter, but everyone, thankfully, ignores him. Well, except for Nan, who mutters something back that luckily I can't hear.

When it comes time for Milo to say his vows and Shane says, "I, Milo," Milo barks back at him.

"Did you teach him to do that?"

Eden's eyes are huge. "No. Did you?"

I shake my head.

When it's Cressie's turn and Shane says, "I, Cressie," Cressie barks back at him. Eden and I stare at each other, until someone in the audience bursts out laughing. I turn to find Sonya and Quinn, dissolved at their own hilarity.

"Very funny," I say.

"Shocking what these two will do for peanut butter," Sonya says, barely able to get the words out through her laughter.

When the exchange of dog tags is complete and it's *actually* time for the groom to kiss the bride, there's a lot of tongue and a lot of hooting and hollering from the audience.

In the spirit of the original event (and the law), we sit down for the catered meal that Eden and I originally planned—with one addition. Eden has asked the caterer to include hot dogs as a menu option. ("In keeping with the theme," she says.)

Cressie and Milo eat their (dog-friendly) meals at the bride and groom's table. Well, the bride and groom's dais. We had to remove the table and chairs. There are limits to everything.

Using a recipe from Pawsitively Perfect and lots of additional guidance from Eden's vet—who's also in attendance at the wedding—Nan has baked a dog-friendly, all-organic wedding cake for the canine attendees. They gobble their slices up like high-powered vacuum cleaners. She's also baked a huge human-friendly version, and she serves up slices to the guests. We eat ours at a more measured pace and take to the dance floor.

I'm dancing with a buoyant Hanna when Milo uses his teeth to tear the white rose necklace from around Cressie's neck. The flowers go flying into the midst of the dancers. To keep Amanda Wilder's daughter Anna from being struck in the face, I shoot my hand up in the air and catch the flying flowers.

Everyone in the room turns to look at me and my handful of bridal...bouquet.

The Hott brothers and their significant others wear knowing looks.

I don't harsh their mellow. Let them believe whatever they want to believe. That Grandfather is a magical matchmaker, that Eden and I will get married and have thirty-seven children, that I'd actually even *invite* them to my wedding.

No way they're invited. If I get married, I'm doing it in secret in an exotic location and I'm not telling anyone. Can you imagine the shit my brothers would give me if they knew I'd succumbed?

Not gonna happen.

Eden and I also dance. A lot, since Paul and Eden had booked one hell of a DJ. We might as well enjoy her talents to the utmost.

Eden slips into my arms with perfect ease, like there's never been a question that she belongs there, like her bare skin was always meant to be warm and alive under my hands, her body pressed to mine. Between slow dances, we dance with Wilders and Hotts, with my siblings and Hanna's friends and their kids, with neighbors and Nan and, yes, even Weggers.

The dogs eventually flop themselves at the edge of the dance floor and regard us over their noses, like exhausted professors.

The music slows again, and Eden sidles up to me. "May I have this dance?" she teases.

She settles her head against my shoulder. I draw her close and lower my nose into the strawberry scent of her soft hair.

And it's not my wedding, but holding Eden in my arms before God and all those assembled feels pretty damn good.

EPILOGUE
EDEN—SEVEN MONTHS LATER

Being more or less a member of the Hott family means that weird stuff is *always* happening.

For example, this morning we're trying out one of Natalie's new concepts for resort activities, breakfast s'mores.

It's 8:00 a.m. on a Saturday, which is what time you call a gathering if you want to find out for sure who the morning people are—and aren't.

Rhys and I are both doing okay. Both of us would have been happy to stay in bed longer, but we can do this.

Preston and Quinn are busy poking an enormous campfire, trying to get the flames to settle down and coals to form.

Sonya is *not* a morning person. She is currently sitting on a stump, hunched over in misery.

"Seriously?" she whines when Natalie hands her a long-handled sandwich press and a tortilla. "Fully grown adults are going to wake up at the crack of dawn so they can make their own breakfast?"

Natalie grins. "If we call it Cowboy Breakfast S'mores, they will."

There are three presses, a giant stack of tortillas, and bowls filled with toppings—Nutella, peanut butter, chocolate chips, bananas, marshmallows, strawberries, graham crackers. The idea is you put a tortilla on the press, load on your toppings of choice, fold your tortilla over, close the press, and stick it in the fire.

"I'm going classic," I tell the assembled crowd, tossing chocolate chips, marshmallows, and graham cracker crumbles into my s'more quesadilla.

"You warm enough?" Rhys asks. He drapes a quilt over my shoulders. It's one I made recently, squares from Rhys's stash of T-shirts going all the way back to childhood. The other side is flannel, and it's warm and soft around my shoulders. But most of the warmth is coming off Rhys himself as he wraps an arm around me.

For several months we kept our own places, but just recently we moved into a new apartment together, and we're looking for a place to buy. I still get scared sometimes that this relationship—like so many other ones in my life— will blow up in my face, but I've learned that the best thing to do when I get scared is to tell Rhys I'm freaking out. He's good at listening, talking me off the ledge, and reassuring me—with words, but also with his body.

I wouldn't have guessed things could get even better between us, but the more I get to know him, the more I see what a fundamentally good man he is—the kind who takes care of people, who anticipates what they need and makes sure they get it.

Rhys has been working with Matias, Evelyn, and Chun

since the beginning of the year, and we've all become good friends. He loves his new job. He has presided over the dissolution of quite a few marriages in the last few months, all of them relatively peaceful. But he's actually been transitioning himself more toward the child-advocacy side of the firm's work, and even though it can be extremely stressful, seeing kids in difficult situations, he loves that he's able, so often, to make a difference.

I spend a lot of time with the other Hott wives and girlfriends—Ivy is now on the "wife" side of that equation, and Natalie and Preston are engaged, so it won't be long for her, either. I still tell them I'm never getting engaged again—

But we all know I don't mean it.

"Hey. I have a question for you all," Quinn says.

Quinn's more talkative than Tucker, but he's still not one to draw the conversation in his direction, so everyone turns with curiosity to hear what he has to say.

"You know how Blue Iron's been under EPA monitoring for water safety violations for basically the last decade?"

"Yeah," Preston says. "From the uranium days."

"I heard through the lab grapevine—"

"There's a lab grapevine?" Shane demands.

"If there's a bakery grapevine, there's a lab grapevine, right?" Ivy says.

"Good point."

Quinn waits patiently for silence, then continues, "Blue Iron just hired a consultant to—"

"Well, hello, Hott family and friends," a voice says from behind us.

We all turn.

"Hi, Attorney Weggers," Sonya says. Given this family's

history with Weggers, her voice is admirably warm. "How'd you know we were out here?"

"Did a little sleuthing up at the lodge, and they sent me down here." He sounds pretty damn proud of himself.

And the truth is, it's hard to hate him, now that Rhys and I are living our happily ever after. Maybe he and Rhys's grandfather even deserve a tiny—tiny!—bit of credit for it. Not that I'd ever admit that out loud.

I wonder if any of the other couples here feel any scraps of fondness for our blowhard friend—or his late client.

"How can we help you?" Natalie asks.

"I'm looking for Tucker," he says.

Beside me, Rhys goes rigid. "He's not here."

"You wouldn't happen to know where he is?" Weggers says. For the first time, I notice the sheet of paper he's clutching in one of his hands. "I have something for him."

We all shoot each other glances, but it's not like we have to lie. None of us has seen much of Tucker, and when we do, it's always brief glimpses. Nothing as dramatic as the night when he fled the party at Hanna's—but not a lot of warm full-family togetherness, either.

"I haven't," I say, and we all take turns echoing it.

"I've been hunting him for weeks," Weggers says, seeming not to grasp how disturbing his wording is. "Can't find him anywhere."

I have to imagine that if Tucker doesn't want to be found, he probably won't be. He is, after all, professionally trained in surveillance, among other things.

"Can't help you," Natalie says. "But let me send you off with a Cowboy Breakfast S'more." She presses one into his hand—the one not clutching Tucker's letter—and then gently steers him toward the parking lot. "Nice seeing you, Attorney Weggers! Good hunting!"

When he's gone, it's quiet for a minute.

Then Shane says, "Anyone else picturing Wile E. Coyote and Roadrunner?"

ACKNOWLEDGMENTS

Readers: I'm sitting here thinking about what I want to say to you and, as always, it all feels so *inadequate.* Fifteen years ago, I started reading romance novels, and shortly after that, I started writing them. And now I've written more than twenty-five of my own, and you just keep reading them, and it's the loveliest thing ever, because although I'd write them no matter what, it makes me SO STINKIN' HAPPY that you like them, too. So thank you!

A huge thank you to my early readers, Kate Davies, Rachel Grant, Christina Hovland, Adele Knight, Susannah Nix, and Brenda St. John Brown. You helped make this book one of my favorites I've ever written, and you're all a part of it, too!

So many thanks also to the author friends who support me on a regular basis—those I've already mentioned, as well as the authors in RAM Rom Com, ECRW, my various Discord servers, and many, many more, including but not limited to Jen Pitts, Kitt Henley, Julie Farley, Emily Smiley, and the other writers of BARN, Kris Kennedy, Liz Alden, Christine D'Abo, Gwen Hernandez, Audrey Nelson, Jessica Auerbach, Cheryl Cain, the Good Eggs, and my romance and indie roundtable peeps. Writing, more than anything else I've ever done (except child rearing) definitely takes a village (or three), and I love all of mine.

Thank you to my agent, Emily Sylvan Kim, and my sub rights agent, Tina Shen.

Thank you, Mandi Andrejka of Inky Pen Editing. The longer we work together the more I adore you and your style—and your style sheets. May it long continue.

Thank you, XPresso Book Tours, especially Giselle, for the release blitz.

Hugs and kisses for my not-author friends who support my imaginary worlds with so much love and patience: Aimee, Darya, Ellen, Elizabeth, Lauren, Molly, Soomie, and Tracey.

To BellGirl and BellBoy, whether you are cohabitants or out there conquering the world, you are always in my heart. In fact, you are my heart, walking around in the world, so please be careful with it and always obey the speed limit. I love you so much.

To Mr. Bell, I am never kidding when I call you my own personal romance hero. The day you knelt in front of Valentine Hall and asked me to submit (to the literary magazine!! Y'all have dirty minds) was the meet cute of my happily ever after.

Any errors of fact or insensitivity relating to representation are mine and mine alone. If you note any, please let me know so I can fix them and learn to do better.

ALSO BY SERENA BELL

Wilder Adventures

Make Me Wilder

Walk on the Wilder Side

Wilder With You

A Little Wilder

Wilder at Last

Hott Springs Eternal

Hott Shot

Hott Take

Some Like It Hott

Running Hott

Hott, Hotter, Hottest

Under One Roof

Do Over

Head Over Heels

Sleepover

Returning Home

Hold On Tight

Can't Hold Back

To Have and to Hold

Holding Out

Tierney Bay

So Close

So True

New York Glitz

Still So Hot!

Hot & Bothered

Standalone

Turn Up the Heat

ABOUT THE AUTHOR

USA Today bestselling author Serena Bell writes romantic comedies with small towns, big hearts, hot nights, and all the feels.

Serena's books have earned many honors, including a RITA finalist spot, an RT Reviewers' Choice Award, Apple Books Best Book of the Month, and Amazon Best Book of the Year for Romance.

When not writing, Serena loves to eat dark chocolate and spend time with her college-sweetheart husband and two hilarious kiddos—all of whom are incredibly tolerant not just of Serena's imaginary friends but also of how often she changes her hobbies and how passionately she embraces the new ones. These days, it's quilting, board-gaming, meditation, and long walks with good friends.